*33 Moments of Happiness*

# 33 Moments of Happiness

ST. PETERSBURG STORIES

*Ingo Schulze*

TRANSLATED BY JOHN E. WOODS

*Alfred A. Knopf*
*New York*
*1998*

THIS IS A BORZOI BOOK
PUBLISHED BY ALFRED A. KNOPF, INC.

www.randomhouse.com

Originally published in Germany as *33 Augenblicke des Glücks*
by Berlin Verlag, Berlin, in 1995.
Copyright © 1995 by Berlin Verlag

Stories 4, 5 and 26 were originally published in *The New Yorker*.

Library of Congress Cataloging-in-Publication Data
Schulze, Ingo.
[33 Augenblicke des Glücks. English]
33 moments of happiness : St. Petersburg stories / by Ingo Schulze ;
translated by John E. Woods.
p.   cm.
ISBN 0-375-40029-X
I. Woods, John E. (John Edwin)   II. Title.
PT2680.U453A611213   1998
833'.92—dc21   97-36894 CIP

Manufactured in the United States of America
First American Edition

*For H.P.*

L et me explain it to you: A year ago I made good on a long-cherished wish and took a train to Petersburg. I shared the compartment with a Russian fresh from the hairdresser, her husband and a German named Hofmann. The Russians took us for a couple, and as the translator of their questions and my answers, Hofmann presumably let them believe that was the case. I don't know what all he told them. They never stopped laughing, and the woman kept patting my cheek.

It stayed sultry all that night, too; the conductors' shirts were splotched with sweat, the compartment windows were dirty, steamed over and unopenable—ostensibly there was air-conditioning—and when the stench wasn't of disinfectants, it was of the toilet and cigarettes. Lowered like drawbridges between the cars were steel plates that banged together tarrara-tarrara-ping, tarrara-tarrara-ping, modulating to tarrara-ping-bong, tarrara-ping-bong when the train braked, until the bumpers finally started banging in unpredictable, unrelenting collisions, so that I could not sleep and was still lying awake the next day, even after the heat let up. When Hofmann wasn't talking with the Russians, he would lean his head back into his pillow and gaze out the window, where amid swampy fallow fields and bleak forests, little houses emerged here and there, blue and green and pressed askew into the earth, with stacks of firewood shining pale behind burned-off meadows and whitewashed fences. Often all that was left of a gatekeeper's little yellow flag was the wooden pole held out in salute.

The second evening, in Lithuania already, Hofmann suddenly invited me to the dining car. Sitting across from me—with his dark blond hair, nearly gray eyes and a scar under his chin—he seemed quite sure of himself. He ordered without a menu and wiped his silverware on the red curtains. But when asked how a German businessman, which he claimed he was, came to be traveling by train, he lost all his jauntiness for a moment. He gave a strained smile and fixed his eyes on me. Instead of answering, he began to ramble on about his work at a newspaper. But above all, he said, along with having a passion for karaoke, he was a lover of literature.

The further we moved away from my question, the more freely and easily he spoke—and, it seemed to me, the more fantastic and incredible his stories. He showered me with wide-ranging and elucidative suggestions of things I simply had to read, all the while heaving great sighs and congratulating me on my ignorance. "What all you still have before you!" he kept saying. We ate and drank a lot, it was dirt-cheap, and whatever was meant to happen happened—tarrara-tarrara-ping. . . .

I awoke with a hellacious headache. The sun was glaring; the train had stopped, a station named Pskov. Hofmann's bed had been stripped, the mattress rolled up. No one would or could say where he had got to. Easy come, easy go. I felt awful. And was still feeling awful even after I discovered, tucked behind my handbag, the folder lying before you now. I knew neither how it got there nor what I should do with it. At first I was going to give it to the conductor, because who knows what trouble not-knowing can get you into. But then I began to read.

Among the things we had talked about, Hofmann also spoke of some sketches he wrote every day and sent back to Germany from Petersburg. In writing them—he did not say for whom—he had yielded more and more to his inclination to invent rather than to research. Because for him, Hofmann said, something fabricated was no less real than an accident out on the street. He likewise must have encouraged business acquaintances and friends to describe for him certain episodes— which is not hard to get a Westerner to do in Russia.

Perhaps Hofmann succumbed to his weakness with me as well, and preferred invention to giving truth its due. I don't know and can say little more than that for the past year I have tried in vain to forget him. "And what," you will ask, "does this have to do with me?" When you spoke so candidly of your own plans, the idea came to me that someone like you should see to it that this folder gets published. Edited, it would surely provide diverting entertainment. And if Hofmann is still alive, he will come forward. I see no other possibility of my ever finding him again.

I beg you, please lend these fantasies your name! Because publishers will not accept a book without an author. They need photographs, interviews, they're hungry for faces and real stories. What would be a welcome outcome for you would be burdensome to me. For one thing, I don't feel I'm up to it all, for another, I would not like to put my own job in jeopardy. Whereas you are a person of literary ambition, are skilled at dealing with texts and have friends who would be happy to be of help to you. Perhaps you may even earn some money from it.

Freiburg im Breisgau, 25 June '94

I have provided this letter, in slightly abbreviated form, as a preface, because it relieves me of all explanations. I would nevertheless like to note that material considerations were secondary in my having assumed an editorial role. I would gladly have refrained from this task had I not been convinced that the sketches collected here go beyond their mere entertainment value and bear within them the possibility of inspiring an ongoing discussion concerning the value of happiness.

I.S.<br>Berlin, 10 June '95

# 33 Moments of Happiness

1

You run across women like Maria only in magazines and commercials. Each evening in the lobby of the Hotel St. Petersburg, where I stayed early on, she would shift from one arrangement of white armchairs to another as if she were moving about in a furniture store. Sometimes she would disappear for five minutes, but she always came back, and she was always alone.

On my way to the hotel bar I spoke to her, and so we entered as a couple. Maria grew livelier and even more beautiful. She had in fact been waiting for me. The bartender ignored other guests to serve me, and within Maria's line of sight, I returned to our table full of success and without sloshing a drop from the glasses. Her fingers got absentmindedly tangled in the silver chain above her décolletage, and her long nails drew streaks across that incredible skin, which re-emerged no less pure from under her red dress just above the knee. I lit her cigarette for her with her lighter so that she would not be distracted from what she was saying about Margarita and Lolita, about the difference between Zoshchenko's and Platonov's use of language, and my palms lay flat on the table while

she recited Pushkin and Brodsky as if she were planning a menu according to the vintage of the wines.
She had time for me, as if there were no soccer heroes
or singers, no members of parliament or captains waiting for her, and I knew: Petersburg, that is her dark
eyes. They would stand like stars for me above the
city, no matter what else might yet await me.

"Tell me about yourself," Maria said, pressing her
hand against my arm and cautiously kissing my fingers. I had appeared in order to rescue Maria. She did
not know who her father was. "An Italian perhaps," she
said, pushing her black hair up at me with the back of
her hand.

Maria would look for an apartment for us, we could
live together and awaken every morning in each
other's arms. I would fulfill her greatest wish and buy
her a car. Together we would drive through the city
and to the sea, go dancing, shop for shoes, visit her
mother and travel, first to Amsterdam to celebrate our
wedding with her girlfriend and then on to Italy.

We sat together for two hours, the bartender gave
us his blessing, and I would have loved to ask him for
two golden rings. Why had Maria picked me of all
people? She let her hand rest on my knee, then took
my forefinger and let it trace up and down her collar-
bone, and I kissed the little hollows on the side of her
neck, so that she lifted her shoulders and closed her
eyes.

I felt embarrassed to offer her money, but she simply nodded the way people nod.

After five minutes had passed, Maria followed me up
to my room; after twenty, she was out of the bed again.

*"Miliziya,"* she explained despondently. She was beautiful down to the hollows of her knees, and in searching for her dress she moved about the room with no more concern than if her things were hanging in the wardrobe.

While I played with the taps, Maria sat on the toilet and promised to arrange for a taxi early the next morning. We would meet again and drive to Pavlovsk.

No sooner had she left me than someone banged on the door of my room. The woman who monitored my floor was holding Maria firmly by the wrist. I explained that everything was all right, that nothing was missing. Then the door banged shut.

Every morning and evening for two weeks, I sat in the white armchairs waiting for Maria. But she did not come. I asked the bartender about her, asked the taxi driver who had exchanged whispers with her, the floor monitor. Maybe someone had abducted her, maybe she was no longer even alive or an old lover had returned from Siberia. For a long time I drove from my apartment to the hotel every evening. None of the other women or girls could match Maria. No one knew anything about her.

Nine months later, we met again at the entrance to the Hotel Europe. Maria had moved up two stars and was hungry. We sat in the courtyard, drank coffee and ate bockwurst. Within an hour there was scarcely a seat left. Like students, we each paid our own bill, exchanged three good-bye kisses like Russians, and Maria resumed her work like a woman in love.

2

"Seryosha, come home! Seryosha, do you hear me, come home!" Valentina Sergeyevna squinted. Another hour and she wouldn't be able to see her hand in front of her face. "Seryosha!" Valentina clapped her hands. Two hens ogled her in profile and then went back to pecking.

"It can't go on like this!" Valentina exploded, and sat down at the kitchen table. "For weeks I've heard not one word out of him, not a good morning, not a good night, he won't look at me, just drinks the water tap dry and goes to bed, the meat is falling right off that boy!"

"Better than eating the cellar bare every night," Pavel replied, spreading the butter thick on the bread and pushing it onto her plate with his thumb.

"Let's eat!"

Valentina reached for the teapot and filled both cups. The frizzy hair in her armpits pushed its way out from under the short sleeves of her apron.

"If he was your grandson, you'd do something," Valentina said.

They began to eat.

"Oh go on, every mouth is one too many."

"Fascist," Valentina whispered.

Pavel hauled back and struck her on the chin. A bite of pickle flew into Valentina's lap. Before she could even start crying, Pavel had stood up. He pushed her forehead back with his open palm and spat on her half-open mouth. He hesitated another moment. Valentina's face was cramping into a pucker . . . some butter was stuck to her upper lip. Then he left.

Pavel sat on the chopping block beside the shed for a long time. His cigarettes were still in the kitchen, his slippers still under the table. The clouds were turning blue in the evening sun. Pavel had to think this through.

"In an hour it'll be as dark as Lenin's asshole," he said to his big toes.

The distant noise from the Petersburg–Novgorod highway was part of the quiet by now. Only if someone honked was the road there again. Without slipping off the chopping block, Pavel scraped up some pebbles in his left hand and sat back up. Two hens were pecking between the fence pickets, their rumps raised high.

"Fire!" Pavel shouted, and threw the first pebble.

"Whooee!" It banged against the fence, whose pastel blue pickets he had tipped with white.

"Two marks lower, three to the right, fire!" The pebble whistled between pickets and disappeared soundlessly into the field beyond.

"Fire!" Pavel ordered.

"Too low, fire! Sustained fire!" He wasn't even aiming now.

"Whooee, whooee, whooee, whooee, ooreeeeee."

The hens ran clucking, flapping along the fence, but finding no openings, they plumped themselves up as if in a storm—and in the next instant drew up small and tight, pivoted in the corner and waddled back.

"Shut up!" Two more shots, and Pavel's left hand was empty. The hens scattered.

"Little shits! Enemy destroyed!"

Pavel was hungry and felt like killing something. But even five hens didn't lay enough, and winter was coming on. In Valentina Sergeyevna's vegetable garden he pulled up a kohlrabi, broke off the leaves, rinsed the rest in the rain barrel and split it open with the spade. He gnawed at the two halves by turns.

"Yuck!" Pavel spat and sat back down on the block. He chewed each bite till all the juice was extracted, then stuck out his tongue with the woody remains and wiped the back of his hand across his lips.

"A fat ass, a juicy ass, a white ass," he said, arousing himself and pressing his thighs together. Without any haste, he raised his right forearm above his left and squashed a gnat. "What are you wriggling around for!" Pavel scolded. He was gradually feeling better. He rubbed between his legs. The kohlrabi was sticky. He pressed the backs of his hands against his groin and spread his legs wide.

"Commando retreat!" He rubbed again, waited and pushed his knees apart with his hands—his organ was pressed against the taut fabric of his pants. Pavel was pleased with himself. He put his legs back together, hurled what was left of the kohlrabi at the fence, managing to hit the old chicken feeder, and placed both hands on his erection. Pavel grunted as if dozing off. Another bright streak appeared in the clouds above the woods. A buzzard circled in the gray sky. "Bang, bang, bang, bang!" Pavel took aim and kept a firm grip on his barrel. With each "bang" his hips twitched. "Keep it loaded, Pasha, keep it loaded. And stay dry, Pasha, bang, bang, bang, bang!"

Pavel was amazed to find himself standing beside the chopping block. He sat back down again now, but without letting up. "Rat-ta-ta-ta-ta-ta-tat."

Here came Seryosha out of the woods. He was running. Pavel saw the pointy knees rise and fall below the tall grass like a tedding machine. In the six weeks since his arrival, Seryosha had indeed become very skinny. He had taken off his shirt and was holding it in his hand like a sack. Even from a distance Pavel could see the boy's ribs. Only Seryosha's head had grown larger.

"Moving target," Pavel muttered, squinting an eye and crossing his right leg over his left. That way he could still feel himself warm and firm against his thigh.

"Uncle Pasha!" Seryosha crowed, waving at him with his free skinny arm and then brushing the hair from his brow. He pushed open the lattice door to the chicken yard as he ran.

"Uncle Pasha!" Seryosha gasped, running up to the man who had moved in with his grandmother two years before. Pavel stood up, his torso bent forward, and shoved Seryosha away. They had never hugged.

"Uncle Pasha, I've got it, look here!"

And directly before Pavel's bony feet Seryosha spread

out his shirt, in which lay a handful of coarse powder, dark, mixed with some larger lumps. Seryosha coughed.

"I'll explain it all to you, Uncle Pasha, everything, the whole truth!" Seryosha gushed, never once taking his eyes off his treasure.

Pavel looked down at the boy's cowlick, at his skinny neck, his shoulders, his sweaty back and the bit of butt-crack above his belt.

"Sit down, Uncle Pasha, please sit down, and I'll explain it all to you, the whole truth, ten minutes, Uncle Pasha, five, please!"

Pavel nodded, blinking the way he always did when he didn't understand something, and sat back down.

"Try it, Uncle Pasha, it tastes so good, it tastes wonderful!" Seryosha held a little crumb directly up to Pavel's lips. He took it between his fingers, shoved it into his mouth and chewed.

"Crunchy," he said.

"It is, isn't it!" Seryosha looked up, happy. "And sweet, sweet as sugar."

Pavel chewed for a long time and swallowed hard.

"I'll tell you the whole truth, Uncle Pasha, you first of all. Everything." Seryosha sat down beside his shirt. Two tiny creases appeared at his belly.

"Have some more, Uncle Pasha, please, help yourself."

Pavel picked out two little clumps with his left hand and nibbled at them.

"Like sunflower seeds," he muttered, and wiped his wet lips.

"It's so nice here with you both, Uncle Pasha, but when I think about leaving, when I think about Petersburg, I have to run to the can. It just wipes me out, Uncle Pasha, you know what I mean?"

Pavel stared at the crumbs between them. This morning, holding fast to the washbasin, Valentina had presented her rear to him. She had almost missed the bus for Novgorod.

"There I sit and I can't move I'm so worried and scared," Seryosha continued, "and then my poop turns hard and after a while it's cold and like something that doesn't belong to me but that still has to do with me, Uncle Pasha, it's horrible!" Seryosha studied Pavel's face. "I didn't want that anymore, Uncle Pasha," Seryosha began again. "I didn't want to have to poop anymore! Everybody knows that feeling, don't they, everybody, but nobody ever says anything about it, no one wants to say it because it's so horrible, right? But why, I asked myself, am I, why is everybody so scared of it? It comes out of my own body, it's a piece of me, and so it can't be any worse than I am!"

Pavel nodded.

"I've known that for a long time," Seryosha said, beaming, "but today I tried an old pile, it was my own, and it tastes good, Uncle Pasha, doesn't it? It tastes sweet! Do you know what that means, that it tastes sweet? It means I don't have to be scared anymore, no one has to be scared anymore, isn't that wonderful, Uncle Pasha?"

"I know about that," Pavel said, and stood up. "Come on!" he washed his hands in the rain barrel and rubbed them dry on his pants.

Seryosha carefully folded up his shirt. He tried to hug Pavel again. Then they both went into the house.

Valentina Sergeyevna was already in bed. Pavel stood at the door to the room, waiting for his eyes to grow accustomed to the darkness.

"Something wrong?" Valentina Sergeyevna asked.

"I've spoken with the boy, he's all right." Pavel loosened his belt and let his pants drop. "We'll all have breakfast together in the morning." He stepped out of his underpants and walked over to the bed. With one jerk he flung the blanket back. Crouching there on the sheet, Valentina Sergeyevna raised her white rear into the air.

"Come, my Hitler, come," she whispered, and buried her face in the pillow.

How often we had gazed up at the round-arched windows, their red velvet curtains wrapping the rooms like a precious gift. How often we had tried to imagine the triumphant view from the second-floor balcony across to the Anichkov Bridge, or, depending on the turn of one's head, down or up Nevsky Prospekt or to the quay under the poplars below. Our eyes might have followed the flatboats as far as the Sheremetyev Palace or, in the opposite direction, to the Fontanka curve. Stepping from these rooms to stand at the balcony's wrought-iron railing was like reviewing a parade and would inevitably evoke ovations from the throng lingering at our feet, waiting for the lights to change. There was no denying it: Whoever might appear on this spot in the city, high above the heads of the people, would possess a charisma that otherwise only birth endows. And it was from here that the sign adorned with the name of our newspaper was to shine.

The owners of the apartment had mounted delays, had mounted the most incredible delays for six months, and it looked as if what I had always feared would prove true: People like us entered such chambers only in our dreams or as guests. But then the forty thousand dollars had arrived, and at the end of April we pulled the curtains back from the windows.

I could see it all before me. I planned the middle room, with its view of Nevsky Prospekt, as the reception area for advertisers, writers and readers. I intended the corner room, where my desk would have its spot beside the door to the balcony, for layout. The journalists would have to make do with the smallest room. The bath and toilet were cramped. But the kitchen offered sufficient space for meetings and discussions.

What I had not expected, however, was that the foul odor in the stairwell would end at the door to the apartment, as if there flowed from our new quarters the fresh, unobtrusive scent of light, of warmth, of the sea and a seemingly unidentifiable floral extract, a scent that either had persisted in these walls over so many decades, and thus told of the fragrance of young noblewomen, or arose out of our own enchantment with the apartment. Perhaps, however, this scent also came drifting in through the windows, beyond which the cooing of doves blended with the first rustling of leaves and the slapping of waves against the quay.

And thus there existed the finest conditions for creating something every entrepreneur—if he is not a scoundrel and a cutpurse—desires, that is, for his employees to regard the firm as their second home. Contrary to my own wish that we hire painters, all the others spoke in favor of taking on the task of redecoration themselves, on the weekends or holidays, of course. I bit my tongue, for from the viewpoint of modern management, to throttle initiative from below would have been unforgivably foolish, particularly since it meant saving money.

Despite our usual Thursday night shift, we gathered on Friday afternoon at three. Even the writers had come. That was all the more remarkable since over time it had become the established practice for them to report in and briefly discuss their columns by telephone, and they were increasingly less willing to enter their texts into the computer themselves. They quoted my motto that the purpose of any article was to fill space between ads. Which is why they never knew if their articles would in fact appear. By June, or July at the latest, they were to be contracting on a fee-for-service basis. That would allow for the hiring of an additional secretary. I had been given a free hand in regard to employees, since fifty dollars a month more or less made no difference.

There were so many of us that there were too few

washable rollers, buckets, putty knives and brushes. It was Saturday before we could go to work in every room. On the following Friday we moved into the kitchen. I gave Tanya and Lyudmila money to buy dishes, silverware, glasses and a coffee machine—an investment, I thought, that would pay off. No sooner had they returned than, as if by prearrangement, everyone unpacked something to eat—and in no time the table was filled, and we drank and talked on into the night.

I attempted to keep a clear head amid all the turmoil, and was determined to maintain this mood for as long as possible. Never before had there been so many suggestions for optimizing workflow and for improving the paper. We set as our goal to publish the next issue from these rooms and used Wednesday, which was an important day for production, for moving in and washing windows. No one was amazed that despite an abnormally high number of ads and a lost day of work, we were finished earlier than usual. Indeed, we could have left for home before midnight on Thursday had there not been problems with our laser printer.

We had finally caught fire! A new life was to begin now at last. I arrived at work around ten and discovered, as always, not only Tanya, our secretary, at work—she had just turned seventeen—but all three other places at the computer occupied. Where before no one had felt responsible for the telephone if Tanya happened to be out of the room, it was often the case now, even more than I liked, that the journalists or the girls from layout, Lyudmila and Irina, would pick up the receiver. The joy and the commitment of each individual employee could be felt even on the other end of the line. Tanya, meanwhile, was spending half the day roving shops and markets, looking for good deals on meat, vegetables, honey, cheese, eggs, butter and the ingredients for borscht, solyanka, pelmeni, pizza, roulades and turnovers. As a secretary, she had practically become superfluous.

I did nothing to stop it, since our midday meal was the indisputable high point of every day. It not only tasted fantastic, but it was cheaper as well, and regular nourishment did everyone good. If there were leftovers, they gave them to me, and that way I managed a second warm meal. Last but not least, *v konze konzov,* as the Russians say, the collective, the team, was forged into a unit by our shared meals. Although, God knows, work was not the only thing we talked about, editorial sessions took care of themselves in this way, there was excellent integration between the ad department and layout, and every suggestion, no matter whether it came from within our operation or from readers, writers or accounts—every suggestion was picked up, developed and seemed to be put into practice all on its own. Even our fee-for-service writers quickly grasped the change in climate and were now only too glad to appear between three and four in the afternoon. As was only fitting, most of them had taken to embellishing our meals with expensive produce that could be had only at exorbitant prices or by waiting in long lines. Which meant that they were not simply tolerated but expectantly awaited, because they might bring an eggplant or some meat or fish one time, and pelmeni the next. An agreement was even reached between smokers and nonsmokers, and was faithfully observed, with no disruption of either work or the cozy atmosphere or, better, shall we say, the homey- ness. The one was based on the other, with the accent merely shifting with the time of day. Our circulation increased noticeably. The firm's management in Ger- many congratulated us on the jolt that had charged the entire team, spoke of the expected upswing and gave me a free hand in awarding bonuses—within appropriate limits, naturally. Rarely had a job given me such satisfaction. Each evening, as the sun stood like an emblem above our building and the Beloselsky- Belozersky Palace opposite took on a red glow, I would smoke a cigarette out on the balcony and gaze proudly down on Nevsky Prospekt at my feet.

This golden age lasted barely three months. In early August I was seized with an uneasiness that at the time I attributed to a combination of causes. Above all, however, I was probably somewhat overworked. For even when the vacation season had reached its peak, the expected summer hiatus never happened and our circulation sank hardly at all, making night shifts nec- essary again—the first in our new quarters—and I postponed my vacation once more. To be sure, it was unwise for me to consider myself indispensable—as I had for a good year—even though the mood of our now smaller team remained relaxed and good.

Sonya's husband, a colonel in the tank corps, had died two years before, whereupon her daughter Polina had moved into the apartment along with her moody, unemployed fiancé—and Sonya was now spending

nights in the office now and then, since her last subway train had left long before in any case, thus sparing
herself a three-hour commute back and forth. When I
arrived of a morning then, she had made tea, dusted
the rooms and washed the dishes.

At the end of September, with vacations now past, I
postponed my own yet again. My uneasiness had not
vanished, on the contrary, it had grown. Although we
were once again at full force and had no greater number of pages to put out than in the months before, the
night shifts continued. After any vacation period there
is an especially great need for talk, and it takes time
for everyone to get accustomed to work again. It is no
different in Germany, either. But when the night shift
began to spill over into Wednesday, it was clear to me
that I must act, particularly since evidently no one
other than myself was upset by this development. I
laid out a schedule that I kept elastic enough but that
nevertheless ended at seven o'clock on Thursday evening. Everyone was to bear some responsibility for
that now.

In the middle of October, when I went to put a new
cartridge in the printer and opened the supply cupboard, I could not believe my eyes. There lay neatly
arranged tablecloths, napkins, bed linens, hand towels, handkerchiefs, dust cloths, cosmetic bags, ladies'
stockings and underwear. Behind vases, place mats, a
mocha service and dessert forks, I found our paper
supply and finally the cartridge.

I took the four ladies aside and demanded an explanation. But they did not understand what there was to
explain. That they had often spent the night here,

indeed were required to do so, I surely knew as much. My new schedule would not change any of that, either, and a little coziness was so nice. All the rest was self-explanatory. They did offer, however, to lay the underwear and whatever else women need for personal hygiene behind the bed linens. I did not even mention the state of the bathroom, which they kept very clean but which somehow reminded me of a beauty salon. Of course, I had nothing against the fact that street shoes were kept in the toilet and that the women ran around in our editorial offices in sandals or house shoes. But whereas at the beginning it had only been four pairs, that number had rapidly doubled.

After this discussion I could not rid myself of the impression that they were whispering about me, and giggling.

However often I summoned up for them the image of earlier days or adroitly promised bonuses set at the very limits of possibility, the extension of working hours grew worse from day to day. Mealtimes, however, had stretched to the point where just about nothing got done between three and six. After that, tea was made and pastries passed around. To be sure, they fulfilled their daily quotas, but that had nothing to do with the number of hours worked. And if I did not want to drive the women home in my own car—which would have taken at least three hours of my time—I could not object to their spending the night in the office. It was too great a risk simply to shove them out the door. Besides, my hands were tied all the more, since all of them, from the secretary to the editor, were paid not by the hour but for punctual

delivery of the paper and in proportion to our circulation. Punctual meant Friday morning at seven. That
now brought them anywhere from seventy to ninety
dollars a month. But you truly could no longer call it
working.

I likewise met with no understanding from Boris
and Shenya, the editors, and Anton, our photographer. As long as the women were doing their jobs and
could pull off keeping house—the turn of phrase
alone said it all—I should be content. The only reason
they themselves didn't spend the night was because
they had families and cars. But since there was nothing
that drew them home, the laxity spread to them as
well. They regularly interrupted their work now to go
to the banya. When they returned, they first had to
have a drink or two—and then they usually fell asleep
at their desks. The women pampered them like heroes.

And yet the newspaper they produced was something to be proud of, even if it did occasionally lack
that final careful touch. I simply didn't know where to
apply the leverage.

What objection could I have to a refrigerator, to a
jury-rigged shower, with a curtain, to carpets in the
offices, to the fold-out sofa they put in the waiting
room, to the bookcases and the reproductions of
views of Petersburg?

One morning early in November, I arrived somewhat earlier than usual and found the women busy
rehanging the red velvet curtains, which I had person-
ally thrown in the garbage when we moved in. The
only sign left of the white blinds were hooks above
the windows. At last the moment for intervention!

The curtains were new, hand-sewn, the material chosen to match the old ones, at least in terms of color. Blinds, I learned, made the room's atmosphere too cold and impersonal. It had taken them only two weeks, they proudly declared, only two weeks from measurement to purchase to the last stitch of the needle. The blinds had been in the way while they were doing the hanging, but naturally they would be put back in place. But couldn't they have told me about it beforehand? It was meant to be a surprise, really it was, a surprise. How could they know I wouldn't be delighted with the curtains, who could have imagined that—not being delighted, even scolding? Sonya's eyes welled up with tears. They had paid for it all out of their bonuses. It wouldn't cost the firm a thing.

Of course, as the boss one always stands alone somehow, excluded from the lives of the others. It's normal, it's justified, and yet this was a new experience for me in Russia. Then again, they accused me of distancing myself more and more from their circle. I no longer accepted invitations, was always the first to get up from the table, wore a glum face, never laughed at a joke, was constantly looking at the clock and certainly no longer praised them for anything, even though the articles, the design, the ads, the service and sales were unrivaled anywhere in the city. Or was I having problems at home?

I am a passionate devotee of the banya, love good food and, it goes without saying, am glad to join in an interesting conversation. But I am accustomed to organizing work as efficiently as possible, in order, then, to enjoy my free time—in the sauna, for all I care, or around a table with others. There is truth in the old adage "Work hard, then play hard," even if it does sound simpleminded.

I was in a dreadful position. Either I went along with this nerve-racking slow motion and just about never got out of the office and home to sleep, or I could just let things slide. And yet a captain should always be the last to abandon ship.

The women no longer went home even on weekends. They cleaned house, did their laundry, took afternoon walks and ate ice cream; some evenings they took in a concert or a movie, sometimes they went dancing. It was always just a short trip back to the office.

Puzzled by their husbands' absence, Boris's and Shenya's wives made a practice of checking on them unannounced. Relieved and happy, they then proceeded to sit down in the kitchen, chattering brightly and praising the cozy atmosphere instead of taking their spouses with them. They, in turn, having finished their work for the day—or having put it off until tomorrow—now began simply to wait for their wives' visits by playing a game of chess.

The other residents of the house took part in the rollicking life of my staff, and would ring the bell pretending that they had run out of salt or lost their keys and had to wait for the wife to return. Of course, they were offered tea, and as long as there were guests, it was considered impolite to work. And when the wife finally did appear with the key, they would chat away for another brief two hours, not without offering their journalistic services as contributors before leaving.

Over time, the honoraria we paid to the neighbors and their relatives would have covered the cost of renovating the stairwell.

Meanwhile I toiled on, in order to imply by my example that there was another way of doing things. I even took over my own typing, which cost me an immense amount of time, what with the Cyrillic keyboard. But it proved a fiasco, like all my other measures. Even counterproductive. Rolled eyes and shrugs were the friendliest reactions. Tanya pointed out my mistakes, and Anton, our photographer, did not think it appropriate for the boss to get involved in work he did not understand. He quoted me: Doesn't matter when you put a newspaper together, what matters is it's good and it's on time.

Whenever I tried to offer an answer, it was as if every thought had been blown from my head. So I found no good argument when they proudly presented a portable television, just to get the latest news, of course—and we were a weekly! The black tomcat that at first had a bowl at our door was now sleeping in the kitchen—it was winter. Or did I want him to freeze to death? The neighbors even rang the bell if Blintchik (that was the cat's name) was sitting outside our door.

One Sunday in early December, I had forgotten to send a fax and stopped by the office in the morning. There was whimpering coming from the waiting room. All four ladies were standing around the sofa, on which an old woman was lying. They hissed at me to be quiet, for heaven's sake, the doctor had already been notified. Irina's grandmother had come for a visit and was not feeling well. She had groaned the whole night, they had hardly slept a wink. The grandmother died on Tuesday—not in the office, thank God. But the women were so distressed that her death came close to seriously endangering the publication of our next issue.

I did not know what to do. My eyes burned, my hands were sweaty, my lungs felt pricked with pins. And when Sonya—whom I had once regarded as my confidante—suggested to me that I really needn't do anything more than sit in the kitchen, drink tea, smoke or go for a walk, and truly had nothing whatever to worry about, I freed myself from her embrace and dashed out of the room. Unfortunately, Blintchik was slinking through the office door just as I slammed it shut. The cat let out a horrible screech and the women came running with a wail.

Less angry than at the end of my tether, I finally reported the situation to the firm's management in my weekly fax. I formulated it cautiously, hinting at the problems. But I had to do it in order to protect myself against the day when the men from Stuttgart would be standing at my door. How would I explain our chaos to them, let alone that I myself was a victim of it?

That same evening—just imagine, it was a Friday— I received a call. I was then connected with the CEO.

"Quiet!" I bellowed across the room, and prepared myself for the worst.

Schafer, with his M.B.A., was not a man for small talk, and after first having to remind himself why he had called, or so it seemed to me, he said curtly that I would be receiving the needed moneys by courier. I should make all the preparations so that the purchase could take place before the year was out—"or do the Russians backdate, too?"

I asked if there was not some confusion here, since I had not asked him for money.

"No? What do you mean?" he replied. The paper wasn't doing badly—and it was never wrong to buy real estate. I was to purchase another apartment but see to it from the start that the work was organized according to Western standards. Efficiency, the basis of leadership in the marketplace.

"Why else would we have sent you?" I heard him say with a laugh.

"And our apartment?" I asked in some agitation.

"Hand it over to the women. Or maybe you want to throw them out?"

I said I didn't; he wished me a pleasant weekend, a merry Christmas and a healthy and prosperous New Year. I wished him the same.

I hung up, and was greeted by the expectant faces of the staff. I said not a word, however, opened the door to the balcony again for the first time in months, stepped out into the peacefully drifting snowflakes and lit a cigarette.

How festively the palaces all around us were lit. How the endless Nevsky shimmered, how it glistened. Gradually the lights blurred. I felt Blintchik rub against my calves.

4

Russia—all you can do is leave it! All week I had been wondering why I was doing this to myself, why I was in this city and not in Paris or Italy. It was as if the people here had only recently come in from the village and didn't know how to walk down a street. They plod along, yelling, shoving, elbowing, spitting. No one says "Excuse me." They pay no attention or just bellow swear words. You have to kick them! And no sooner have you worked your way free than they push you onto a bus or into the path of a car. Or you save yourself by standing flush against a wall like a beggar and don't know what to do next. And everywhere, like some peculiarity of the climate, is this stench of old farmer cheese, embedded filth and cigarette smoke. At the airport, on the bus, in the hotel, on the street—you can't escape it, only the blend changes. Sometimes there is a little gasoline in it, or garlic, or toilet bowls. From courtyard doors drift odds and ends of meals, stairwells reek of piss. In grocery stores the odors hang so heavy that yesterday's heat is still sticking to them. And when it comes to people, you don't know if they have taken on the stink of their surroundings or if it's coming from them.

Except for the bread and tea, hardly anything is edible. Every bite bloats in your mouth, and is another sin against your body. Even the milk is musty, the champagne sugary, the beer sour. No matter where you look, there is nothing that is not dented, defective, mended, crooked, scruffy, askew, loose, dirty, as if it all came from a dump and had just been crudely patched together again. Only imports shine.

The madness of the czars is the only culture they have, but they manage to ruin even that, crap all over it. And all the while they talk about Pushkin, fate and the Volga. Their metal roofs are the hulls of shipwrecks; doors and windows hint that the creatures housed inside do not speak a language—you think you can hear snarls, whimpers and howls. Russians in general seem to have been so conditioned by some lifelong experiment that apathy marches in step with an astounding ingenuity for humiliating others. Everything is contrived to cause people the greatest possible unpleasantness, whether it's a lack of benches, mirrors hung too low, repairs that go on for years or the shopping, which requires standing in line three times for a pat of butter. Functioning toilets are to be found, if at all, only in hotels. Be it a floor monitor, a waiter, a travel guide—they are all permanently offended, foul-tempered, testy, gruff. They speak without even looking up; if you ask them something, they squint as if they are about to spit at your feet. If a woman is beautiful, she can be bought; if a car is new, the owner is a criminal. Never, not in any other country, have I felt so vulnerable, so defenseless. I knew: If something happens to me here, no one will help me. If

I stumble, they'll trample me down, if I scream, they'll rob and strip me. They can spot foreigners at a glance. As if we were a different color. There is hardly any opportunity in daily life to mix with Russians and just stand aside for a moment and watch—and that's what makes travel worthwhile.

For all that, the weather was warm and clear. But the old women, their bodies wrapped in coats and scarves, stood on scraps of cardboard, as if they still had to protect themselves against the cold as they held out bread, sausage and eggs in plastic bags. Beside them littered paper stirred whenever pigeons landed. One of the money changers had taken off his reflective glasses and was sunning himself. A man drained the last drops into his mouth from a beer bottle held high above his head, staggered, stumbled and then knelt down on the warm asphalt behind the kiosks. Others were already lying there asleep. Across the way, under a portico, some schoolgirls were sitting. They pushed the short sleeves of their blouses up over their shoulders and leaned back like the attendants of Aphrodite. A little farther on, in a circle of the park, a redheaded accordion player was singing in front of shaded benches. A woman with a parted wig banged out the rhythm and raised her fists at the end of each verse. "Anarchy, anarchy!" she would cry, until he took up his song again. Listening to them was a woman in black, who suddenly stood on tiptoes and without moving her arms stretched her face toward a chestnut blossom.

At Gostinny Dvor I bought a poppy-seed pastry, and it tasted so surprisingly good that I ate it on the spot. I asked for another, and it, too, was truly excellent. It was fun to give out rubles and actually get something for them. Every second stand offered the same wares, which was practical if you had forgotten something. I watched a saleswoman for a long time. As if blind, she moved her hands across eggs set on tiers of cardboard. If she gets a customer, she first takes the sales slip between thumb and forefinger as if picking up a butterfly by its wings and then slides it down over a giant pin. From there her hands float back across the rows, the eggs already appearing between her fingers like a magician's white balls. Eight eggs, and the motion is repeated. Then her hands come to rest again on the tips of the eggs, as if earth's gravity were transmitted through her palms and fingertips.

On the subway escalator Petersburgers glided past me. Not a woman without a hairdo, makeup and a nice outfit. And the men, one step below them, gazed at them as if at something precious. On the platform was a convivial shoving throng, a kind of collective forward motion. If I could not finish a step and was about to fall, I was promptly able to regain my balance against strangers' shoulders or backs.

When I got to the vegetable market, I walked between rows of vendors who waved to me as if they were fanning themselves. I tried some watermelon and tasted the honey. But their politeness to me was equaled by their cruelty to a beggar woman, whom they drove off, striking at her with canes the moment she touched a fruit. She let out a groan, burying her face in her hands. There was not a spot on her that was not bloodied or scabbed, her black coat was shiny and dragged in the dust. I took two steps toward her, put a ten-thousand-ruble note in her half-closed hand—and retreated before the pungent odor. But at least no one would drive her from his stand now.

She looked at the note for a long time, then stuffed it into her pocket and gaped at me. Instead of heeding the waving hands, however, she bowed before me, blessed me, thanked me, wept, blessed, thanked, babbling with a heavy tongue, her eyes staring wide.

As her fingers brushed my arm, I winced. Slowly she sank to her knees before me, touching my ankles and pressing her brow to my sandals. If I didn't want to step on her, I would have to hold still. I could feel her lips now between the straps. In her gratitude she grasped my calves with both hands, digging in her nails until I swallowed hard in pain. My knees buckled, and I swayed and had to brace myself on her shoulders to keep from falling. In the meantime, the vendors had come out from behind their stalls. But with a shake of the head I stopped them from pulling the old woman away from my feet. She bawled, coughed, yammered.

Without loosening her embrace, she worked her way up my legs, kiss by kiss. To calm her, I patted her head. In the next moment, however, she pressed her face to mine—I tottered and, grabbing at her hair, fell backward and would have landed hard on my back if two men had not caught me and gently lowered me to the ground. Coughing, she crawled on top of me. Although I was having trouble breathing, I tried to calm her and hummed a lullaby. But there was no help for it. Gurgling from exertion, she stretched her neck forward and kissed my chin—and for a moment our lips touched. Then, with a whimper, she rolled off me.

I was close to tears. The voices of the bystanders sounded affectionate and kindly. A young woman in a suit bent down, looked into my eyes and said something in Russian. Others patted my legs, placed kisses on the sides and back of my neck. Filled with the wish to do good, they pressed more closely around me, gave me apples, pears, radishes and *matryoshkas*. Two vendors knelt down, loosened my sandals and washed my feet with their spittle and hair. The melon vendor opened my shirt, button by button, and pressed his heavily ringed hands against my navel. Could I now refuse the others as well without offending them? So I nodded, still uncertain whether I had correctly gauged their mood.

With that they lifted me up stoutheartedly, carried me tenderly to the melon stand and laid me belly down on the quickly cleared wooden table. While they were stripping off my shirt and pants, the melon vendor removed the cap from a black felt marker, checked the color on his thumb and now began writing across my shoulder in short, firm strokes— evidently printed letters. Just when I had become accustomed to the peculiar charm of the strokes, they turned more supple, and I thought I recognized numbers, until suddenly three, four solid flourishes sent a shudder through me—presumably his signature. The melon vendor kissed me between the shoulder blades and crouched down so that I could gaze into his dark eyes. Now I even had his telephone number.

No sooner had the next man—a grandfather who had been selling bundles of chives—reached for the marker than others now began to write letters and numbers on my legs with ballpoint pens. I first tried tightening my muscles to provide as smooth and firm a surface as possible, but then, when several people began writing at once, I got a cramp and gave that up. All the same, I was now enjoying the way they stretched my skin between thumbs and forefingers. The woman in the suit pushed the hair from the nape of my neck. She wrote with an easy, swift hand. I thought I detected exclamation points. It all took place in a happy, free and easy atmosphere, and since there was evidently not enough room, someone pulled off my underpants, too.

Before me rose a mountain of apples, plums, cauliflower, pumpkins, radishes, potatoes, grapes and other fruits of the earth. Right beside them was a pile of the best that the kiosks had to offer: from cigarettes and soft drinks to canned meats and toothpaste, all the way to brassieres and a stewpot.

Finally, the crowd grew so large that they had to turn me over on my back. But now I didn't have to crick my neck to see those sweet faces above me as they pointed first to suitable places to write, then motioned back and forth between themselves and what they were writing, so that I could imprint on my mind the connection between the address and the person. In one or two cases, I gave an encouraging nod to someone who was still hesitating, offered armpits or opened an elbow. So some of them ventured to go as far as my wrists, a few even to my fingers.

At about half past four I indicated that it was high time for me to return to my hotel, since departure was at six—it was already too late for a light supper. A few of them, who had called their friends and neighbors, begged me to be just a little more patient. But there was really nothing I could do.

And now they all said how sorry they were I had so little time left. There was no one who did not expressly invite me home yet again, who didn't want to show me his or her dacha, Lake Baikal or the Arctic Ocean. I fought back the tears, such vast hospitality was embarrassing, for I well knew how little they themselves had to live on. Yes, they even called a second taxi, because not a single gift was to be left behind. Naturally, I promised to come again very soon.

Every morning, when the noisiest time was over, Anna Gavrinina would immerse herself in the melodies of Pushkin, Lermontov, Blok, Mayakovsky, Mandelstam and other poets. Her lips, her forehead and eyebrows mirrored but shadows of the stirring

intonations that seized her mind. Most of all, however, Anna Gavrinina loved to read Gogol from a book
with a black leather binding, only the corners of
which were visible in its newspaper wrapping.

During her ten years as doorkeeper of the Tass
Building on Sadovaya Street, she had made work easier for the employees of that institution, coordinating
keys for those who were entitled to them and provid-
ing information as to who had entered the building,
who was momentarily absent and for whom one
would have to wait yet. Anna Gavrinina would rather
have vanished into thin air than allow any unautho-
rized person to pass through her gate—and she
achieved this solely by virtue of her authority. She
might still have been considered girlish had she not
grown somewhat heavy about the hips.

Ever since the new director had issued his order
that the four women were no longer to provide their
service for twelve hours, but for twenty-four, Anna
Gavrinina had been looking for a new job. That was
not easy at age seventy-four.

At the same time, barely a week after taking over
his new position, the director had brought foreigners
into the building. Anna Gavrinina made a special
effort to make things as pleasant as possible for these
Finns, Americans and later even Germans during their
brief stay in her sphere of responsibility.

Upon sighting one of these foreigners through the
panes of the entrance door, she hastily opened the box
at her right knee, snatched a key from its hook and hid
it in her fist while thrusting out her forefinger. That
was her way of designating the spot for signing in,

while with the other hand she held out the ballpoint. She said "Good morning, mister," or simply *"Päivääi"* or even *"Guten Morgen, mein Herr,"* and opened her fist like a magician. It tickled whenever a foreigner took the key from her open palm.

She had refreshed her German with a dictionary and now brought the two gentlemen to a halt with a loud *"Achtung,"* something she had once been forced to learn as an expression of respect. Unsettled by the word's effect, she avoided the Germans' eyes and looked down at her doorkeeper's desk, where a calendar with a color illustration of the *Aurora* was displayed under plate glass. She would have liked to say something, but the only thing she could think to do was to present them with her little dictionary. She wanted to be a good hostess and hated shortcomings with all her heart.

To be sure, Anna Gavrinina never accepted gifts herself, not even from Germans. What reason could foreigners have to give her presents? It was not Women's Day or Victory Day or even her birthday, the date of which no one here knew in any case. After all, Russians never gave her anything. And that her colleagues accepted such items, indeed spoke of nothing else and even got into arguments over them—she noted all that in silence at every change of shift, the reason for her disdain merely confirmed by their gossip. She did not want to hear any more about it. The gentlemen should lavish their pralines, coffee, or sausages wrapped in transparent foil on the masses. . . .

One day, however—this was after she had become quite accustomed to foreigners—as she was starting her shift, she found on her chair a package wrapped in beautiful pink paper.

"For you," Polina, three years her junior, said as if doling out their food coupons. Standing there with the pink cube in her hands, Anna Gavrinina was immediately wary. Polina shrugged. She herself had actually only been given it by Antonina, the youngest of them. And having offered that information, she left Gavrinina alone. It was Sunday.

Anna Gavrinina had already eaten the second of the sandwiches she had brought when, to her own amazement, she suddenly pulled at the pink ribbon as if at a shoelace.

She was startled by the recklessness with which she had done it, without a thought to what would happen next. She moaned softly, the way she did at night sometimes when she couldn't sleep. Then she laid her book aside and unfolded the paper. It was exactly two in the afternoon.

What she now saw, she had never seen before. Or she had forgotten it. Inside a clear box and bedded in soft pink cotton lay a tiny dark bottle, no bigger than her two thumbnails placed side by side.

Only a shuffling sound in the stairwell frightened her out of her reverie. No one, no editor and no photographer, and definitely not Lilya Petrovna from the Teletype, was to know anything about this. Anna Gavrinina pushed the little bottle onto the shelf under the counter where only she could see it. She didn't want to decide just yet and began, as she did every Sunday, to polish her nails. To dry them, she laid her palms on the desk, not far from the object that she had to think about.

It was well past four when Anna Gavrinina dabbed the perfume on her neck, behind her earlobes and at her wrists. . . . Lost in the fragrance, her eyelids almost closed, she heard a song she recalled now for the first time in a long while. As she sat there, only her shoulders moved. "Ah, Netotchka," she hummed, "sometimes life is beautiful!"

By way of distraction, Gavrinina turned on the television. The fragrance, in its fresh and gentle way, dominated the entrance to the Tass Building. But how long would the contents of this little bottle—which itself must surely be worth a fortune—last, even when used with her customary frugality? She shuddered with unfamiliar happiness at the idea of diluting just one drop of the perfume in water and thereby prolonging this fragrance until the end of her life. She had made her decision and now dozed off, exhausted from the excitement of the last few hours.

The racket, a clanking and rattling at the entrance door, startled her awake, but without any sense of time or place.

Dobrovolsky, the photographer, was making all that noise at the double doors with his large hands and fumbling with his key. The perfume in its little clear box, along with the pink paper and ribbon, was gone.

Dobrovolsky did not even try to deny it, but was putting whatever energy he had left from fighting off Gavrinina into turning the key in the lock and escaping. "What do you need the stuff for?" he gasped. "I thought you didn't accept gifts."

Anna Gavrinina, who now recalled every detail of her happiness, set up a wail that resounded through the old building. The echo of her voice bounced off the walls of the entrance hall, raced up stairways and along corridors.

She threw herself at Dobrovolsky, whose hands had apparently now attached themselves permanently to the doorknob and key and who was protecting his face by ducking his head between his arms. Plunging a hand into the left pocket of the thief's jacket, Anna Gavrinina felt a cigarette lighter—and a little bottle. She would never let go of it again! She clutched both the perfume and the lighter so hard that Dobrovolsky, who was holding her by the wrist with his left hand, was unable to open her fist with his right. He crushed his broad thumb against each of Gavrinina's knuckles; she groaned in pain but did not yield and snapped at Dobrovolsky's arm with her teeth. For that he gave her a blow to the temple, yanked her around, trying to bang her closed fist against the wooden door, and . . .

At last, there on the far side of the glass door, they saw the new director.

He had come to show a colleague from Moscow, with whom he had studied at one time, the new furnishings in his redecorated office.

With her left hand and a kick Gavrinina opened the door and, sobbing, raised her arm to the director. To the stern demand that an end be put to this circus at once, Gavrinina and Dobrovolsky both gave loud assent, without either abandoning his or her position.

He went on crushing her fingers, while her dark red nails clawed into the balls of his hands. She was back to defending her left hand with her right.

The director, taking affront in the presence of his Moscow friend, grabbed hold now with both hands. But even he could not loosen the knot. He was instantly and painfully caught up in the struggle, so that all three were like a savage, raging rat's nest there in the entrance of the Tass Building. Without anyone letting go and amid repeated interruptions of curses, the following explanations were offered: Dobrovolsky the photographer had bought this perfume for his wife at Lancôme's on Nevsky Prospekt, which he was ready to prove at any time, and that lighter there, only the tip of which was visible—everyone here knew it was his. He had wanted to show the perfume to Gavrinina, but she had gone completely crazy and in a fit of senility had claimed the gift as her own, although she had no use for it whatever. Anna Gavrinina wailed and stammered that the perfume belonged to her. The director only had to smell her neck or behind her earlobes, or here, here on her arm, and the truth would come to light.

But as if he had memorized his role in what little leisure time he had, the new director barked at her, asking whether she knew whom she was dealing with here . . . and what it was she had just asked him to do—and joined in trying to bend back her fingers. Gavrinina was no match for this attack. She gave up, and from her opened hand both the lighter and the little bottle dropped to the floor. The glass burst. Gavrinina fainted.

The ball of her right hand was bleeding so badly that it had to be bandaged as she lay still unconscious on the tile floor. Then they sent her home.

She did not appear for work again, and no one knew what to say. She had vanished into thin air. Only the fragrance in the entrance still reminded the photographer and the director of Anna Gavrinina. But by autumn it, too, smelled like the rest of the building, and they were both rid of an unpleasant memory.

I finally gave in to Oleg Davidovitch's entreaties. I was tired of his calls pressuring me to spend the weekend with him and his family at their dacha. We had met only twice, with someone introducing us both times, had tried both times to have a conversation, and both times had fallen silent, twirling our empty glasses in our hands.

Although he was the boss of the largest car dealership in Petersburg, Oleg Davidovitch—I was asked simply to call him Oleg—did not have a dealer's car.

"What am I to do?" he asked, giving a melancholy smile. What was he to do with two shiploads of Jeeps and Chryslers stuck in customs?

And so he ordered daily general cleanups, had flags, pennants and posters hung first here, then there, and played with his stopwatch. And he made plans for his weekends. Which is also why he never forgot to phone me and praise an outing in the Russian country-side. One simply had to experience it: that air, what berries and mushrooms, and then the colors of the foliage. . . .

I first saw Natalya Borissovna, Oleg Davidovitch's wife, sitting between their two daughters, ages eleven and twelve, in the backseat of a black Volga. She was very beautiful and said nothing, while Ira and Anya demonstrated their knowledge of English, which they were acquiring in a private school.

"You know . . ." each of the girls' perfectly intoned sentences began, and Oleg Davidovitch, who spoke no English, seemed to relax at the sound of their voices.

We had been driving for two hours when Natalya asked, "Do you prefer Tolstoy or Dostoyevski?"

We turned off the highway. There were hardly any other cars, and after another hour, with asphalt long since behind us, the road turned to sand. Despite the occasionally hard ride, the girls had fallen asleep in Natalya's arms, and with his head pressed to the wind-shield as if in fog, Oleg Davidovitch stared at tracks overgrown with grass and wildflowers. Through the open windows I could smell the resin-rich air, warm and bright as only early September can be. When a jolt that could be felt clear up into the headrests silenced the motor, I listened to the encircling still-ness. It was as pure as the sky, and yet just another way to hear sounds. I would have loved to get out. But then the car swayed ahead again between birch trees, so gently that I thought I could feel the grass at my feet.

Oleg Davidovitch talked about his father-in-law, whom I would soon meet. Boris Sergeyevitch spent the snow-free months at the dacha and lived on potatoes and dried mushrooms, which were his favorite foods anyway. In addition to which, he had a supply of cheese. Natalya pointed over my left shoulder to a cottage emerging at the far end of a clearing. The back of her hand accidentally grazed my neck.

Boris Sergeyevitch, a monstrous alarm clock in his left hand, put his arm around his only daughter and then greeted me as the long-heralded guest. His face had a few creases, but they were so irregular that I took them for scars. Oleg Davidovitch unloaded the luggage, deftly clutching under his arms whatever he could not grasp by a handle. There was nothing left for me to carry. When I went to remove the key from the trunk, Boris Sergeyevitch shook his head. "No one ever goes this far astray!"

He knelt down and placed the alarm clock under the car.

"To keep the martens away," Natalya explained, and, linking her arm in mine, led me up five wooden steps to the verandah. I admired the wood carving of the ornate shutters, the flower boxes and pots of plants that were set out along the railing and sent tendrils all the way down to the meadow. Boris Sergeyevitch banged his fist against the planks. "The only good work is your own work!" Then he showed me the dacha. In addition to a large room with a kitchenette, there were just two small bedrooms. One of them was his, and Natalya, moving like a ballerina, carried the girls' things into the other. Ira and Anya ran hand in hand down to the brook that meandered past nearby.

That evening we roasted potatoes on an open fire. Boris Sergeyevitch taught his granddaughters how not all birds go to sleep at once, but rather each species at its own time.

"Now the finches have fallen silent," he said, "and soon the robin redbreasts will follow. Then the buntings." He cut slices from a cheese and nibbled the tidbits from the blade of his heavy pocketknife. The trees merged into blackish masses. The first stars appeared in the dark blue sky. Here and there a robin still chirped. Somewhere an oriole called mournfully. Boris Sergeyevitch talked about the price of yogurt, sausage and cars in the Brezhnev years.

"Are there a lot of old people in the city?" he asked. I nodded.

"Do people have to eat if they want to live?"

"Yes!" Anya and Ira replied both at once.

"And where do these old people come from, if everything was as bad as they claim? From other countries perhaps?" He was thinking of building a fireplace inside the dacha, Boris Sergeyevitch informed his daughter, so that he would never again have to set foot in the city.

"And when the road is open again come April, you'll have frozen to death or the wolf will have got you!" Natalya's blanket had slipped from her shoulders.

"Bah!" With his heel Boris Sergeyevitch thrust a log deeper into the fire. "Our kind can't freeze!"

Oleg Davidovitch, who was wearing a cap because of the cool evening, reported how he had found a job for Grandfather one winter—as a doorman in a foreign-exchange hotel.

"Not a week, and he was fired!" Oleg Davidovitch said, laughing and massaging his knees.

"Why not, why shouldn't I tell about it?" he cried, turning to Natalya. Boris Sergeyevitch had performed his tasks as spelled out in the job description. He had allowed no one into the hotel who could not prove he was a guest, and had only grown more furious with each raise in the bribe.

"Ran me off, go ahead and say it, they ran me off!" Boris Sergeyevitch bellowed with agitation. "The dogs!"

"No matter how well you feed the wolf, he always has his eye on the forest," Oleg Davidovitch said, and pushed the hair back under his cap.

"Dogs!"

"Papa, please!" Natalya rested her head on her father's shoulder. The girls tossed hot potatoes from hand to hand.

Suddenly there was a rustling in the forest, the black treetops bowed low to the sky, something was coming toward us—the gust tore into the fire. The children screeched, Natalya ducked, Boris Sergeyevitch fell back, his legs twitching. I had jumped up. Oleg Davidovitch shoveled sand onto the flaming logs. The girls were standing behind Natalya now, blowing the ashes from her hair. Then they went to wash up in the brook. Until they returned, we smoked.

"That was autumn," Oleg Davidovitch said. Now we men walked down to the water.

Upon returning to the house, Boris wished us a good night and vanished into his bunk. It was already dark in the children's room. Three wooden cots had been set up between the table and the window, and Natalya was lying on the middle one, reading a magazine held over her head with both hands. The sleeves of her nightshirt had slipped down. She had wrapped a towel around her wet hair. I thanked Oleg Davidovitch and Natalya Borissovna for their hospitality. And the first evening came to an early end.

I cannot say how long I slept or what awakened me, whether it was the men's snoring, the moonlight or the splits Natalya was doing. She was lying on her back and gazing at me, as if she had nothing to do with the leg that reached from her cot to mine. Her toes were stroking my shin and knee. Without moving, I watched the inside of her thigh as her foot inched higher and higher. "Don't be afraid, no one will wake up here," she said as loud as if we had never stopped talking, and threw her blanket off.

Oleg Davidovitch only needed to stretch out his arm to grab me. He grunted, sniffed and pursed his lips in his sleep. Natalya, her hands on my butt now, paid no attention. Oleg Davidovitch found his rhythm again and went back to snoring. I held her head. Her hair was still damp and smelled of smoke and shampoo. The cot squeaked dreadfully. And yet the greater my fear that he might wake up, the deeper I felt her fingernails dig. The cot did not collapse under us, or at least we just managed to avoid that.

Taking deep breaths, Natalya rubbed my back. Then she fell asleep. I was crouching between the cots and was pulling her blanket up over her shoulders when I thought I saw Oleg Davidovitch wink across at me.

The next morning we had breakfast on the verandah. It was as if I had never not been part of the group. Evidently no one had noticed anything.

No sooner were we done than Boris Sergeyevitch shouldered his best basket, inserting strips of felt under its straps. Oleg Davidovitch pulled a club, its handle smooth and shiny with use, from under the stairs. I was to accompany them. Natalya stayed behind with the children by the brook. As we said good-bye she slipped a little knife into my breast pocket, for mushrooms.

There was not even a footpath worn across the meadow strewn with buttercups. There were scattered birch trees. Yet when I stopped to turn around, we were already entirely surrounded by tree trunks glimmering white against the yellow-orange of their foliage and the dark green of the grasses. Pink gossamer drifted over our faces. I could feel Natalya's foot and her hands, I knew what would be on her mind as she built little dams with the girls or read to them.

I kept close behind the old man, the thick veins visible on his calves. I never heard him breathe, but he did spit now and then. Whereas Oleg Davidovitch was panting all the heavier behind me. Whenever I turned around, he lowered his eyes. His stalking gait, as if his legs began just below his shoulders, struck me as odd, and the smile that usually greeted my every glance had vanished as we set out.

Gradually beech, ash and oak became mixed with the birch. We walked through dells whose slopes were covered with ferns. The ponds at their deepest point attracted every animal imaginable. We passed boletus mushrooms larger than any I had ever seen. I could not help myself, I stepped out of line to harvest a couple splendid specimens. Both men acted as if they had not noticed. I quickly caught up again and passed Oleg Davidovitch. He did not honor my find with so much as a glance. There were hardly any birches now, but the trees stood more densely. It seemed to grow dark in the middle of day. A lark had been silhouetted against the sky as we set out. Now I was startled by the cries of crows taking flight. It was not long before the old man had to bend aside branches and boughs with both arms for us to make any progress at all. As they snapped back from his shoulder basket, they almost struck me. I threw the mushrooms away. Oleg Davidovitch wiggled his hands in annoyance: I should move on and not keep turning around.

If we had any goal I was not aware of it. At some point we stopped to rest, right beside three large anthills. We had no provisions. The old man unfolded some sugar cubes from a dirty handkerchief and laid one on each anthill. "When the sugar is gone, we'll move on!" Propping his basket against a pine tree, he sat down between two roots and closed his eyes. Oleg Davidovitch stretched out beside him. The ground was damp. The first ants were straying up my arm.

I awoke only because Oleg Davidovitch was tugging at my pants leg. With a finger to his lips, he pointed with his other hand at a fox, padding along among the trees nearby, his pointed muzzle close to the ground. I saw one last wag of his rusty red brush, and then he was gone.

"He's heading straight for the trap!" Oleg Davidovitch dusted off his pants as he stood up. He was smiling again at last. There was nothing left of the sugar cubes. And the old man was nowhere to be seen.

I had trouble keeping up with Oleg Davidovitch, and when he suddenly stopped I bumped into him hard. There he was again, the fox. But there was a sheep trotting beside him now. It tossed its head and, seeing us, shied and galloped clumsily down the little slope that we had just made our way up. The fox scurried soundlessly after it.

"That can bode no good," Oleg Davidovitch said. Then, making a funnel of his hands, he put them to his mouth: "Haaahooooo? Haaahooooo?" "Haho, haho," I called somewhat awkwardly in the brief pauses. He laid an open hand behind one ear and began circling like a radar dish. We listened and called again and again, until the old man appeared, not very far off at all. He was trying to run but limped, and since it was an uphill climb, he made only slow progress. He rowed with his arms, he fought for air and pointed with his thumb back over his shoulder.

"Wolf, wolf," he managed to bark, "just now, a young one!" A short club rolled around in his basket as he cast it aside. Oleg Davidovitch stepped on a branch, broke it off and tossed it at my feet. Then we ran off after the old man, slid down the hill and landed near a boulder. The old man motioned for us to stay close behind. Above all, not one word! Every step had to be planned now if we wanted to get out of this forest safe and sound. With his club he pointed to a spot in the underbrush, a stone's throw away.

I had never before seen a wolf in its natural habitat. Its pelt was partly black and thick, partly a lustrous gray. It was trying to bring its muzzle around to a hind paw, which was caught in the trap and bleeding. Only after we had crept closer did it pick up our scent and fling itself around. The trap, which held it pinned to the spot, rattled.

The old man moved tentatively forward, each step smaller than the last, trying to get as close as possible to the circle in which the animal was still able to move. He let his club whistle in the air a few times. Blinking excitedly, Oleg Davidovitch jostled up close beside him. The old man's first blow landed on the young wolf's snout. With a gurgling sound the animal snapped and sunk its bared teeth into the wood. The old man tugged at the other end of the club, but suddenly he stumbled, let go and screamed. Oleg Davidovitch yanked him back by the shoulders. In the next moment the old man reached for my branch, grabbing it with both hands. The wolf let out a yowl. As if in a convulsion, it laid a trembling paw across its bleeding eye. Oleg Davidovitch struck a blow that began from his hip. The wolf lurched to one side, could find no footing, then managed to stand up again, panting, rattling the iron. Now the men flailed away at it, taking turns like two blacksmiths, aiming at the muzzle, ears, hind legs, spine, neck, ribs. No matter how savagely the wolf tossed about, each blow found its mark. I heard only soft whimpering and the thud of the clubs descending on the twitching animal. The blows kept up even after it was long dead. Then the old man pulled out his heavy pocketknife.

Oleg Davidovitch sent me back for the basket. It had grown darker now. When I returned, the trap was open. Next to it lay something small, bright red, bloody. The old man tossed the pelt into the basket. Oleg Davidovitch hoisted it onto his back for him. They both seemed nervous and in a hurry. "Quick, before the bear comes!"

I laughed to disguise my own revulsion. Angered by this, the old man spat at my shoes. His hand took a swipe at the air in front of my face. Oleg Davidovitch handed him the short club, and he limped off.

It thundered in the distance. A storm was moving over the treetops toward us. When the rain finally burst, the lightning and thunder were very close. The old man was spitting more and more often now. He cringed at every bolt of lightning. If I stopped for even a moment, Oleg Davidovitch pushed me on ahead. I saw everything around us as if through a scrim. We could have drunk from the air. My shirt had become heavy. I was just reaching for the knife in my breast pocket when a bolt struck right overhead. There was a cracking up in the branches, twigs and leaves plummeted, tree trunks scraped, birds screeched, and from far off came growling as if bears were indeed leaving their dens. And then, with a ghastly roar and a thud, a bolt shook the earth. A broken branch struck my neck and shoulders.

The growling ceased. No lightning, no thunder, the pelting rain stopped. The silence was terrifying.

As if searching for something under a tree trunk, the old man lay on his belly, his basket beside him. His arms were spread wide, the palms of the hands turned up. The pelt was draped over his shoulders. Oleg Davidovitch was standing beside the corpse. His lips trembled, he wept, now and then he wiped his sleeve across his eyes and nose. Or was he laughing?

"Let me be," he said, without turning his eyes from the ants searching for a path through the brown pine needles. I heard rustling in the treetops, smelled the churned-up soil and watched now as a gray woolly beard began to cover Oleg Davidovitch's cheeks, chin and neck. Soon he would sink to his knees, stretch out on the ground, there to be covered like a stone by moss, grasses, shrubs. Then I noticed his right arm moving slowly higher. Above the bloodied ball of his hand, his extended fingers, as if pushed by a gentle breeze, were playing an instrument only they could feel—and it seemed to me as if each chord struck was meant to echo into infinity. I turned around and ran.

Night had fallen when I reached the dacha. The full moon coated everything in its chalky light. Bruises and scrapes told me that I must have taken a number of falls. My knuckles were bleeding. Apparently I had run without stopping. My lungs hurt and I could barely keep back my nausea. All I could see of the house was its silhouette, the windows were dark. I still hadn't noticed anything when I took the few steps up to the verandah and broke through a rotted plank.

I first missed the reflection of moonlight in the windowpanes. They were broken. The shutters were missing or dangling askew. The door had been forced open. I could feel the moss under my hands. I could see stars through the rafters. I thought I had stumbled on some house deserted during the war. But here were the five steps, the carved flower boxes. Natalya had leaned against this post and laughed as she said good-bye. The brook had become a mere trickle, flanked now by the mountain ranges of its former banks.

Finally, I saw the Volga. It was only a few steps away, just where Oleg Davidovitch had parked it. I groped my way back down the stairs, limped over to the car, huddled against its taillights and wept. I stroked the metal with my cheeks, my hands, and breathed in the delicate fragrance of gasoline. The ticking of the alarm clock was calming. I carefully took the key from the trunk lock. The Volga started. I was amazed at the resolve with which my right hand released the brake and pulled the choke, at the assurance with which it pushed the gearshift forward. Lights and wipers both worked, there was even a spray of water. My body remembered all the necessary motions. The car pulled away, I shifted to second gear, turned on the brights and steered for the clearing. I knew for sure now.

7

I've already told this story so often, Valentina Sergeyevna said. First to the director, then to the mayor, and he sent the newspaper to me. Then came the other papers and television. Foreigners, too. The story just grows and grows. I lived it all, from the start, and I'm truly the only person who has any right to claim that—I saw it all happen with my own eyes. I've thought so often now, Well, it's finally over, this is the end of the story. Then it just went right on.

I think about it a lot and try to keep up with things so that I can offer a true picture, because people are constantly wanting to talk to me. I have nothing against that, just the opposite, because the director still wants to let even more of us go. But they ask for me so often—so he would have to tell them where I live, since they all want to hear it from me, from Valentina Sergeyevitch, and then I could tell them that I really didn't want to leave, but that he threw me out. As time has gone on, I've gotten used to speaking. That comes all by itself. Sometimes I even make a little money from it, the only one of us twelve who does—two at the cashier's desk and ten responsible for security. I'm fifth in seniority. When I started here,

eight years ago in July, Konstantin Dmitritch was still
deputy director and Yelena Ivanovna was our boss.
She hired me and never threatened to let anybody go.
There was no glass over the icons back then. That was
first done on Konstantin Dmitritch's orders, because it
didn't end with just one scribble, but people kept
scrawling more and more names on the icons. It was a
plague. Even though we kept an eagle eye out. Nothing could possibly happen. And then suddenly there it
was again, another scribble. I was afraid to even check,
was forever finding some new scrawl. Like up in lookout towers. Once the metal even got bent. That's why
there were no bonuses, for anybody. They just pecked
and pecked at me and didn't even apologize when the
whole thing got cleared up. Konstantin Dmitritch
took a closer look himself, and what did he discover?
Always the same names: Vanka and Anton, Anton and
Vanka. Always written different, sometimes just two
letters, $A$ and $V$, $V$ and $A$, a monogram. Vanka was the
janitor, and our furnace man was named Anton. Konstantin Dmitritch didn't catch on right off. They said
they weren't the ones, and so he let them go for
drunkenness. Afterwards the glass got put on. Konstantin Dmitritch has threatened to let us go, too. All
you do is close one eye, and he's standing there. But
what's there to guard? It isn't our fault nobody comes.
Used to be, the collective farms came. Oh well.

May 11 was a Wednesday. We had no visitors at all,
because the hotel was being renovated, so not even
foreigners. When I saw him I knew right off he was a
tractor operator or the like. Sometimes you really
have a sixth sense. I said to myself, He's definitely not

local. But we were all happy to have somebody visiting our museum. He stopped in front of every picture. You pay attention to people like that, I didn't know him, though. Alya Petrovna winked at me, the way she always does when she likes some man. She kept on winking and winking, that's how caught up he was in the pictures, and I said to myself, We'll see if he doesn't stay longer in here with me. I gave him a good look, from top to bottom. I was sitting like always, right here. And he was standing there, in front of that picture across the way. So that I was watching him from behind, and then he stood over there, and I could get a look at him from the side. A strapping man, straight as a rail, around sixty or so, definitely not a drinker. And I said to myself, too, that I'd gladly exchange my Pasha for him. Time passed, and it was clear to me that he was staying at least as long as with Alya Petrovna. And while I'm watching him, from the side, he takes another step forward and—he just cringes, his whole body cringes, like when there's a loud bang. Then he stood still, gave me goose bumps, I was so startled. What's he doing? Slowly, very slowly he bent forward, like he was bowing. Can't he read the description, I ask myself, eyes that bad, but by then he already has one knee on the parquet, then the other, and is kissing the glass, crosses himself two, three, four times and starts muttering, but not so you could understand a thing. Of course, I don't know what to do. This has never happened, this is unique. I didn't say a word and just went on sitting there, to keep Alya or Georgiyevna from coming in. Let him kneel, I thought, let him go right on kneeling, he's in good hands here.

It was eerie all the same, a grown man kneeling in a museum and mumbling. And then he slides forward, toward the glass, inches closer and closer. By God, I swear I stood up at that very moment. He's way too close, even with the glass. So I stand up—and it happens. A horrible noise, let me tell you. It went faster than I can describe it, the way his head fell forward, his forehead hitting the glass, bong, and then again, bong and crash. Good God, I thought, this will get me fired. And he's kneeling there, glass everywhere, and kissing the icon, and his lips are bleeding. Alya said I was screaming, till she grabbed hold of me. The glass was broken, no help there. His lips were bleeding, and then he kissed it again, and his lips weren't bleeding anymore, I'd swear to that in court! At first, very badly, and then not at all, after the second time, truly not at all. All of a sudden. And he was weeping, the tractor operator was weeping, and he wasn't drunk!

Alya fetched Pyotr, the new janitor, but he ran to the police and they got hold of Konstantin Dmitritch, who was working at home. The tractor operator prayed and wept, wept and prayed and knelt there like a fool the whole time in the broken glass. And then, faster than you could even see him do it, he kissed the Madonna again, not Her feet, no, on the face, stood up, and the women all ran off like he was some black savage. They don't want to hear about that now. But I had to stay behind. He bowed to me, I bowed back, and then him again, then me. And now he started in: During the night, a woman had appeared to him, she had called him, a tractor operator, to the district capital and waved to him. Actually, he had wanted to wait another night to see if she would come again, because you couldn't get off work just like that in May. But then he hadn't been able to close his eyes and couldn't stop thinking of this woman. So come morning he had got up and caught the train here. For two hours he had sat in the *stolovaya* at the station, staring into every woman's face and calling himself an ass for trusting his dreams. And now he had found her again: our Madonna with the Savior on Her lap. I just wanted to kiss Her hand, he said, the hand She waved at me, that golden hand. And the instant I touch Her hand, my lips start bleeding, he said, but Her hand is warm and soft, nothing like gold at all. And I knew, he says, if I kiss Her on the mouth, then my lips will stop bleeding. And that's how it was. The policeman wouldn't let him kneel in the broken glass again. But nobody could stop him from weeping. There was not a fleck left on his lips. But the Savior on the Madonna's lap was bloody.

Then they took the tractor operator to Konstantin Dmitritch's office. I had to sweep up the glass, as a punishment. He threatened to throw me out, Konstantin Dmitritch did. If this wasn't grounds, he said it twice, if this wasn't grounds. Thursday was quiet, and I said to myself, Valentina, if Konstantin doesn't call you in today, nothing's going to happen tomorrow. And that's how it was.

That Friday three women came in. They greeted me like a neighbor, crossed themselves, knelt in front of the icon with the missing glass and prayed. I thought, This can't be, but then I thought, too: Thank God they can't break it again! They kissed the golden hand, the Madonna and the Savior. What could I do? I sounded the alarm. Everything went faster than on Wednesday, and the women paid a fine.

They were back on Saturday, laid an envelope on my chair, and everything went as usual. They crossed themselves, knelt down and then crowded forward around the icon to kiss it—I gave the alarm. Scared now, they huddled together and prayed until the police came. At first they were going to take them to jail. But Konstantin Dmitritch talked the police out of it and just banned the women from the museum.

On Sunday a bus arrived from Dubrovka. I counted exactly forty people, thirty-seven women and three men, who wanted to see our Madonna. Neither the policeman nor Konstantin Dmitritch could do anything about it. My Pasha sure would have come up with something. The visitors for the Madonna paid the entrance fee that Konstantin Dmitritch set—we started at seven thousand, half of what I was getting paid at the time, and that went for everybody, no discounts. Not even for veterans. Konstantin Dmitritch stopped running around and shouting and summoned a policeman—who took the tickets.

Did we ever have visitors now! Soon it was a hundred a day, then a hundred and fifty, up to three hundred on weekends. By June at the latest, we were taking in a million rubles a day, Sundays two to three million, depending on the weather.

But don't go asking me about the miracles. A person can't have eyes everywhere. Anyway, they often didn't come true till later. And then, too, suddenly people were reporting so many things about us. A blind woman could see again, and another one could walk. Even run-over cats were coming back to life. All I ever got out of it was the botheration when somebody fainted.

I never kissed our Madonna, not even in secret after closing, like Alya. Alya said our Madonna was warm and soft, just like a person. But Alya didn't become a believer, even if she did like incense. The fire warden said candles were forbidden, of course. When we saw somebody unpacking a candle, Vassily, our policeman, would blow his whistle till the candle got put away. Cameras weren't even allowed in the museum, but that really affected only tourists. Konstantin Dmitritch banned singing as well. So they hummed. Do you know what that's like? That humming in your ears the whole livelong day. I could still hear it when I dropped off to sleep.

I've already told all this to the mayor and then to our paper. There are lots of pictures of me and Konstantin Dmitritch. Konstantin Dmitritch went on trips and gave lectures. He often met with the priests who came to visit us now, too. Before long there was one standing beside me every day, listing out loud, over and over, all the miracles our Madonna had performed. For Easter they were even planning some big event with the patriarch. We were supposed to help out with security.

Yes, and then there were all the people who wanted to buy our Madonna, starting with the tractor operator on down to Russians from America, and some from Finland. Of course, the Jews were hot for it, too, just like always when there's something shiny. But we were a state museum after all. And art belongs to the people.

By now the miracle in hall eight had made us so famous even beyond the Leningrad area that there were demands that we close our museum.

The art historians were embarrassed because they couldn't date our Madonna, they could find no mention in the archives of when the museum had come by the Madonna and from where. Some of them said that it was not painted by human hands but had fallen from heaven, as the true portrait of the Mother of God. And therefore it belonged in a church. But the mayor and Konstantin Dmitritch didn't believe that and opposed the idea.

We got bonuses again now, and there was something going on every day. And I was a little bit famous, too. And that's how things would stay, I thought. The city was getting something out of it, our museum was—and this time, so were we.

But one morning the Madonna and the Savior were gone. I mean their faces had disappeared, were all black, clear to the edge. When I reported it to Konstantin Dmitritch, he was very nice to me and said that it was damage wrought by time. And then he said that we could forget about our showpiece, and left. That made a strong impression on me. I don't know what to say. It didn't matter to people. More and more came, till the line for hall eight wound through the whole museum, and I was normally an hour late getting home. They knelt before two round black holes and prayed and kissed any spot they could find on the metal.

When I thought about the future, my only thought was that someday not everybody who arrived each morning to see the icon with the two black holes and the golden hand would get in to see it. I assumed we'd soon have to start giving out numbers. That's what I thought about the future.

And now I'm certain you want to hear what I have to say about the robbery. But all I can say is, one evening it was still here and the next morning it was gone. I wept, I had gotten so used to our Madonna, it was so beautiful when so many people came. When I heard that it was in the cathedral, I was relieved. Everybody thought: The police won't allow that, the state won't, that's robbery. The fairy tale about it making its way to the church on its own because it belongs there, that it fled from us to seek protection there—you can't tell the police a story like that. But they don't lift a finger, and even the mayor just says that he knows all about it and Konstantin Dmitritch has started some things that he can't talk about. Of course, the news was all over town right away, and there were crowds standing clear outside the church. Everybody was saying it was a miracle. But nobody was allowed to see the Madonna. Not till Sunday, they said. That Sunday, with everybody waiting, they said She wished to be shown only on Easter and Pentecost. You can imagine how people liked that. Porfiri, the priest, couldn't even finish before they collared him. There was no help for it then. And now he has to stand there on Sundays and hold the icon out for people to kiss. I'd say people were better off when the Madonna was here with us. A lot of people say that.

Konstantin Dmitritch just keeps getting more and more famous, since we were the first museum with a Madonna who performs miracles. The others can say what they like. But for me it's meant that my job has been on the line—still is! For even if what they say is true, that Konstantin Dmitritch goes to church and crosses himself, he hasn't got any better. He still wants to let me go. Vanka and Anton have forgotten me. They're rich now and even more famous than Konstantin Dmitritch, because they're the only ones with a photograph of our Madonna, one from earlier, when it was still all in one piece. You can even see the scribbling: Vanka and Anton and *A* and *V*. The tractor operator works for them and sells the copies. He gets room and board in return, doesn't want anything more than that. They can charge as much as they want for their little pictures, people still buy. And the art historians are already calling our Madonna the Anton-Vanka icon, for simplicity's sake, or so they say. Well, we'll just have to wait and see what comes of it all.

In the bottomland between the new high-rises, the fog held on longer. Only the screeching of the gulls found its way across to where the new blocks of buildings must be, lost now in the mist of sea wind and frost. At times you heard buses approach and the jolting of empty trucks. As long as you could see the gulls, they circled silently, screaming only when they were in the fog again.

Petyushina had been watching this for twenty minutes now, ever since the way to the bus stop—the path between the long block on Artists' Prospekt and the first block of a new, still nameless street—had been obstructed. The gulls flew so low in this canyon that everyone ducked his head at the beat of their wings. And then you heard their cries emerge again from the fog.

"Whenever it freezes," Petyushina said bitterly. She had an empty bag wrapped around her wrist. "Whenever it freezes, this happens! It's a scandal!" she cried, and looked around to see if someone might not be nodding in agreement. But they all stood there in silence, watching the spectacle taking place between the twelve-story buildings.

"We should call the police!" Petyushina began again, and took a few steps.

"Will you stop!" a fellow up toward the front called out, the only man not wearing a cap. The wind blew a strand of hair off his forehead, but it fell back when he tilted his head to one side.

"Are we going to call in the police or not?" she asked again, turning to her right, where the crowd was densest.

"Pooh! You can see for yourself how hard it is for them on ground like this, the way they skid. They won't easily find their feet on this!" scolded an old man only a few steps away, whom Petyushina recognized from the subway station where every evening she sold sausage, bread, eggs and other things.

"You were here last Monday, just four days ago, weren't you, when we all voted and decided no police?" The old man spat.

Petyushina put her blue-and-white woolen mittens to her mouth and coughed.

"But maybe they won't shoot?" a woman to her left interjected.

"That's what I'm saying!" Petyushina added. "Don't always assume the worst, times have changed!"

"Let them live, let them live!" scoffed a man in his mid-forties right behind her, and batted at the tassel on his cap. "Our police obey every order, splendid lads, really, splendid! Get it into your head, my girl, you're not in France or Denmark!"

"What do you mean France and Denmark?" asked a young woman clutching fast to several folders.

"If Mitterrand's dog runs away, every Frenchman checks his backyard to see if the pup isn't pissing on a tree, and the Danes are no different if it's the queen's dachsie," the man in the tasseled cap replied. "And you want to get our police involved? That's my point!"

"Just be patient," an alto voice admonished Petyushina. "Enjoy the sight, the elegant movements, such noble creatures!"

"Yes, and if it's too much, then just go round by the other route!" Petyushina exploded. "But we can't go back, clear around the block, then the swamp, the ditches, that fence, all those bushes, across to the kindergarten and up the street, all to get to the bus stop. Those people on Pereshovski are just waiting for that! Ask Alya Mikhailovna! They took everything she had, everything!" She coughed again.

"Do you have a job to get to, or do we?" the same woman asked now in a shriller voice, ducking and watching the gull fly on.

"You try living on a pension!" Petyushina cried in outrage. "Can a person live on a pension, or does she die on it, dearie? Just try buying a pair of boots with it!"

"Shut up, or I'll tell about the profit you make on your sausage and bread. Thirty percent!" the old man shouted, holding his forefinger under her chin. "Thirty and more!"

"Tell everybody," she sang out, and clapped her hands, "tell them all, for heaven's sake, please, go right ahead—"

The old man gave Petyushina a slap on the back of her head that made her dentures jump. "What do you need a bus for anyway!"

"Well, finally!" said the woman with the alto voice, who had put a couple of yards between herself and Petyushina.

"So we still do have some men in the state of Denmark!" The guy without a cap grinned.

"You can just go and—"

"Ohoho," said the guy without a cap, and laughed.

Petyushina wept softly and balled up the bag in her hands like a handkerchief.

"You act as if there's nobody here but you!" a man called out, and flailed his arms so excitedly that it looked as if he were trying to fly.

"There are maybe a hundred people here, but four

or five start acting crazy, and word gets out that the people from Artists' Prospekt are rowdies, but ninety-five of us standing perfectly still, not saying a word, not turning our heads, simply enjoying the sight, nobody ever says they saw that!" Outrage choked off his voice. His outstretched arms would not come to rest.

"That's life," Petyushina sobbed. The gulls screeched. Slowly the fog began to lift.

"Somebody should call a television station," suggested a new arrival who had worked his way to the front.

"You don't get it, don't get it at all," someone said calmly. You could see the bus stop now.

Then came the whistle. No one knew from where. And now the Great Danes turned in their tracks and raced to the corner of the building, from behind which two girls appeared, leashes slung around their necks. They grabbed the two strongest animals by the collar and—swung themselves onto their backs. In the middle of this splendid pack they vanished into the drifting swathes of fog.

Everyone watched for a while, and then they all went their separate ways. Most hurried across to the bus stop. Others went back into the buildings.

"Despite everything, it's always beautiful," Petyushina said, tears welling in her eyes again. She looked for the old man. And there he was, waiting for her, and he patted her on the shoulder.

"I knew it would turn out all right." He spoke softly and laid his brow against her head. "Just don't lose your nerve, girl, never give up. That's the least they expect of us, isn't it?" Petyushina nodded fervently and used the bag to dab first her left, then her right eye, while her other hand reached for the old man's hand on her shoulder.

It was a little while before she could see the gulls again, floating with widespread wings on the updraft, directly above Petyushina and the old man. The early morning sun was so bright that they both had to shield their eyes with one hand.

9

The only time of year that Irina and Anatoly went for a walk every day was in September, during those hours when darkness settled over a lively bustle even beyond the boulevards and at the same time still held some residue of warmth. To Irina and Anatoly, such evenings, so rich in the play of clouds, had for some time now seemed a kind of vacation, the only one still left to them. No wonder, then, that in those rare hours they recalled the beauty of their former everyday life, which had allowed them to end each workday without noticeable weariness. In their evenings they had been enthusiastic actors at the Workers Theater, and had even been spared a trip by trolley or subway, because the company had supplied them with a car—and three weeks' vacation in Sochi, every July. That was over now. Even television held their interest less and less. So they still had plenty of time to devote to their personal mission, to their inclinations and wishes.

Emerging from a side street onto Sadovaya, near the Egyptian Bridge, Irina and Anatoly usually strolled along the canals. They both especially loved the Griboyedov, whose railings reminded them of an endless chain of Greek lyres. Arm in arm, light coats open or buttoned, but still without scarves, they alternated banks at each bridge, if some construction site did not block the way. They were very fond of bridges, so fond, in fact, that they never spoke when crossing one.

Most pedestrians overtook Irina and Anatoly, who gazed about calmly, keeping an eye out. Anyone who saw them would never guess the fire their marriage still possessed after thirty years. Irina and Anatoly recalled their youth, but without any knowing smiles. Not eight weeks after first meeting in the corridor of the School of Economics, they had married—above all, for the key to the dacha in Solnitchny. In the weeks before, they had spent their nights together in Yusupov Park because neither had a room and it would have been impossible for them to remain apart after those first embraces. They had always seized the moment, and yet could plan ahead as well—for the children, too. With a grin, Anatoly called it their kitchen dialectic, and the future had looked brighter than the day at hand.

Although Irina now had to carry quite a few pounds

more on her little feet, and her heavy upper arms quivered as she went about her kitchen work, to Anatoly she seemed a woman of touching beauty. He was a man who looked into a mirror only to shave, but he had nothing against Irina's tugging at a belt loop when his trousers drooped too low, while at the same time reaching under his shirt to tweak the little hairs on his belly.

They had been living together so long and had shared a common path so often that despite a considerable difference in height, they walked in step. Between themselves, they called their walks "patrols." The bag dangled at Irina's arm like a limp flag. But if she happened on a good bargain, it swayed like an overstuffed coal sack in Anatoly's hands, which never showed marks from the straps.

At Sennaya Square they walked past the booths on both sides, discussed what was being offered, made a side trip to the fruit market, dickered but in the end did not buy, and did not leave the accordion player in his uniform jacket waiting in vain for a coin. But smoked sausages, easily sliced cheese, yellow apples or whatever else was once such a rarity in state shops could never induce the two of them to waste their time standing in line. They had always preferred to do without. Only for tickets to the Mariinsky Theater were they willing to put up with almost anything.

Usually Gorokhovaya Street, or Apraksin Alley at the latest, marked the invisible turnaround point for all their walks. Beyond them began the noise from Nevsky Prospekt, which they avoided. Coming from Fontanka, they neared the market that branched out like an archipelago among the dilapidated buildings of Apraksin Dvor. They did not go far into it, but lingered among currency and weapons dealers, whose singsong sounded like some special, muted promise in the ears of the passersby. After dark they grew louder and made their offers more clearly.

Irina pulled a reluctant Anatoly from one dealer to another, inquired about the exchange rate for the dollar and the markka, asked to see small but not too expensive pistols and before long became involved in a conversation with a young woman who produced three such items from under her trench coat.

"Finally something for women, too!" Irina said, and when that did not help, she pulled Anatoly over by his coat lapel. "Take a look at least!"

The young woman, who after only a few sentences suggested that they simply call her Sonya, spoke to Anatoly in a lighthearted, clear voice. The only thing that revealed her uneasiness was the way she kept brushing back one strand of shiny hair behind her left ear. For Anatoly, she evidently did not even exist, even after Irina called her "little daughter" and Sonya reciprocated with the promise of twenty rounds of free ammo. The women would have come to an agreement if Anatoly had not declared this sort of deal unnecessary, dangerous, indeed suicidal. Before Irina could even reply, he dragged her away with him. Sonya ran beside them for a few steps but then stopped and watched them go. Irina tore her arm out of Anatoly's grip and said spitefully, "Do you want to or not?"

They all decided to settle the matter somewhere else, in a building entryway or along the Griboyedov.

"By the canal," Sonya proposed when Anatoly, who was ahead of them now, nodded toward a courtyard entrance. They walked across the stone bridge, turned left and came to a halt behind a tree, perhaps thirty yards from Gorokhovaya Street. Anatoly rested their bag of purchases on the railing and put on his gloves.

Sonya never gave him more than one pistol at a time. The weapons kept disappearing under her coat, Anatoly kept asking to see them all for comparison. Her hands in her pockets, Irina kept a lookout.

"Well, get on with it!" She smiled at Sonya.

"This one here!" Anatoly decided.

Sonya laughed.

"Well, what's wrong, have you changed your mind?" Anatoly asked. "You have the money!"

Without turning her head, Irina eyed the bridge and both banks. Then she dropped her wallet.

"Oh my," Sonya cried, and bent down. Quick as lightning Anatoly grabbed her by the ponytail and flung her against the railing. He threw his left arm around her sagging body, propping it against his thighs. Then he rammed Sonya's head against the iron, again and again, until finally it fit inside the upper triangle between two Greek lyres. The railing had a dull ring. Anatoly could feel the skull give. He yanked it back and let go. Irina used the tip of her shoe to scrape some of Sonya's hair over the bleeding mouth. While she pulled a bottle of vodka from the shopping bag, Anatoly searched Sonya's vest, found a fourth pistol and threw them all, along with the bullets, into the canal. Irina poured vodka over the body and tucked the bottle under one arm.

"Beast!" She spat and put her wallet away. Anatoly nodded, clapped his gloves together to remove long clinging strands of hair, pulled the gloves off and laid them on top of their purchases. Through the inside of his coat pocket he reached for his trousers, hiked them up, and although he noticed that his shirttail had slipped out, he now thrust his arm under Irina's and gave her hand a loving squeeze. He picked up the bag. It was time to go home.

**10**

Ivan Toporyshkin, the father, orders for all the guests at the table. Suddenly the waiter says, "That really doesn't taste very good."

Everyone at the table looks up at him.

"It doesn't taste very good," the waiter repeats, and exchanges glances with all the guests, including Ivan Toporyshkin, the father.

Pointing once again to the dish designated number 3012, Ivan Toporyshkin, the father, says: "I want it!"

"It doesn't taste good, though," the waiter says for the third time, and jots down number 3012 and goes to the kitchen.

Now all the guests, including Ivan Toporyshkin, the father, start laughing. They laugh so hard that their faces touch the napkins folded at each setting and the manager has to be called.

"It doesn't taste good!" Ivan Toporyshkin, the father, splutters, and every face is in its napkin again.

"What impudence," the manager says. Finally, however, the whole story comes out, the waiter is called and fired. A waitress arrives with the meal, including dish number 3012.

"Number 3012 doesn't taste good," Ivan Toporyshkin, the father, says, laying knife and fork back on the table and reaching for his napkin. The manager is called and the waiter is rehired.

Every time I hear stories like this one, I gather renewed courage.

11

The snowstorm had been so sudden that neither buses nor trolleys were running, and Olga Vladimirovna had to walk all the way home from the subway station. She hugged her bag of bread, pulled her shawl tight—there were always those leaky spots between the neck and the coat collar—and took little quick steps. She expected the cold to attack her toes and back first.

At this hour the Krasnoarmeyskaya was empty and

seemed wider than Nevsky Prospekt. In the well-lit container shed a woman trolley dispatcher sat smoking, framed by green curtains. At Izmailovsky Prospekt, Olga Vladimirovna walked catercorner across the entire intersection. Instead of feeling cold, she was warmed by each new step. She walked more slowly to keep from sweating.

Passing Trinity Cathedral and already under the chestnut trees of Moskvinoy Prospekt, Olga Vladimirovna heard something behind her—like a bell ringing. And then suddenly once again—a short, bright sound. As she walked on, she looked back over her shoulder, checking to see that her shawl hadn't slipped—and stopped in her tracks. She pulled her coat collar tight and swallowed hard. The streetlights swayed on the wires overhead. Branches and shadows seesawed. Olga Vladimirovna turned all the way around.

"Have you been standing there long?"

"I think so, yes." His voice easily, effortlessly overcame the few yards between them.

"How did you get here?" His house shoes were covered with snow. He did not reply. "Do you like it here?"

"I don't know," he said. Now she took a few steps toward him.

"You're dressed rather poorly."

"Do you think so?" He gazed down at himself in amazement. Peeking out at neck and legs from under a coarse gray bathrobe—held together with one hand at his belly, with the other at his chest—was a white nightshirt, its collar edged in blue. Snow was melting on his balding head.

"Here, take my cardigan. I'm almost too warm from walking."

"I don't need a sweater. Please, don't trouble your-self," he replied.

"But it's a very lovely one!" Olga Vladimirovna coaxed. She unwound her shawl, unbuttoned her coat, slipped out of the sleeves and took off the cardigan beneath. The bag of bread she had been holding clamped between her knees fell in the snow.

"You're right, a lovely cardigan," he said, and pressed it to his nose. "Warm."

Olga Vladimirovna laid the cardigan around his shoulders, buttoned it over his hands—there it was again, that ringing sound—and tucked the empty sleeves into the pockets, from which she quickly extracted a few slips of paper.

"Have you all got enough to eat?" he asked, jutting out his chin. Olga Vladimirovna nodded and put her coat back on. He stood there as if chained to the spot. "Always?" he probed more deeply. The snow was sticking to his wreath of hair now. Drops trickled from his bald spot down into his face.

"Yes," Olga Vladimirovna said, "even fruit and dried mushrooms." She wrapped her shawl around him like a head scarf, so that only his eyes and mouth were visible.

"Do your women grow old?" he inquired, and plucked at the shawl with his lips. She said they did.

"And your men?"

"Many of them do," Olga Vladimirovna replied after a brief pause for thought.

One question followed another. Did she have an apartment, was it warm and did it have running water, room for a bed, a toilet, did she love her husband, and what about her neighbors, and where had she been born. Olga Vladimirovna answered each question in detail.

Suddenly he said: "I can work, too!"

"Of course you can work." He was her age, perhaps a bit younger.

"But you're shivering," he said in surprise, jutting out his chin again. "Your teeth will be chattering soon."

"Do you want money?" she asked.

"Sleep," he said, taking a step toward Olga Vladimirovna, and would have slipped and fallen had she not grabbed his shoulders. Then she picked up her bag of bread, clasped the corners of her coat collar with her other hand and started on her way again, past the great rusty gate—and heard it again, short and bright.

The only footprints ended at her feet. Was he standing behind a tree, or out in the street? Then she spotted him leaning against the wall of the building, next to the gutter spout, the shawl between his teeth and tightly buttoned up in her cardigan. But dangling below it was the bell. Olga Vladimirovna walked on, and by the time she saw the illuminated sign for the Hotel Sovietskaya appear above the row of façades on the other side of the street, she no longer heard the ringing.

## 12

D id you see that? Bad business!" Mitya said in a voice that seemed too high, too lacking in resonance for his bulky body. Falling silent again, we walked on side by side. He was smoking, his hands resting on his cameras. They hung at his hips like Colts. Their broad straps crossed at the front of his denim outfit, which every few yards got dusted by a snow of cigarette ash.

It had taken almost three months to get access to Mitya, and before he agreed it was already June. Starting from Moskovskaya, we had spent hours moving back and forth across the city, by subway and bus, even making a few treks on foot. I had asked no questions and followed Mitya, who never turned around even in a crowd, as if it didn't matter if I was behind him or not. In the subway, two stations before Gorkhovskaya, a young woman had sat across from me, dozing. Her calves were so swollen that she could only close the zipper halfway up her boots. Green, yellow and blue splotches covered her legs clear up to her short skirt, so that at first I thought she was wearing colored stockings. When she raised her head for a moment, you could see her smeared lips. Her eyes were blank. Just before the doors opened, the tip of a foot knocked her on the shin. She got ponderously to her feet and vanished among the people on the platform.

Mitya seemed to know everything and everybody in this city. I was to handle him with care and not ask questions. I'd been told that was the best way to get him to talk. Although it was past eleven, the sun was still so dazzling above the flat roof that amid the tangle of supports and cables the sign's blinking bulbs offered nothing legible. The glass door opened for us, music boomed in the distance, and out of the darkness came a cowboy—dressed in red and blue—wearing a hat.

Mitya gave the wide brim a snap of his fingers and shoved me through the door. It was cool inside. A dwarf, about as flat and inert as a cardboard cutout, pointed the barrel of his Uzi toward the cashier.

"Oh, oh!" he said, spotting Mitya, and hurried over to him on his bowlegs. I counted out the fifteen dollars for each of us on a counter that vibrated with the bass coming from inside the building. The dwarf let out a laugh, and as I turned around he bowed my way, took a couple of steps toward the curtain and pushed it apart in the middle.

"Oh, oh!" he said again, and bowed low, his Uzi clutched to his chest.

We walked down a corridor carpeted with felt mats and lit by the occasional bulb at foot level. It ended at a steel door that opened to reveal another corridor ending in a steel door and leading toward the music. I had to turn around to make sure Mitya was behind me since I couldn't hear even my own footsteps. There was an odor of sawdust and sweat; the ceilings, draped in white fabric, seemed high. After four or five such corridors, I again felt hard flooring under me. We were standing in a large room. Women were sitting under sunshades, alone or in pairs. A disco ball threw garish spurts of light across the empty dance floor.

"Move, move!" Mitya pushed me toward some stairs that ended in a gallery at the front end of the room. He was in such a hurry that he trod on my heels, and we took the last step up side by side. Two Vietnamese women were washing glasses behind the bar. They barely glanced at us.

Each table at the railing was separated from the next by a massive column—it was like sitting in a box seat. The sunshades hid the women completely. The only things moving were the hands of the Vietnamese and the dots of light that picked up speed and grew larger as they left the ball and rose up the walls to the ceiling.

"We're the first," Mitya said, never taking his eyes off the room. He had calmed down again and even smiled when the two Vietnamese brought us each a brass tray with two slices of white bread and cheese and a Snickers bar. This was served with a glass of sweet sparkling wine. With the two women still standing beside the table, Mitya took the slices of cheese from the bread, pushed them into his mouth, chased this down with a gulp of wine, tore the wrapper off the Snickers, took a bite, then shoved the rest in after it. As he slurped his glass empty, he crumpled up the wrapper with his other hand and deposited it on the plate with the dry bread.

I wanted to gain Mitya's trust, scout his home terrain and learn how he came by his photographs. I wanted to see what sort of person puts his life on the line every day. For it was Mitya who showed up, again and again, at just the right moment, who never lost the thread and whom commissars honored with a kind of love-hate. I admired his Indian-like ability to follow a trail. Without Mitya—as everyone whom I told of my plan had confirmed—the Mafia would vanish from public awareness. You could thumb through a text without reading it, but you couldn't miss his photographs.

"Do you have a guardian angel?" he asked, squinting and never taking the cigarette out of his mouth.

"I'll depend on you," I replied. Women flitted to and fro under the sunshades.

"You're no kid anymore!"

"I know less than a kid would here," I answered, happy at least to be talking.

"What do you want to know? I'm single, thirty-two and without a real job."

"But you're a fighter, Mitya, you take on the Mafia!"

"I don't fight the Mafia."

"Sure you do, with your weapons, you fight them with your pictures. . . ."

"I can't fight something that doesn't exist!" When I burst into laughter, Mitya shot me a quick look and went back to staring at the sunshades.

"It's just crazy to say that it doesn't—"

"There isn't any Mafia!" he interrupted me gruffly.

"I'm the Mafia, you're the Mafia, these people here are the Mafia, everybody's the Mafia, that's how it is, period."

"And your photos?"

"I'm a photographer."

"And so who kills these people, Mitya? Two, three, four a day, yesterday seven dismembered corpses in the trunk of a car, allegedly still warm."

"How should I know?"

"But you'd like to know who it is, wouldn't you?"

"Not on your life!"

"But then why do you chase after these people?"

"Who says I do?"

"Mitya, you don't show up just by accident. You're quicker than the police."

"Because they call me."

"Who calls you?"

"The people who tell me where something's happening today."

"Who are they?"

"The ones who want money."

"Money? From you?"

"Only after the photos have been published." Two couples were slowly climbing the stairs.

"And you don't know these people?"

"They're always different. Some of them want too much."

"First it's fix on a price and then: where, when and what's happening?"

"More or less."

"And they all know the great Mitya's telephone number?"

Raising his head, he looked at me.

"Listen, pal, you need to read something other than your newspaper sometime. What I'm telling you is staler than yesterday's toast, and you're amazed." Mitya leaned over the railing as if he had his eye on someone in particular, and added, "Anybody seeing us together is going to up his demands—publication in the West."

"So why are we—"

"I had to come here."

"So you do know?"

"No. Ambiance doesn't count anymore. All the same, you wanted—"

"—to not end up like Hofmann," I quickly filled in.

"Who?"

"You know."

"Not much."

"Have the sketches ever resurfaced?"

"Hofmann'll lead us to them." And with that Mitya gave me an odd look.

"But if it's all just made up!" I cried. "Somebody's invention! Pure fantasy!"

"Bullshit!"

"It'll be reinvented today or tomorrow. Maybe it already happened yesterday."

"Yes, the things people can come up with," Mitya said, brooding, but at the same moment pulled his right hand from under the table and, as if making his grand opening move, laid photographs in front of me. At first I was confused by the notion that he must have been holding these postcard-size black-and-whites in his hand for some time already.

But then I took a closer look. "But these are of me . . . ?"

"Right. Four variations on doing you in. First à la tourist: intersection Nevsky and Liteiny. Stabbed and robbed on the street. Classic motif. Likewise the next variation: subway, Sennaya station. Prussic acid in the face. Foreigner collapses, dead. Number three: businessman leaving a bank, sniper, silencer on the weapon." Mitya's tone of voice, his gestures, that smile would have been right at home in a travel agency. "But now the really tasty treat: countryside, nothing but countryside, peaceful green, the fellow has vanished. Don't get up."

"Mitya, if this is supposed to be a joke . . ."

"Maybe it is a joke, maybe."

"But you know, Mitya, you have to know! I'm just a guest here."

"Shut up!" For the first time Mitya looked me directly in the eye.

"I don't know if this is about you or about me," he whispered, and squinted. "Whether it's about the photograph, and so about my job, or about you. Get it?"

"Why are we here?" I cried in bewilderment.

"Shhh! Do you think it would have been any safer at home? It was the best we could do, the very best for you, pal." His forefinger touched me just above the heart. "And for me." His thumb was bent back toward himself.

"And in case something does go wrong . . ." And with that he unbuttoned his jacket, pulled back the left side and revealed a pistol.

"A Makarov?" I asked, but instantly recoiled from the hideous grimace he was making.

Instead of answering, Mitya clawed at his collar with both hands, ripping his shirt open, his eyes bugging, his lips pursed to a funnel, and blood shot out, a fountain of blood, spurted upward and then sprayed. He tried to speak, eyes huge, a second wave came burbling up, lips, tight together only a moment ago, opened, no words, only splashing blood, and then— then his head sagged forward, a third surge poured out over the ashtray, setting butts afloat like little ships. The second shot came through the table from below, striking exactly between Mitya's head and the rapidly soaking slices of bread.

I wiped the spritz from my mouth and could not help laughing, although I was enraged. For Mitya really should have noticed at the last moment, definitely should have understood, felt the pain as he realized that it was not he who had duped me, but vice versa.

"Sorry," said Ada. "Sorry," said Ida. The waitresses were nowhere to be seen, and that was a bad sign.

"Let's get out of here," I suggested. They both nodded and covered the room. I had never carried a weapon, on principle, for I held in superstitious reverence the adage: All who live by the sword shall perish by the sword.

No sooner had I stood up than Ada and Ida buckled like two little calves and fell to the floor. The bullet wound glistened red and black on Ada's forehead. Ida had been struck in the ear and was bleeding like hell. In the next moment I was lying on the floor. Sadness gripped my body, numbing and paralyzing me. Never before had I been so aware of my love for both the shy and perfectly beautiful Ada and the brave and delicate Ida. Neither had escaped that anguishing training that is the gods' price for a life lived without illusion yet filled with joy. Few were those who held the course. Yet those who did shared with one another their deepest emotions and boldest thoughts. So clearly could I hear Ada and Ida singing Brahms' "Lullaby" that for a moment I thought they were both alive. I wanted only to lie there and listen until everything was just as it had been before.

In truth, however, I did not hesitate for a second. I crept over to them, kissed Ada and Ida on the neck, took possession of the Browning and the Heckler & Koch—Adieu, Ada! Adieu, Ida!—then crawled under the table on my belly and snatched Mitya's Makarov. It, too, was still warm, as if Mitya wanted to place some final greeting in my hand.

Flat on the floor inside the railing, I searched for the gunman, the treacherous, cowardly murderer. Never before had I found myself in such a situation. And yet, well stocked with weapons now, I instinctively knew what to do. I could not get Brahms' "Lullaby" out of my head, but it spurred me on. He who acts always puts his life at risk. But I had no choice as long as someone was moving around down there who was working with a silencer.

Something new had been added, a kind of laser that flashed bright green runways through the darkness—a torture for the eyes. Which was why it took a whitish flicker and a shot that struck the table before I spotted the node of the silencer. Trying to get a better look, the figure emerged from the protection of the fringed umbrella—like Liza Minnelli, with a pageboy and oversize eyes. Before she could pull back, I found the bridge of her nose in my extended sights and took up the slack in the trigger. Once the shot was fired and her head snapped back and her fine-boned body fell to the floor, I noticed my mistake. Instead of settling accounts with Ada's Browning or Ida's Heckler & Koch, vengeance had come by way of Mitya's Makarov—without a silencer, of course. And so I handed the whole barn the ultimate big bang that automatically shot me out into a daredevil universe. The music stopped, absolute silence, then screams, and a few seconds later everything was bathed in glaring light. I myself was so shocked and confused by the new situation that I fired a second shot.

It's never too late, I told myself. It can all still turn around! I crept out from under the table and stood up with my hands raised—and was rewarded with a hail of bullets that relieved the wall behind me of its plaster. It was ghastly. I hit the floor again and waved to the room below—and again plaster shattered. Did they think I was a murderer?

Suddenly, as if out of nowhere, a giant of a man stepped out from behind the next column, crouched to leap, stumbled and took a shot from me as he fell. He landed on nose and knees at the same time. His buzz-cut skull, however, was lifting itself between my feet, eyes searching for their tormentor, and he ground his sharply jutting jaw one last time, as if trying to bite off the bitter pain and choke it down. Then he roared, and propped himself on his elbows with his last bit of strength, head swaying, blood gushing from the mouth. My God, the agony the man was in!

I could only watch as he embraced my left thigh and tried to press it against his wound. What strength the guy still had in him! The more desperate he grew, the more painfully he pressed his body against my knee, shin and ankle. I landed several blows with my pistol butt, guessing at the location of the soft spot on his head. And as I kicked at his shoulder with my right leg and yanked the left out from under him, his eyes grew wide, and his chin struck the floor. One soon grows accustomed to this bloody business.

Her mouth contorted, tearing at her hair, a girl stepped out from behind the column, stared at the huge corpse, lurched and sank at its feet. She was incapable of weeping, incapable of breathing, like a baby when it can't get the cry out and turns blue and suffocates. She groped along the parquet floor. I should have killed her and brought a halt to this undignified spectacle. But the murdering had to come to an end at some point.

Now a bullet frisked the vent of my jacket. Just grazed me, I thought. Damn, I need to be careful or other people will be deciding how I die. For of one thing I was certain: I would not get out of here alive.

"Boohoohoohoo," the hulk's sweetheart finally howled, her face contorted even more horribly than before. There wasn't much to it, however, for as I took aim at her, she scrambled nimbly to her feet and dived back behind the column.

I rolled in the only direction still open to me,

toward the bar. Mitya's Makarov was a mean weapon. Every shot from it gained me a few seconds' peace.

As I kicked open the door at the side of the counter, the two Vietnamese women stared at me dispassionately, never budging from their crouching positions, as if answering the call of nature.

Suddenly all three of us were flat on the filthy parquet, hiding our heads under arms and hands: an Uzi was clearing off the shelves above us. I concentrated on the end of the salvo and didn't even feel the shower of liquor, glass fragments and splinters. The light stood above us like an eternal flare. A few shots hit the refrigerator, in front of which I held my head pressed to the floor—in a puddle of beer. Did I still have a chance? Were they closing in so they could take their time slaughtering me? I knew they killed slowly and loved to use the occasion to study tactical variations.

As if by reflex, I held the Makarov above the bar and squeezed twice, even before the infernal Uzi fell silent. Two screams, terrible, bloodcurdling screams, followed. I had hit someone. *That* makes an impression. Silence at last! Among shattered glass and ice cubes the most peculiar cocktails were being mixed with blood.

The Vietnamese whimpered. Red flowers blossomed on their white blouses. I pulled off my jacket and ordered them to wipe the floor with it. They had to be kept busy if I wasn't to waste any additional energy and attention. I carefully pushed the refrigerator to one side and inched forward. There were two bullet holes in just the right spots. The right one allowed me to keep the gallery covered if need be.

The larger one, on the left, gave me a view of the bottom of the stairs, where two fat men lay in a pool of blood, not even twitching. With Ada's Browning I fired soundless shots at their bodies. I couldn't take any chances.

There was another burst of the Uzi. The shots were all aimed very high. These guys were getting cautious. The Vietnamese had to do their job all over again.

The one thing I knew for sure was: I was going to sell us for as high a price as possible.

The ticking of my wristwatch reminded me of a world where I had not needed to lie under a bar with a Makarov, a Browning and a Heckler & Koch, counting my bullets. But I had tasted blood. Give me bullets, enough bullets, or, better yet, a Kalashnikov—and then we'll see who's the better man. I felt a certain respect for my enemies. After all, they had challenged *me*.

The Vietnamese mechanically went on wiping up and paid no attention to wet strands of hair clinging to their mouths.

My plan was simple and not especially original, but would lead to a decision in any case, one way or the other. The problem was bullets: Makarov, three; Heckler & Koch, six; Browning, twelve. Another salvo was unleashed on us. Only a short one this time. Followed by laughter. It sounded blithely relaxed, as if an earlier life were beginning anew. That's how sure they were of themselves already. And I was the first to admit that I didn't have a chance if the other guys made no mistakes.

"Do you know the dwarf?" I asked the two women, not turning my head. "Do you know the dwarf?" I repeated more sharply, aiming Mitya's Makarov at them.

"She's his . . ." said the one with the broader face. We exchanged a glance.

"Take it off!" I barked at the other one. "Make it snappy!" What a pitiful sight, the way the tormented little thing slowly undid the buttons and slipped her blouse first from one shoulder, then the other. She was skinny, still a child. She crumpled the blouse in her lap.

"Tie it to that!" A broom that had survived every salvo in the far left corner was now my most important prop.

"Now scoot, scoot!" I hissed, although I felt sorry for her. But it had to be. Someday she would understand this perhaps. Every second we weren't under fire increased my chances. I allowed myself three deep breaths, during which I gratefully remembered people and things that had once meant something in my life. With no effort on my part at all, the faces of my mother and my father rose before me, of my grandparents, too. I easily recalled teachers of both sexes, my trainer. I thought of old girlfriends and friends, and naturally of my best friend, Karl. I saw my wife with our son, who had died so young, a loss that had caused our marriage to fall apart. And so in a single breath all my dear ones passed before me, many of whom would gather around my zinc-lined coffin and ask themselves if I was really lying there inside, and if so, what mutilations my body had suffered.

The second breath was devoted to those poets, painters and musicians that I viewed as my second family; whom I called my friends and confidants whenever their names were mentioned, even if I had never met them face-to-face. How foolish were all those petty jealousies and one's own desire for fame when the only important thing was to give this world something. One should be glad and grateful for each beautiful thing of this earth, and happy if one had been permitted to augment such goodness, for it belonged to all humanity. Why all this strife, why all this unnecessary pain that we inflicted on one another? How pointless! And on the other hand: What responsibility each human being bears! Just as everything that is good somehow remains in the world, since no fragment of energy is ever lost, in the same way everything bad, mean and ugly never leaves our planet. Yes, I was prepared to die, and yet it was a comfort to me that as grass, as a flower, perhaps as a tree, I would not be lost to this earth.

The third breath was devoted entirely to the present. I forgave my opponents on the other side of the bar. By some unhappy accident we were all entangled in this affair. Many of them had families of their own and would rather be home watching television right now. A few words would have sufficed to prevent all this. Once again innocent blood would be shed.

"Take the white flag and go!" I said at last to the Vietnamese woman. "Go and call your dwarf. But no farther than the top of the stairs, got it?"

But she simply shook her head, her mouth a horrible jagged line, and began to sob. She was so skinny. I had to put the barrel of my pistol against her right nipple. That helped. But I shall never forget the sight of that innocent, emaciated little thing, to whom few good things had surely ever happened in life, stepping forward, quivering with fear but willing to fulfill the task assigned to her. The other woman crouched behind me. She gazed at me with dark eyes as if to say: Don't worry about me. The main thing is, you pull this off!

It was quiet in the room. I carefully broke a chip of wood from the bullet hole on the right and made a rough count of the number of steps that would put my negotiator at the edge of the stairs. I cleared my throat when she had reached the first step. And indeed, she was already calling: "Jim, Jim"—forming the *j* far back in her throat. "Jim, Jim, Jim." Her voice went right through me. There she stood, this little woman with a broomstick clutched to her breast like a rifle, and didn't know what she was supposed to do besides call out "Jim, Jim."

Finally, as if a curtain had been raised on a stage, all the invisible figures with whom I had been fighting appeared. They were climbing silently, step by step, emerging like phantoms from behind the columns of the gallery or simply stretching their necks from wherever they lay. I thought only of saving one bullet for myself so as to escape torture or forestall a shot to the stomach, lungs or bladder. Now the moment had come for me to toss Mitya's Makarov over the bar and out into the room. That would be convincing!

Peering through first one bullet hole and then the other, I stamped on my mind the positions of every Mafioso as he crept forward. On the stairs three heads appeared simultaneously in my sights: up front, the dwarf with the Uzi; behind him, two buzz-shaven guys with pistols. They were all watching so intently that I was afraid they would discover my eyes. Inch by inch they stared their way across their field of vision—except for the dwarf. He never stopped watching his bride-to-be, who kept intoning, more and more softly, her "Jim, Jim."

I held Ida's Heckler & Koch with its silencer in my left hand, Ada's Browning in my right. Step for step as the three moved closer, my negotiator moved back. Two bruisers emerged now from behind the columns of the gallery and crept forward in a crouch.

I was not afraid, on the contrary. The night is always darkest before the dawn. I wanted to live! Between my desire and its realization lay only a little luck and a little dread. Just make no mistakes now!

The dwarf reached the top stair. It seemed to me that they were focusing more and more on the spot where my peepholes were.

"Halt!" the dwarf called out in a high but calm voice.

The cries of "Jim, Jim" died away.

"Come on out!" snarled the hunk in the second row. "Come on out!"

I let the silence reach its zenith, aimed, pulled till the slack was out of the trigger, kept pulling, slowly, very slowly, so as to keep the weapon steady, sucked up all the silence and inertia into myself—and let it rip. The first shot tore open the dwarf's chest, the second hit the guy with the mustache in the belly, the third struck the hunk's nose. Now I was up on the bar. Dodging behind the girl, I started shooting at the gallery, stormed forward, firing away at the stairs until Ida's magazine was empty, grabbed the dwarf's Uzi and threw myself behind the cover of the first column on the right. Some idiot shot at the girl. She fell without a word on top of her dead Jim.

Now I was the boss of the house. The first salvo was for the gallery. I whistled and the other Vietnamese leapt forward. I pulled her to me, pushed her on ahead, followed after her, giving short bursts of fire, and raced like an avenging angel down the stairs with the Vietnamese in my arm. But she, too, was torn from my side. I tailored a row of red buttons on the perp's massive chest, and then my magazine was empty. I was standing halfway down the stairs. . . .

Inside me Brahms' "Lullaby" was still humming along. I waited for the reel of my life to unroll once more, and closed my eyes. Which is why I did not see the man from Chermukin's Brigade suddenly step through the door and open fire. I hit the ground. Everything else around me was mowed down. It was hell.

"Better late than never. Congratulations!" Chermukin came up the stairs and shook my hand. Relief was written on his face. Then he looked me in the eye. "Was it bad?"

I started to bawl, I was so totally wiped out. I trembled with revulsion. Chermukin took me in his arms.

"Calm down, Hofmann, calm down," he said. "It's all over."

Then he led me out into the warm night, where I could finally read the lit sign above the entrance.

"You were magnificent, absolutely magnificent," the

girl with the green, yellow and blue bruised legs cried, and threw her arms around my neck.

"Where did you come from?" I asked.

She gave me a look fraught with meaning and said in a whisper, "Absolutely magnificent."

And now I, too, smiled into the cameras. After all, we had got every one of them this time.

Hello—Mama, Papa—it's me—Pavel—dear Mama, Papa—I haven't been here for a long time. What can I say—suddenly time has slipped away, and before you know it, a year is gone, and another, like you said once: Clap your hands and life is over."

He looked around. The young woman pulled back again. The tall, bare trees shielded them from the sea breeze that had been blowing hard as they left Primorskoye station. After a ten-minute walk, they had entered the cemetery through an open gate and taken a path that would bring them to the main entrance and that led among sunken, overgrown graves reminiscent of sand castles adorned with seashells. Only at the woman's urging had they used the asphalt path where strolling women came in such dense clusters that you might have taken them for a family, or at times for a group of tourists or a delegation. Near the chapel, where there were some new graves, he lost his way, but then he remembered the metal cross so askew that it seemed to be balancing there. He was standing a few yards from it now. Although it was only four o'clock, the sky was gathering to a dark gray. Above the trees darted gulls tinged with a pink light you would never have noticed otherwise.

"Come on!" He motioned the young woman closer. After two steps she halted, looked at the ground and crossed her hands with her shoulder purse in front of her. After he had watched her for a while, he turned again to the grave.

"Dear Mama, I blame myself. If I'd known you were going to die so soon . . . Then everything would have been done the way you wanted, but not right off, it couldn't be done all at once. I disappointed you. And that just leaves me no peace, especially now, with so many new things going on, so much has happened in the meantime, things that would make you both very happy. I've been promoted to technical director at the Institute. They need dependable people. Supplies have to be right there, always on hand and in quantity; otherwise years of work are shot and projects worth millions are ruined. I bought our apartment, it belongs to me, three rooms on Moskovsky Prospekt, plus a fridge and a video—really fine stuff. I don't have to count pennies anymore. If it tastes good I buy it, if I like it I can have it. Half my salary is in dollars. I was in Turkey in July. I have a car."

He carefully extracted a little package from his coat, unwrapped the cyclamens and laid them on the stone beside the enamel portrait of Lyudmila Konstantinova Samukhina, 4 January 1935 to 28 June 1986. He picked a few dry blown leaves off the grave. A web of black cracks, fine as hairs, had formed over his father's plaque, 1935–1969. He alternated clutching his left fist with his right hand and his right fist with his left. The woman put both hands in her coat pockets and rolled her shoulders. Her legs moved as well, as if she were shifting weight from one foot to the other, but her shoes never left the ground.

"But the most important thing is Katya. She came with me. You always said that the woman who finally got me would have no more worries. Katya is not only beautiful but sweet and clever, too; you only have to look in her eyes. She hasn't had it easy. But with me backing her up now, she can do whatever she wants and doesn't have to slave anymore. She can even go to university. And someday we'll have two children, too, because everyone agrees two are better than one. A better day has dawned, Mama. Not for everybody, but for anyone who has ideas and works hard. I'm so happy that Katya is moving in with me. There's enough room, and it'll be so wonderful with the two of us. We eat together, morning and evening, we drive somewhere every weekend. That's very different from coming here every Sunday, coming to see Father and giving him an account of the last week—lies were pointless, because as captain of a submarine he knew it all anyway. Whenever you spoke with him, I would count to sixty, like in hide-and-go-seek, and then again and again, twenty, thirty times over. And each time, after sixty, I would check my watch, like a trainer. I had talent, Mama, by age eleven I had it down perfect. I could have told you when four minutes and thirty seconds had passed, but you always used the egg timer anyway. I walked to school blind, but not like other kids, counting steps. I counted seconds: 192 to the stoplight, 408 to the school door. I didn't tell you about it because what was the point of such advanced skills if you weren't interested in the basic principles. I preferred to count the seconds that it took us from the subway to the grave than to think about what I was going to say to Father. You always wanted to talk with him because you were afraid of Mondays. But with Katya, there's no more fear now. And that's why for a long time now I haven't felt the need to cross myself like I used to without Katya. Everything is going so well now that I don't even remember to cross myself, although it does do me good, makes me feel more sure of myself and calms me down. But it would be a cheap trick—as if I believed in it and prayed every day. That's what women do. But it seems silly for men. Whenever you secretly went to church, I would think: Whatever she's praying there, she could tell me about it, too. You always preached to me: No secrets between people who love each other. Do you want to know that there is something beautiful about the way Germans saluted each other, something liberating, enriching? You don't want to know that. I'm no fascist, but the gesture is wonderful, grand and meant for everyone, for all people. You never tried it! It's no different than the sign of the cross because you're afraid of Monday, believe me, or going down on your knees, people do that everywhere. But it's not good to tell everything, because then everything gets messed up, because everything is a matter of ego or instinct or not really anything in the end, because there's no such thing as selflessness, never a time when you hope everything for others and nothing for yourself. Only people who want to go to heaven believe that. Everything is just basic urges and necessity. If you sacrifice yourself for somebody, then it's because you expect to get something out of it, whether you know it or not. Even God had his reasons for doing his work, if he did it. There's a basic urge hidden behind it, you see, a wish, meaning something egotistical, even if it was just to pass the time, or he didn't know what to do with his hands, and it's exactly the same with Kirov and Jesus and the other heroes of history, who died of their own vanity, their desire for fame, their dream of eternity. That gets you nowhere! Instead of making a good life for yourself! That would have been better for them all, for them all! Believe me! The worst part is . . ."

At this point he started mumbling, but then all at once he fell silent, spun around, kissed her—she turned her head away—on the hair and walked back to the asphalt path. She ran after him and caught up with him when he stopped in his tracks. The first snow of the year was falling very heavy now.

"Well then," she said, and crossed herself.

He squinted into the dark gray of the sky. Then he started walking in the direction of the exit. Every few yards he stomped his feet to knock the snow from his street shoes. Her steps were so tiny that she had trouble keeping up with him without slipping.

At the exit he paid her—laying twenty one-dollar bills and four fives in her hand.

"Are you feeling better?" she asked, closing her purse and holding out her business card to him. "Go ahead, take it!" Then she laughed, because he rubbed his thumb twice across his first two fingers.

"Do you have a cigarette?" he asked, and pulled the card from between her fingers. He watched her search in her purse. With his left hand he shielded the lighter's little flame that she held out among the snowflakes, and patted her hand with his right. "Thanks," he said.

She nodded. "So then . . ."

"Yes," he said, and watched her as far as the cemetery gate, where she linked arms with another woman who had been waiting there. The two supported each other as they walked, and as they turned the corner it looked as if they were resting their heads together.

He tossed the cigarette into the wet street, thrust both hands into his coat pockets, felt her card in each and followed the women. Anyone watching him might have thought that he was sleepwalking.

14

Nail clippers, lighter, handkerchief, key, rubles, dollars, watch, key. Yes, there it was. Müller-Fritsch gathered up his utensils again, put the watch and the lighter in his jacket and the money in his pants and apportioned the rest between his two coat pockets, until only the office key was still lying on the log book. Müller-Fritsch felt in his breast pocket for his blue enameled fountain pen and at the sound of the buzz pressed against the door. He turned to the right, fumbled at his cap until it covered both earlobes and held his head at a slant into the fine snow. That got him a wet neck. I'm a bundle of nerves, over-worked, a wonder I'm not hallucinating.

At half past midnight even Nevsky was dead, the arcades of Gostinny Dvor black, Sadko dark. The only thing left was the Marlboro kiosk and the Chaika on Griboyedov. If there was at least someone to tell, if somebody only knew, how hard I work. Just imagine it, pff, pounding away for seventeen hours straight, wide awake, no notion of the past, the future, even the city a blank. Not even time to trim your nails, not even that, when in fact it's all banging at your finger-nails, banging away at you, clear up into your head, tip tap, keys getting filthy all by themselves, whether you wash your hands or not, a sound like stiletto heels, seventeen hours in a stinking building, sloping floor, damp heat, windows puttied shut, soot, it's the same everywhere, thirty seconds and there's the screen saver, an aquarium or a flying toaster, at noon meatballs disintegrate on your fork, rice as gooey as a potato, sweet tea, the snow, you've got to be born for it, with a gift for suffering, undemanding, historically conditioned, never known anything else, pff, what Russians find tolerable, as the proverb says, is fatal to Germans. You know, nobody pictures that in concrete terms. What does it mean day after day? You don't even recognize the letters of the alphabet! I do something for the German image, my modest contribution to the enterprise, work and more work, work makes a man lazy, I don't even go shopping anymore, when can I? And in return, coffee without milk, bouillon cubes, salami, bread and tea with sugar for my heartburn. I'd settle for some good sausages and tea with lemon or milk. Never in my dreams did I think that I'd land here, not even a vice president, almost like a Russian, that takes idealism, I'm telling you, day in, day out. Do you know what Chaika means? Seagull, pff, sounds like chacha, reminds me of those hulking creatures on Brighton Beach, Coney Island, that was my first concentrated batch of Russians, summer of '91, didn't like them right off, pelmeni and borscht on the boardwalk, vodka on the rocks, Stolichnaya, gold medal 1963, Leipzig, G.D.R., but don't know what a Bloody Mary is, have them repeat "Manhattan": Meenkhkhetten, no way, just don't like them, arrogant riffraff, invaders, wannabe Westerners, souls with a permanent drip, the Concorde under a white full moon at a quarter to six, hung there in the air, toward the west a yellow-brown fog. What are they looking for over there? Hirsch's Knishes, kasha, gray, choppy sea, Café Volna, Café Tatyana, French fries, Frank's Burgers. When the poor play king. Can a real Jew believe in Jesus? Of course not! But why not? Call 718-555-0079. I've got a memory for numbers, break-fast, lunch, dinner. Go to bed with their sunglasses on. And then all that fat stuffed into green jogging suits, skintight, prick wedged against the right thigh, sort of thing you notice somehow, and forever kvetching. Cheeseburger, with a nice Asian guttural, ends up as a cheese pirozhki. Well, enough of that.

At the coat check Müller-Fritsch stuck the nail clip-per in his pants pocket, too, removed his glasses, pushed out his stomach and rubbed his steamed-up glasses, first one lens, then the other, on his shirt. Then he shimmied his arms out of his coat and held it out in front of him. Before anybody notices a cus-tomer here, it'll be New Year's again, chattering their way to ruination, and before they wake up, somebody else is bankrupt. I could write a book, books! Take it as a simple observation. Thank God, Sonya! The corner table, *morituri salutant*, since seven o'clock this morning, not a single Russian has thought about work, and cer-tainly not these guys here, pff, look around, business brass, bored to death without us, well, they've got cushy jobs, but scared shitless the minute they leave their cars. They get paid twice, and their once is more than double what I get. Believe me, not even a Russian

would envy me, at least I haven't noticed one. These
fingernails, must be hexed, three days now, hell, even
longer, just the right hand, except the thumb, but the
index finger, it's growing fastest. Kitchen closes at
midnight, Sonya, goodness, that corner table there,
look at that, lovely as always, such a pretty young
thing, and the teacups, like they're screwed on, but
otherwise elegant, and that hairdo! I noticed right off
that day something fine was sitting beside me, in the
plane, good six months ago now, pff, heavens heavens, coming back in tears, jetting here and there, as
long as the sugar daddies are able and willing to
finance it. Barely recognized her, with the ponytail
and jeans, and that T-shirt, white, just her little rosebuds underneath, you saw those, oh! tasty, tasty,
goulash soup, ah Sonyusha, parsley on top, Sonyusha,
Sonyusha, and served with the left hand: sausages,
four of them and a handful of mustard packets beside
the plate, dig in, stick with it, and with me, your
guide through Russian hell, cheers! Well yes, Lisaveta,
around twenty, pointy shoulders, vocabulary list rolled
in one hand, doesn't even have to look up, immediately obvious, the way she comes on, can spot it just
from her shadow. Tight pants, no ass, bird head, dan-
druff, would rather squint than wear glasses. Learns
quick as the devil, and best when there's beer. Needs
practice, pouts her lips if nobody corrects her. Belongs
more at the Moscow train station, go have a look,
nobody here is gonna take her stuff, pff, no orders for
those goods, or maybe you would, pff. I see you've
caught on. Would love to know what they talk about,
women between themselves, eternal mystery, because

if we're there, it's not between women, obviously, a good ad needs movement, that's what people want to see, legs like that, the way the skirt hitches up when they're crossed, say it straight out, right, the whores' table. Place your order with Sonya, works like a charm, first they disappear to the toilet, come back as if on a date, quicker than sausages. But do they ever dig in again, careful, can shovel down tons, ribs and beer, sossiki, Lisaveta, I'm eating. The operating room, *der, die, das*, masculine, feminine, neuter, chapter 22, "In the Hospital," her sister's broken arm. Ambulance? Neuter, feminine? Feminine. A lot of men like it when whores greet you and come over, without being asked, like girlfriends, your daughter's friend. Our sister's broken arm. Operating room: masculine, ambulance: feminine. Full blouse, red, glitter at the temples, red skirt, would love to see them run, that hurts, and how she wipes her ass, the way she tries to get in between. The others just chicks, drab and underage. Dacha, they all understand that, simply say dacha, Lisochka, her cheeks quiver, chomping on gum, shows her tongue, boots, man oh man. Pay collector's prices, the basis for negotiation. If she isn't something for the Japanese. Don't trust themselves, would rather hang their head over the glass, mum, well, twirl your little glass, mum's the word. Get in each other's way. One blocks the other, and they'll never see equipment like that again, pressed between her arms, that ups the price, fifteen pounds maybe, hanging inside there, by the button's silky thread, dammit Jap, those'll box your ears, yen, yen, doesn't count, especially not with the street bankers it doesn't, but her, I'm telling you, I like

her best of all the Russians. And only dollars or D-
marks count, and markkas, too, sometimes. With their
calligraphic cardboard badges, works of art on their
shirt seams or as a medallion in the hand. Dollars: top
of the pyramid, the question is for how long. They
know what's what, pure joy those guys! No waiting, no
chitchat. Do good work. Nice work. Lisaveta puffs her
cheeks, sort of cheeky, I'm eating, no obligations. The
road, and so consequently, the highway, not a neuter
noun in German, but feminine, *die Landstrasse, die* curve,
*die* turn, *die* incline, *die* U-turn, *die* road signs. Hard not
to con Lorenzen. A grand game, you'd like it, we
determine the rate of exchange: nobody refuses, otherwise you raise the sum, the rate stays constant. After
five hundred it's almost fantastic, your pocket calcula-
tor multiplies in thousands. As good as waiters, snap
your fingers and away we go, no comparison to the
usual crummy service. Service is their destiny, their
passion. Take off their cardboard pins, the way others
turn a sign around in the glass door: closed, all to ourselves. Dig the dreck from under a nail with the corner
of a dollar, no problem with new bills. You are welcome! Student speech, charismatic, objection, tourism,
question of attitude, colonization by other means,
seek, and in finding you will kill. Now who let them
in, still wet behind the ears, every seat taken, and you
thought they'd gone out of style, cuffed trousers?
Look at that: mouth twitching at the corners, the way
he's winding his feet behind the leg of the chair, knees
pointing downward, Russian and a whore, no language
problems, nervous and beautiful, her back, shirtwaist
dress, black, hair pulled up from the neck, zipper tab

flipped up, red scratches, silver necklace, heels, hairs on the nape, smooth for snuggling, brushes it up, raising a pointed elbow, *demoiselles d'Avignon*, worth dreaming about during a hand job. Without a video the Japs sleep through absolutely everything. Ah yes, the dudes, something's up here, given how quick they move, slick as a whistle, sharp no fingers, pull out bags full of bundles of rubles, wide black rubber bands around them, give me a second and start counting, eyes half closed, concentrating, spitting on index fingers and thumbs eight inches away, counters the static, new money, not the worried faces of gangsters, bandits. Under the table, I'd love to . . . Just having it along is comforting. Some people never cut them, just file, every day, instead of shaving, twice maybe, would actually love to here, under the table, but if a nail clipping ends up on Lisa's lap, snipping it off, can't see where, except you find it again in your bare feet, once almost twisted the whole nail off, slipped cutting, on my index finger, a nightmare. I can't bear the thought, probably the only one, twist the nail off, simply just slipped. Now left, now right, and the middle tip makes three, like a paper clip, and it stinks under your toenails, desperadoes, just have to get under it, principle of the crowbar, then even the corners turn out good, with no inflammation, ingenious idea, TRIM, BASSETT, U.S.A., 81, genuine progress, best right after a bath. Little toenails peer up at you like squashed faces. But I think: Why diddle away your time at home? Snipping is good during breaks, but I'm never alone, even when I'm sitting alone, like now, when you snip it off, see, one hand trimmed and the thumb on the right hand: until I get them all the same length. Amazing biceps, huh? Four glasses in each hand, shoulders back as she sets them down, rosebuds, Slavic girls, two marks like always, a lot of money for Russians, ambulance: feminine, operating room: masculine, red blouse, no pleats. That's what they love to do, count it all out again, boundless patience, look away and still have a gentle smile the second time through, know their trade, honest, full of trust and always right in the end. Whatever they're entitled to gets checked with fingers, ears and finally eyes, quite unbiased, tell you their first name free of charge and put the little cardboard pin on again. Adios, amigos! Starting at a thousand, just an office, in pairs, or threes, with sacks and a telephone, open line to the guys outside, this prickling in the stomach, walls of notes stacked on the table, bundle after bundle, counting rhymes, every rhyme results in another hundred, pff, this prickling in the stomach, I sing best when I'm exhausted. Scared shitless, cigarettes, calling cards, smiles, nothing eases it, the things you hear, an umbrella up the ass and out the mouth, managers with one ear, and then the handshake, oh boy, skip out with thin wallets, pff, the gold nuggets in the shirt, friends forever.

Müller-Fritsch laid two mark pieces on the table, paid the cashier for himself and Lisa, flung himself into the coat held out for him and rolled up the collar. "Taxi?!" two voices called at once out of the mist. It was snowing. Müller-Fritsch did not answer. To the left of the exit a child was rocking on a crate, back propped against the building wall, talking to himself, jumping jack, comes hopping in pursuit, the little

match girl, the whole pack, subway, Nevsky, intersection Griboyedov, as cold here as everywhere else.
Kazan Cathedral, Bank Bridge, where they shoot
films, cold here, too, yawning at the sky, a neighing
nag, fogging up my own glasses, middle of the canal,
thin ice, black down there, all drowny-corpsey, ducks
asleep at the edges, where the snow has stuck,
Gorokhovaya, three German shepherds coming out of
the mist: a whistle turns them around, back to the
women, thickly padded in training suits, moving in
step, the leashes looped twice around their necks,
such little boots, follow their tracks, take every turn
with no shortcuts, hiking across Petersburg, a hero of
our times, not even the deputy branch manager, no
one says: Thanks, no boss and no deputy and not
even a Russian, development assistant, martyrdom for
money. Was there, sure, but all I saw was work. Awful
limp, lanky, elongated figure, briefcase. Have you ever
seen anything like it, in the middle of the street, and
kids right behind, two of them, and another, on a line
with them, across the way, watching doorways, and
then another, just ahead, along the railing, gaunt figure, breathing out fog, having a heart attack or maybe
shot, sees nothing but the hunters, skinny legs, every
step a miracle, stops for a few steps, no cry for help, no
gasping, he doesn't see me, fog at his mouth, no pleas,
gasps now, it's all over, anyone who looks around will
freeze on the spot. Nothing changes, keep moving,
follow the curve of Griboyedov and vanish, nothing
more to see, just gasping in your left ear, keeps on,
grabs your attention, listening intently. Who are you,
riding there on a carriage horse, tourist gyp, trotting,

my listening ear, following the sound of hooves, of gasping, what a monstrous hole my ear is, stretched by listening, the animal snorts into the fog, the silhouette of a woman rider stands out sharply above the horse's croup, it snorts over and over, the steam from its nostrils, like pillars of fire, divides the fog, enfolds the street in glowing light. The red queen breathes heavily, heavily, that much I can hear, from hundreds of yards away, I feel her breathe and breathe again. The top button pops from her blouse, and the next one pops, too, and another, and now she's grabbing for my galloping ear, which has grown as big as a plate just from listening and circles her, a sputnik. She snatches the enormous ear out of the air like a Frisbee and thrusts it inside her blouse over her left breast, heartbeat and nothing else.

Müller-Fritsch lay half on his back, half on his side against the canal railing. He stirred, raised his head, his nose was bleeding. The tracks of hooves and feet around him were little depressions filled with snow and could hardly be told apart. Müller-Fritsch tried to get to his feet again, no pain, head clear and light, but his feet cold and damp, fingers cramped, no coat, no glasses, no watch, no fountain pen, no money, no key, no shoes, but still has both ears. Müller-Fritsch takes a few staggering steps, slips, on his naked heels, stuffs the white ends of emptied pockets back into his pants, lets out a groan, lifts his left foot and falls over. Müller-Fritsch watches his breath melting the snow bit by bit from a shiny piece of metal. My nail clippers.

15

When the Communists were driven from power and democrats still governed, a few people did better and many did worse than before. Some, however, had no idea how they would survive the next weeks, the next few days. Among such people were my neighbor Antonina Antonovna Verekovskaya and her three daughters. After Antonina Antonovna had given birth to four children, first a son and then three girls, her husband, who headed a brigade working on some distant natural gas line, was stabbed by his deputy. As Antonina Antonovna said at the time, it would have been better had the man slain the entire family. Seventeen-year-old Anton, her sole support, left the family thirty days after his father's burial and never returned. For the first time in her life, Antonina Antonovna had to fend for herself. True, a sympathetic heart did find her a job washing dishes on the night shift at his factory. But her pay was not much more than the supplemental income a retiree might earn. And so the four Verekovskis eked out an utterly destitute existence. In search of another breadwinner for the family, Antonina Antonovna practically threw herself at any man who had a secure income and wasn't known to be a drinker. Her reputation was quickly ruined. When she began to take money for her labors of love, people made fun of her and no longer associated with her.

Antonina Antonovna's sole consolation was in Russian literature. Putting down her reading, she would always remind her daughters what a luxury it was to have at one's disposal a two-room apartment with a refrigerator, television and telephone, one in which there was also a bathtub with hot running water—and in St. Petersburg besides! How quickly we forget, she would often say, that in centuries past the broad masses of the Russian people never had it as good as we have it today. Another result of her reading, however, was an idea that, though it promised an end to want, would bring Antonina Antonovna to tears. Because she saw no other way out, she was soon weeping daily. Never, however, did a word of her terrible plan pass her lips.

When at month's end hunger drove the girls to the canteen, where they could eat their fill of soup and bread, the working men there never took their eyes off Antonina Antonovna's daughters. But as pretty as these young things were, and though they showed signs of precocious maturity, they did not have their father's intelligence and quick grasp of things. They had the same resigned attitude as their mother, who could find no merit in herself, though she always found it in everyone else. And for that reason the girls had no inkling of what awaited them.

Shortly before Vera's fifteenth birthday—she was the oldest—Antonina Antonovna simply could not stop weeping, and decided to wait until the New Year and put the entire matter to Valentin.

Life for the four of them grew increasingly unbearable, despite Antonina Antonovna's struggle to run a household on very little money—they were not exactly starving, but the bread, potatoes, farmer cheese, margarine, marmalade, tea and sometimes an apple or a tomato were hardly enough for her alone. And there was nothing left for shoes, clothes and sweets, not to mention other things. Antonina Antonovna and Vera shared boots and a coat, Annushka wore Vera's hand-me-downs, and Tamara wore Annushka's and Vera's old things. But what if Vera's feet continued to grow? Even cheap winter shoes cost more than a month's salary. And so, whenever Antonina Antonovna looked at her daughters, she could think of no other plan for what was to become of them . . . and she fell to weeping again, and the girls with her. For despite their simpleness, they knew her tears had to do with them.

More and more now, Antonina Antonovna would sit after work with Valentin in his gatekeeper's hut, and she could not hear enough about his friends and buddies, about hotels. On New Year's Day she would explain everything to Vera, and the coming year would find the whole family happy.

Then the unexpected happened, something no one, and certainly not Antonina Antonovna, would have dared to dream of. It was the fifth of December, in the evening, just before eight, when she entered the canteen and to her surprise ran into the same people she had greeted that morning when the paychecks had been issued. Were they drunk? They were screaming at one another, then embracing in the very next moment, only to start banging on the table again.

Since Antonina Antonovna never spoke when there were more than three people in the room, she asked no questions and waited beside the counter, behind the chair where Dombrovskaya sat shrieking, arms extended, her palms now turned up, now down. What could possibly be the objection to a raise of three thousand rubles? Antonina Antonovna asked herself.

But when she heard that Dombrovskaya had been counting on a raise of six thousand rubles, and that Valentin had expected ten, just to keep pace with inflation, when she saw the despair that had seized colleagues who had pensions besides their pay and only themselves to care for and were better off in every way than she—when she saw, heard and understood that, her fear grew beyond all measure and she fainted.

"Come on, old girl, come on!" Antonina Antonovna neither understood these words, spoken in English, nor recognized the face. Only the voices of her colleagues sounded familiar.

When the director crouched down beside the stranger, Antonina Antonovna's heart was wrenched with woe and she began to weep bitterly. Such misery, she thought, let him see such misery, let him see it! Suddenly she was lifted from the floor, was floating the way she once floated in her father's arms. And everything had grown quiet around her. They were all gazing at her with open mouths and shining eyes. The stranger bore her away. "In an American's arms!" she heard the director whisper.

In the car, sitting in the passenger seat, Antonina Antonovna feared an accident at any moment and tucked her head between her shoulders. There was at least twice as much room here as in a Volga. It was her task, however, to tap on the windshield, left here, now right, and straight ahead again—otherwise she would have shut her eyes. From time to time he looked at her. They understood each other without words and did not crash into either trees or buses. What a shame it was so late when they drove into the Southwest Rayon.

How lovingly the American bent down over the couch that served as a bed for the three girls. They lay together under the blanket, heads tilted toward each other, like in old frescoes. Gazing at the girls with a stranger's eyes, so to speak, Antonina Antonovna was forced to think of her plan. She turned away and sobbed.

Without asking, the American took the three *matryoshkas* down from the shelf, the girls' only toys, and filled them with something good from his pocket.

"It's all over now," he said in his own language, stroked Antonina Antonovna on the cheek and left.

The next morning the girls were amazed that their dear mother was already home and making their breakfast. And did their eyes ever shine when they opened the *matryoshkas*. Antonina Antonovna ran to the bank at once to exchange just one of the many notes. And try as she would to stuff all the rubles into her wallet, there were simply too many. Antonina Antonovna trembled with fear that it might be only a dream.

She ran at once to the factory office to ask for this noble American's address. The secretary received Antonina Antonovna with great joy and led her at once into the spacious main office. But instead of the old director, there sat an American, the only one she knew. He came toward her and put his strong arms around her in a long and heartfelt embrace. And since everyone called him Nick, Antonina Antonovna called him Nick, too. She fell to her knees before him, kissed his hands and invited him to visit her modest apartment again.

He appeared that very evening. There was no end now to their joy and amazement. He liked Vera so much that it was decided on the spot that they would be wed in two years. And that is what happened. Nick and Vera were each other's all in all. Prosperous now and without a care, Antonina Antonovna and Vera's two sisters lived in the adjoining apartment. When Vera died, Nick married her beautiful sister Annushka, and when Annushka died, Nick married the even more beautiful Tamara. Antonina Antonovna shed tears at each wedding. I cannot say how long she lived so happily. For here her story becomes lost in darkness.

## 16

Above the yellow, red and whitish blue blocks of buildings, above the columns of the blue, oxblood rococo and Baroque palaces, rose the dark walls of a huge church; its golden dome and rows of columns stood out sharp and clear.

"What a pinnacle of culture!" Venyamin called out to the photographers, journalists and the cameraman following him, and with all the verve of his small feet leapt over the barrier railing in front of the cathedral stairs. The members of a brass band, who had just begun a pretty slick rendition of "Oh When the Saints Go Marching In," took their lips from their mouthpieces, lowered trombone, tuba and trumpet, and let their eyes wander in annoyance back and forth between Venyamin and his retinue and the open violin case at their feet.

"On our way back, friends, on our way back!" Venyamin said, placating them, and began to labor up the great slabs, each three times as high as a stair step. Not until he was at the portal did he turn around to look for the photographers, journalists and cameraman who followed, taking the path provided for visitors. Although they were younger than he, he could have shaken them off anytime he wanted. Not only because he knew his way around here better, but also because he had greater stamina. And yet if he didn't come up with something soon, being in great condition would be of no help whatever, the whole tour would be in danger of turning into a flop, and the newspapers would not even take note of the anniversary of his exile. As it was, the only one who remembered the past, remembered history, was the blond woman from AP who had put him on front pages back then: Venyamin with arms raised high, one hand balled in a fist, two fingers of the other spread in a V.

The band had just struck up "Oh When the Saints . . ." again when a woman in a huge fur hat on the far side of the railing fell into a skip-step but then found no way to stop herself and check her body's forward momentum on the icy path. And so with arms pressed tight against her sides she was pulled away like a marionette. The music broke off again.

"Where is the pendulum?" he asked, incensed. They had filmed him buying his ticket, then he had to follow arrows that read MUSEUM. In the gloom of its interior, he looked about in vain for someone from security.

"They've removed the pendulum," Venyamin protested, "they've dismantled the pendulum, the earth is no longer rotating on its axis!"

Disregarding the rest, he left the room. His memoirs were selling poorly. That was the only reason he had agreed to this tour. Caught up in such thoughts, Venyamin did not notice the effort demanded of his short legs by the spiral staircase and the little stairway.

He reawakened only at the sight of the iron stairs that led through the air and across the roof—and for the first time in his life realized how close the angels were.

How seductive to picture the earth as a disk, he thought as he arrived atop the colonnade and took comfort in the very immensity of such height. No builder had ever dared raise himself to this same level. From here, even the Great House seemed small, its antennas melting into the gray. Venyamin saw the city crouching below him, not unqualifiedly beautiful, façades in need of stucco, rotting roofs, masses wrapped in rags and warming themselves on one another. The spaciousness of its palaces dwindled from this perspective. The only shiny thing was the new sheet-brass roof of the Astoria and its adjoining buildings. To the southeast, Nevsky Monastery, then the towers of Smolny Cloister, farther to the north the green of the Winter Palace and the angel above Palace Square. Like arrows the Admiralty and Peter and Paul shot skyward—how well he knew it all.

"There!" Venyamin shouted. "There!" Holding out his palm, he directed the others' eyes lower, or, better, closer, to the south shore of Vasilievsky Island, until he thought they had the snow-clad park with its czar on horseback in view.

"Peter the Great, upon his return to Russia from a visit to Europe," Venyamin began, "grabbed the rifle from a soldier standing beside him and rammed it bayonet first into the ground. The enormous impact of the blow snapped the bayonet in two. And Peter the Great then used it to turn the soil. And thus the spade came to Russia. It happened over there."

Venyamin lowered his eyes for a moment. Then he began again with undiminished concentration:

"Peter the Great, upon his return to Russia from a visit to Europe, grabbed the rifle from a soldier standing beside him and thrust the bayonet at the man's privates. From there he slit the man's garment down to its hem. And thus trousers came to Russia. It happened, if you please, over there!"

Venyamin did not let himself be rushed in the least by the attention his escorts were now paying. In a monotone voice he continued:

"Peter the Great, upon his return to Russia from a visit to Europe, grabbed the rifle from a soldier standing beside him and pitched it bayonet first into an oak more than three hundred yards away. Then he knocked the soldier out cold with four blows of his fists. And thus athletics came to Russia. Do you see that stadium there?"

There was no missing it. Venyamin's left forefinger traced a semicircle, the borderline that inconspicuously divided the city as conceived from what had been built afterward, a wreath of factory smokestacks depositing their fumes in low clouds, which drifted past as if they themselves were vapors from some gigantic chimney. Behind them, the ring of modern buildings, which lay in sunlight. "From there people are sent here to Peter," Venyamin declared, "so that they may get a taste of life. Beneath their footsteps the city is sinking back into the swamp."

"Go on, go on, tell more stories. . . ." They were filming again now. "Yes, it's true," Venyamin improvised. "Here in Russia we, too, love to tell the story of a Komsomol named Petroslavsky, who even before he obtained his engineering degree had succeeded in constructing a magic wand. Petroslavsky, being a young man given to self-doubt, could not fathom his good fortune. His family, friends, colleagues and the Komsomol all insisted that he should patent his invention before someone stole the march on him; for in those days scientists around the world were hard at work trying to solve the same problem. Petroslavsky went looking for the patent office. But as sometimes happens, he could not find one anywhere. So he decided to travel to Moscow, since his application seemed to justify such a trip. But the search proved fruitless in Moscow as well. The Soviet government had other things to do than to worry about patent offices. It had to drive interventionists from the land, fight hunger, eradicate illiteracy and promote electrification. And all that at the same time. That seemed obvious enough to Petroslavsky as well, and he decided to use his magic wand to conjure up a patent office and everything that goes with it. No sooner had he done so than he walked right in. A civil servant led him into a bright room, told him to have a seat and handed him a form to fill out. Petroslavsky, who liked the place very much, was soon lost in thought about the impact of his decision to turn his invention over to all mankind, and began hesitantly to fill out, in printed capital letters, the space that asked for a description of his invention. He had just finished the last printed letters when the civil servant took the paper from him and said: 'What a wag you are!' The civil servant left the room and, still laughing, slammed the door behind him. Petroslavsky was in shock, then he began to weep. Suddenly, however, he became so angry that he broke his magic wand over his knee, clutched at his heart and fell over dead. Ever since, we in Russia do indeed have a patent office, but no more magic wands. All right?"

The blonde from AP gave him a thumbs-up with her left hand without looking up from behind her camera.

He turned energetically in profile. "I love the sea. The sea always means freedom and good air!" They moved to the west side. "The wind comes from here, and as you can see, behind the nearest factory, there is the sea."

Venyamin paused and rubbed his hands. To the right, that is, in the north, banners of smoke were moving from left to right, and in the south, from right to left. The angels had come to rest on the corners of the cathedral's roof and were dividing the air. And there it was, just above the hem of the angel's robe: the little flap through which a Holy Ghost could slip in and out. How long would it have been closed now? . . .

"As the Holy Ghost was moving through bare ruined choirs and *stolovayas* during one of His processions, the janitor in charge of the cathedral colonnade—an Old Bolshevik who had escaped to the roof after Mayakovsky's death and served his people from there in a kind of tolerated exile—locked the little doors on the angels' robes and threw the key from the roof. He had had enough, you see, of angels flying off at night, and sometimes even during the day, which was an offense to all atheists, including the Bolsheviks among them, and a refutation of the scientific worldview that now reigned in the city—and, ultimately, a threat as well to his own exile. The angels are inert now, their soulless bodies feel neither cold nor calls of nature—except when a Holy Ghost, while searching for some little hole to slip into, brushes against their bodies, and then they whimper a little and, being very hollow, look forward to Pentecost, for they have never given up hope. What became of the colonnade janitor is not recorded even in Baedeker. Presumably, fearing for his life, he slipped into one of the angels—which would also provide a scientific explanation for their whimpers. He is still waiting to be rehabilitated and is said to issue ultimatums in which he threatens to open the little doors again for a Holy Ghost. Then there would be no holding back the angels, that much is clear. But perhaps it is only one of the many threats people make when socialism's dead inventory grows more rapidly than its living one. In this case, however, I believe he made a fundamental miscalculation. . . ."

To fight off the cold, Venyamin wrapped himself in a continuation of these thoughts, shuffled backward along the west side and disappeared into the darkness of the spiral staircase.

Since the earth is once again a disk, Venyamin thought, developing his premise, the angels will soon be flying back as well, and the construction workers will receive their just deserts in the beyond.

He had barely emerged from the cathedral's exit when a red armband began to wave at him from behind the barred corner window of a guardhouse. A spotlight was peering down at him from the roof. Venyamin stood there as if in a daze. Through the reflecting windowpanes he saw only the red. Slowly his posture stiffened. He was no longer aware of the marble under his feet, that's how light he felt, how clearly he knew what was to be done. The door to the guardhouse opened—at first Venyamin saw only a dark brow. The woman guarding the exit was wearing felt boots. On her arm there was a red glow. Instructions issued from her mouth.

Venyamin took a deep, regular breath and watched as she moved forward—stay calm, slip in under her gaze. Her arms flailed, her head shook. The red was on fire, creeping nearer. He had to find the spot. There was no other way. Wait . . . wait, he had the spot, wait . . . the nostril, on the right, that quivering there. That was it, that crease, deep and shaped like a little hook, the origin of all evil. It moved out from there, spreading in concentric circles up to the brow, down to the chin. Everything ugly came from there.

And now the angel approached as well. Its bolt struck her in the face. Her hands flew up, her legs stumbled back, the red followed, shrill sounds.

Ripped from his thoughts, Venyamin was freezing. He would not be jumping over the railing again.

"That's what I love you for . . ." the blonde from AP gushed, and linked her arm under his. "The way you stood there with your head thrown back . . . that was it, I think. It had something so . . ." Just as she was about to utter the word, Venyamin tossed a coin into the open violin case, and the brass band struck up a deafening "Oh When the Saints. . . ."

17

Ladies and gentlemen, read this letter, read it in its entirety, for it will assist you in avoiding a serious mistake. I ask you most sincerely, indeed I beseech you, if that word is still used nowadays, to help a simple man whose life has become a nightmare through a combination of absurd circumstances and whose only hope rests in you. Save me! Without my faith in you, ladies and gentlemen, I would already have ended my life. What other choices do I have? Either prison and forced labor or the madhouse, I'm told. And yet even if I should escape ending up in one or the other of those, I am sure all the sooner to run upon the sword of vigilante justice, the worst fate of all. For it asks for no explanations. Help me, ladies and gentlemen.

The testimony of witnesses and evidence provided by various experts have removed all suspicion against me. Nonetheless, I am being held here; nonetheless, I am mocked, belittled and abused, and, to be candid, even my lawyer returns my gaze with hesitation and a remarkably dubious look in his eye, despite the fact that even those who wish me ill can offer no motive for the crime I have allegedly committed.

I wish briefly and succinctly to share with you everything I know. These are essentially the same things to which I have already testified before the court of inquiry. But as my detention has gone on, one or two other things have occurred to me about which it would pain me to remain silent—and therefore these notes contain at least the possibility of contributing to a true understanding of my case, and I shall report it all as truthfully and with as little bias as it is possible for any single individual to do. Please forgive my poor handwriting, but I am so accustomed to using a typewriter—surely you have heard of my literary works—that I have almost lost the art of writing by hand. Moreover, the light provided in this cell is not the best.

I shall proceed now with the actual presentation and so begin a new page.

Report concerning the events of 23 February 1993 in Banya No. 43, Fonarny Alley, St. Petersburg, Russia.

At approximately 6:40 p.m. three persons arrived, none of whom was unusual either in behavior or appearance.

I was working the coat-check room at the time. To that I would add that I assume this job whenever my office work permits. Despite frequent changes of personnel, I have thus far not succeeded in finding the right coworker. That is, however, not my topic for today.

The three gentlemen purchased six bottles of Baltiskoye beer, rented six towels and paid with a five-thousand-ruble note. They left the change—three thousand fifty rubles—on the table without a word. I picked it up and put it by itself in the lockable desk drawer, since I regard such moneys as my property only when a satisfied guest has left our banya.

What I did observe about these gentlemen, however, was that all three seemed to be freezing. I would contend that two of them were even shivering, and the third kept his blue lips pressed tightly together. In comparison, moreover, to other guests who leave their coats with me, I counted them among the better dressed. Nevertheless, I demanded that they deposit with me their watches, wallets and glasses—two of them wore glasses. We keep our customers' valuables in a safe, to which only the person on duty has the key. Except for Gypsies, everyone gladly avails himself of this service. I repeated my demand, noting, however, that we could assume no liability for any damages that might be incurred. Without so much as a reply, either by gesture or facial expression, the man whom they addressed as Volkov attempted to push me aside. When that proved unsuccessful, the man they called Vanka instantly reached over the shoulder of the man in front of him and pushed me back down on my chair. Crude and pompous conduct of this sort is to be observed in the population with increasing frequency nowadays. Whoever will not listen must feel, I thought, and let them pass. I can no longer be offended by such things, since I know that all kinds of complexes contribute to such patterns of behavior. The only mitigating circumstance these gentlemen could have offered was the excitement everyone feels upon entering the banya.

Not five minutes later, such a clamor erupted in the changing room that it even drowned out the television. The Gypsies again, I thought, and I was right. But it was not their usual jabbering or haggling—if anyone can tell the difference in their case. I still see in perfect detail two of those galoots hopping about on one foot while trying to pull on a sock. They were naked except for their velvet caps and wristwatches. But they were hopping about not in order to keep their balance, but out of fear.

The three gentlemen had forced them to remove their underpants. That, in my opinion, did not take much, since Gypsies are cowardly and yield even when they are in the majority. I took it for a successful practical joke, until all the other guests began silently but hastily to force their way in—and force is indeed the word for it! They were pressed so close together that each was shoving and pushing the man ahead of him with his hands; everything was quiet, the only sound that of slapping shoes. An undignified sight, a panicking herd. Among them I recognized several who had paid only just now for two full hours.

"I'm not going to sweat with Satan!" fumed Rosenstock, a man I knew well, as, shoes in hand and shirt still open, he pattered hurriedly out into the vestibule. After the Gypsies had departed under the orders of their honcho, the only voice was that of the man on television. Soap dishes rattled, bottles rolled, still half full, across the tiles. The men did not dry themselves off, and the moment they had all their clothes on, they went scurrying out. No one looked me in the eye, let alone demanded his money back. Only the professor and Jesus were not among them.

I must concede that nothing better occurred to me in this situation than to wipe down the adjoining massage room. I felt powerless, and for the first time I was happy that my petition to privatize the banya had been turned down.

How many customers are we going to lose forever now? I asked myself—and came to the decision to act.

Granted, I hesitated at first to join any battle in which I was outnumbered, no matter with whom, for anyone not fighting explicitly for himself is no match for his foe. Then, however, with no clear notion of the consequences, I crossed the coat-check room and walked down the corridor, passing the Oasis Dining Room, where through the kitchen hatch I saw Georgy Mikhailovitch busy at the grill.

"Where are you going?" he shouted. "Wait!" I heard the slap of his old shoes and stood there at the end of the corridor outside the basin-room door. To this day I do not know what had gone on behind it up to that point. Presumably fear had spread from one guest to the next without anyone being able to say that anything in particular had occurred. Indeed it often happens that way: suddenly everyone is gone, and everyone thinks there has to be some reason for it.

"Hold it, hold it, hold it!" Georgy Mikhailovitch rasped, spotting my hand on the door handle and waving the greasy towel he used for hot shashlik spits.

"For heaven's sake, stay here!" He grabbed my forearm and pulled me back; his huge mustache, on a par with Gorki's, bobbed even when he wasn't speaking.

"Don't you know who went in there?" Georgy Mikhailovitch closed the door to the Oasis Dining Room and leaned his back against it. I do not know why I permitted myself to be treated in such a manner, since, after all, Mikhailovitch is my subordinate and a couple of years younger as well.

"You don't know who that is, do you?" he snapped at me, and crossed himself, something so unusual for him that it alarmed me.

"Has everyone lost their minds?" I shouted back at him.

"Stay here and help me, stay here, do you hear?" he warned in a calm voice, as if everything were explained now, and pressed a damp dish towel in my hand.

"Tell me!" I barked at him. But instead of answering he continued to instruct me in that same self-important tone. "Better yet, go back up front. Send everybody away. Lock up!"

He gave me a wink and pulled two bills from his pocket.

"*Dollary* have arrived, *dollary* . . . don't do anything stupid!" Georgy's tone of voice was outrageous. But there are situations when one's own feelings are tied in such knots that one remains silent.

Shura, an ex-student and Georgy's lazy assistant, was already hard at work. After pushing three square tables together, he had wiped the crumbs onto a tray, scrubbed the tabletops and rubbed them dry with towels.

I was still standing near the entrance, watching the two of them spread white cloths over the shiny tables, when the door burst open. We all flinched, especially Georgy. It was the professor, naked, skinny, with a potbelly, his swim cap pushed back, his whole body glistening. The birch switches in his hands—he was wearing mittens—dragged on the floor. When he moved they seemed to be grafted on to him. He and Jesus were priests, who would still be flailing their arms in the acrid air long after everyone else had already fled down the steps before the heat. They celebrated a mass of the flesh, they consecrated the banya. The professor's sensory responses were especially legendary. No one could absorb as much warmth under the skin as he, and no one, not even Jesus, let his body shiver so violently from the cold that the pores would scream for blazing heat. And when thrashing his back with hot switches, only the professor could transform unbearable pain into pleasure that cleansed the body from all superfluity and set it free to enjoy a lightness otherwise achieved only with drugs or Eastern philosophers.

Naturally, there were some customers who vanished whenever he appeared. He needed only to wave his switch and no one could defy him.

"Dima, they want you!" The professor sounded exhausted.

"O Lord, O Lord!" Georgy groaned, and crossed himself yet again. Shura gave me the cigarette he had only just lit.

"Come on!" The professor stroked the hollows of his knees with the switches.

"They can't be kept waiting. . . ."

As he walked his penis flopped like a garden hose between his thighs.

I had expected to find the three gentlemen on the bench across from the entrance. Not a soul. There was only the trickling of showers in the basin room.

"They're absolutely freezing," the professor mumbled without turning around to me. The switches in his hands rotated incessantly.

As we reached the door, Jesus flung it open from inside, tore off his gloves and cap, reeled

past us and to the steps, took them in two strides
and plunged into the water. The spillover drain
gurgled and smacked. Steam rose above the
basin.

"Let's go!" We scurried through the wooden
door and into the heat.

The three gentlemen received us with a loud
"oh" and "ah," but then went on with their conversation, bracing their hands beside their thighs
and hunching their shoulders. Yes, they were
shivering. And even when the professor opened
both stove doors with the ladle handle and
poured more water on, nothing appeared to
change. Whereas I found the air down here so
hot that I had to crouch low.

I can neither call their attitude toward me
unfriendly nor do I wish to conceal my own
empathy for their easygoing conduct, even if the
dubious aspects of their nature did gain the upper
hand later on. Their holsters lay beside them.
Semyon, as they called the tall one, finally came
down off the steps, laid his right hand on my
shoulder and apologized for their churlish
behavior upon arrival and for having driven off
the Gypsies, but they really had no use for Gypsies. What were they to do? He praised the professor and Jesus as masters in the field who had
made every effort, but who were likewise powerless against the gravelike cold in this damn
banya. I did not contradict them, although even
the professor was crouching now in the heat. It
was inexplicable to me how they could stand it

up there. The one whom they teased by calling him Stenka took over the spokesman's role from the tall one and shook his head with great certainty. He did not wish to argue, I had only to take an unbiased look: goose bumps instead of sweat. Without my ever getting a word in edgewise, he asked me to organize a couple of women for them, so that they could at least warm themselves up a little that way. Yes, those were his very words. They spoke of warming up. And with that I was dismissed.

A request of that sort, ladies and gentlemen, is not as unusual as some of you may presume. It has happened now and again that when renting our banya for an evening or afternoon, sport clubs, work brigades or ship's crews have expressed similar desires. Moreover, such commissions are in great demand among the girls. They earn good money while they party, and the men smell at worst of bad breath.

Georgy Mikhailovitch took childish glee in my being included in the preparations. Shura's Belomor had gone out in my hand. He offered his lighter and I finished smoking while I phoned for girls. So things took their course and promised to end in a lovely evening. And these three might even become regular guests!

I helped out here and there, wiped a few glasses till they sparkled—one normally didn't dare hold them up to the light—inserted napkins in tumblers, checked the silverware, which was used only seldom, smoked and read the paper. I

was in a gala mood somehow: the white tablecloths, the tidiness, the special aroma from the
kitchen. My mind was at ease.

At 7:20 there was a knock on the door to the
men's section. I had already got to my feet to
open up when from the basin room came screaming that in its falling tone was more like a moan,
perhaps even keening. Georgy turned off the
radio. The voice grew softer, then crescendoed
again and broke off. The girls, fearing that others
had been let in before them, rattled at their door
and called for me.

Under the pretense of announcing their arrival, I entered the basin room. Jesus was lying on
his belly on the tiles, his left hand groping about.
Stretched out beside him, the professor lay with
his forehead pressed against the rounded-off
stones that embellished the stairs and basin like a
grotto. His long gray hair, his thick eyebrows,
his potbelly as it rose and sank, and his penis
dangling over his right thigh lent him something
of the look of a satyr.

Shura was already kneeling beside Jesus. In
one hand he held the hose for cold water, with
the other he was propping up the man's forehead,
the way one does when a person is about to
vomit.

I heard laughing and the slap of birch switches
coming from the banya. Cold air drifted like mist
through a window hatch and dispersed under the
low ceiling. Gathering above the basin in narrow,
dense swatches, the vapor hovered above the

water and transformed the room into a landscape whose horizon was veiled. I took the hose from Shura's hand, began at the professor's feet and moved upward—the hair on his chest swayed like algae. In order to bathe his pulse in cold water, I directed the jet again and again at his wrist, which he managed to turn by himself. Shura dragged Jesus out and helped me carry the professor, who whispered: "Devils, they're devils. . . ."

We laid them both on red upholstered benches in the niches across from the lockers. From the next room we could hear an urgent rustling, zippers purring and soles scuffing. Irina came out—we had worked together for a long time—hastily greeted me and asked me to let one of her girlfriends join in, who was celebrating her eighteenth birthday today. That, of course, violated our agreement—what was to stop the other two, then, from asking to bring girlfriends along? But who is in a position to deny these girls anything, especially when they're standing before you in nothing but their underwear? They are, of course, no common prostitutes, but have all had some ballet experience, more or less. Even barefoot they seem to float.

They pulled back in alarm at the sight of the professor and Jesus, with Shura kneeling between them, opening bottles of beer. And yet I could tell them no more than that their customers were Russians with an apparently ample supply of dollars at their disposal. Then I led them to the basin room and asked them to wait.

The trio was still sitting in the banya, laughing, cursing, pounding one another on the chest and thighs and making fun of the professor and Jesus. What limp dicks, who couldn't hold out for half an hour, but then that was to be expected in this lousy banya, which never got really warm, let alone hot. Their nostrils weren't even shiny. They were cursing away happily, as if this were some kind of sport. Each outdoing the other, the three fell into a rhythm that they reinforced with blows to their dry bodies. After telling them what there was to tell, I waited outside with the girls.

From experience I knew the peculiar nature of those first minutes in which the girls had already left one world but had not yet arrived in the other. Each of them took a stout pull on my bottle of kirsch, which I let them pass around twice, and now the door opened. Towels draped like napkins over their left forearms, the three came goose-stepping out. All of a sudden, Pyotr—who was repeatedly called "our Pyotr"—began swinging a towel above his head, faster and faster, all the while emitting drawn-out whoops, like a child playing Indian. The other two followed his example, and we laughed. "Quick, quick, take your pick, quick, quick . . ." The three broke into a rhyme, moving in step toward the girls. I left the room.

Busy with kitchen work—as usual the radio was playing—neither Georgy nor I heard anything out of the ordinary. Besides, the presence of Irina's girlfriend, who had taken Shura's place helping us, prevented us from commenting on what little we did hear with anything more than glances. Despite all her assurances to the contrary, Tanyusha was perhaps fifteen, at most sixteen. But her shyness, which was at variance with a certain definiteness of character, lent her a very womanly beauty. Like the others, she wore only panties and a short chemise and seemed happy to have been assigned work of any sort. I followed the quick movements of arms and hands as she cut sausage, ham, cheese and pickles into thin slices and laid them in fanned sequence around the edge of the platter. She filled the bread baskets and opened the jar of preserved garlic, skinning the shimmering cloves to decorate the platter by alternating them with pieces of tomato and little hot peppers.

When Tanyusha asked to be allowed to examine our spice rack, we could not believe our ears. The same girl who until now had barely looked up from her work preached a sermon unlike any ever heard in Banya No. 43.

"Don't you regularly clean the table, the bowls, the silverware, the plates and cups, the glasses and tumblers? It doesn't look to me as if everything is washed daily in hot water and toweled dry, either in the morning or in the evening. You see—sieves, grills, pots, pitchers and pans have not been properly scrubbed down. They should be stored, upside down, in a clean spot. Foodstuffs are to be kept covered at all times and in all places. The floor, the walls, benches, both large and small, windows and doors are to be swept, wiped off and scrubbed. Doesn't anyone here know that? I imagine you can't even tell me how many plates, knives, forks and spoons you have, and that you'd even have trouble telling me the number of pots and pans you have. Don't you have a freezer for keeping meat and fish in sufficient quantity? Where are your supplies of wine and beer, where are your spices?"

I am unable to describe the impression these words had on me, let alone on Georgy.

Without defending himself, without uttering a word, but occasionally swiping his sleeve quickly across the top of a jar, he piled all his spices and herbs in front of her. Tanyusha found his supply of cream, mayonnaise and yogurt on the top shelf of the refrigerator and thanked him in her own way. Quick as a wink, she had prepared a dozen different sauces, in colors from yellow to green, red and white, even blue. She crushed basil with her hands and peppercorns with a few strokes of the mortar. Even raisins and capers long forgotten in the cupboard found a use.

She was exerting herself so much that her breasts bobbed under her chemise. She would frequently suck at her little finger, splaying it from her sauce-smeared hand to taste a sample or to brush back a few strands of hair.

When Georgy sat down with me for a cigarette, Tanyusha performed nothing less than a tour de force. In a matter of minutes she had filled so many skillets, pots and pans that when he returned to the stove there was hardly anything left to do but lend a hand here and there. And Tanyusha went about it all with the same agility as if she were executing dance steps, spins, leaps.

What all did she not conjure up out of our meager supplies. She revealed her competence simply in the way she inspected the chickens that had just been thawed—bending joints, examining claws, giving thighs another singe above the flame while plucking at pinfeathers and making sure to pull back the neck skin before chopping off the head. And as for ingredients, she did not restrict herself to pepper and salt and a bit of paprika. Carrots, parsley, onions, lemon juice, mushrooms, tomato paste, herb roots, eggs, pickles, tkemali sauce, marinated fruit, dill, prunes, tarragon, coriander, port wine, bay leaves, butter, berries, bouillon, etc. etc.—it all had to be standing at the ready for Tanyusha. She braised, boiled, roasted, breaded, fried, baked—chicken on the skewer, Grusinian tabaka, chicken Kiev, chicken soufflé, roast chicken and mushrooms, chicken in clear gravy, stuffed chicken, chicken fricassee—pots, pans, skewers, casseroles, roasting pans, it all was in a turmoil. Meanwhile vegetable and fish sakuski were created, one cold soup of kvass and another of cucumber, a milk soup, cheese omelets, Russian cheese dumplings, scrambled eggs and herring, a noodle casserole, galushki, pelmeni in cream, pumpkin-apple zape-

kanka, creamed cabbage and—for me, the pièce
de résistance—a borscht the likes of which I
shall probably never eat again. And all the while
Tanyusha not only maintained her grace and
charm but also worked with tender loving care,
as if nursing a patient or cuddling a child.

Heavy blows to the door, as if feet, heads and
fists were striking all at once, put an end to our
carefree labors. Singing and humming, with
Yeronimov as drum major strutting at their head
and brandishing a towel, the three marched
in, white towels wrapped around their hips.
Tanyusha screamed and rushed to the girls, who
were crawling naked on all fours between the
men and being dragged by their hair and jerked
from side to side as if on leashes. When the trio
spotted Tanyusha, they clicked their tongues and
watched alertly as she hurried from one girl to
the next, pressing a handkerchief to Irina's bloody
nose, touching her fingertips to Vera's swollen
eye, now wiping the sweat, makeup and snot
from Marina's face with a dish towel. Softly, very
softly, Tanyusha spoke with the women, who did
not so much as whimper or weep. They stared at
the floor as if dazed. It was quiet. The borscht
burbled. A short cough from Irina, however, sufficed for her to be pushed to the floor again.
Blood spurted from her nose. The grace period
was over, Tanyusha was shooed back, the three
men sat down at the table, clamping the girls'
heads between their thighs. While I filled the
glasses with vodka, Menshikov explained wordily

that they wished to see no one but Tanya. And
with that they raised their hands, fingers fidget-
ing, and reached for the appetizers.

Through a crack in the closed hatch for dirty
dishes we could follow what was happening. And
if Stepanov's tone of voice had been a pleasant
surprise, I was now astounded by their exquisite
manners, which revealed a well-disciplined childhood and which cannot be assumed nowadays
even among educated Russians. Who still holds
his back straight, elbows tight against the body,
and chews without smacking his lips? True, none
of the three took things from the cold-cuts platter with the serving fork, but they did place each
slice of meat, cheese or pickle precisely on their
bread and cut off little bites that were practically
wooed by knife and fork before being speared
and vanishing into their mouths. They spooned
borscht without dribbling over the edge of the
bowl and even used napkins. Plus there was
the kindly, almost paternal way they treated
Tanyusha. They not only took the filled soup ter-
rines from her as she served but also passed
empty plates back to her, heaping compliments
on her. They even tolerated her shoving bowls of
water under the table. Tanyusha served ladle
after ladle of milk soup, cucumber soup and
borscht, all the while frequently admonishing
them to leave a little room for the dishes yet to
follow. They thanked her for her solicitude with
a toast, for which they stood up and held glasses
together, as if waiting for a photographer's flash.

Tanyusha, forced now to sit down with the trio, spoke too softly for us to understand her. Suddenly, however, the man called Afanasi and the one lovingly titled Mormuno, shouted for Georgy and me. Tanyusha had sprung to her feet, but they held her fast by both hands, like a child caught stealing red-handed. I immediately realized which way the wind was blowing when in a trembling voice Alfonso asked to which category of exploiters we belonged—were we slave drivers, parasites, pimps or simply lousy, stinking little fascist extortionists? Close to tears, Tanyusha looked up as if begging a thousand times for forgiveness. But now Fyodorov likewise broke in and cursed us as bloodsuckers, as the disgrace of the nation, as proletarians with delusions of grandeur, as Communist scum, as men with no ideals and no dignity, etc. etc. I cannot even recall all their slanders. The three pulled and tugged at the girl as if trying to force an answer out of her.

I said nothing, because it would have been pointless to argue against such scurrilous tirades. But when they began to manhandle the poor little thing, I decided to take action. I managed to gain a hearing and spoke about how we would of course pay Tanya for her work, for her exemplary and creative work; it was just that until now there had been no opportunity for an exchange about the matter; but there had not been a minute in which we were unaware of the perspectives that Tanya had opened up for us and that could not be valued too highly; needless to say, we were ready and willing to create for her a position commensurate with her talents and abilities; indeed, we would beg her to allow us to do so. I also added that the atmosphere among us here was harmonious and that, putting aside all false modesty, Tanya should be open and honest in naming the conditions under which she would be willing to work in our collective, for we would bid her a hearty welcome from this moment on, and if there had been a misunderstanding here, if anyone should doubt our integrity, I would be the first to clear up this regrettable misunderstanding, here and now, not with promises but with actions and a contract with my signature and official stamp.

The trio's faces twitched, they winked. One after the other they burst into laughter, till they were all banging on the table in glee. Tanyusha blushed. Perhaps my voice had sounded anxious, perhaps I had not understood the true basis of their accusations, perhaps it had only been a joke—I shall probably never know. They laughed and laughed, until even Tanyusha lost her self-consciousness and could no longer restrain herself and—although I could see her embarrassment—snorted and spluttered, holding her right hand to her mouth. Georgy stood motionless beside me.

And with that the whole affair could have come to a happy end. Even the fact that they were laughing at my expense was secondary. The main thing was that they were laughing. I was breathing more easily now.

Then the towel around Tanyusha's hips loosened and fell to her feet. The trio was at once speechless. She quickly bent down and tied it again, but that did not end the devilish silence!

Both the one they also called Chandauli and the one they frequently addressed as Carpaccio grabbed Tanyusha by the hands, kissed the fingers and the backs, and in this fashion worked their way up to her elbows. Changorok, however, waving Georgy and me back into the kitchen, stood up, came around the table and puffed himself up in front of her.

As I peered through the crack, Bessmertny was holding Tanyusha's towel in his left hand. His right lay at her neck. His thumb stroked under her chin. She kept raising it higher and higher.

Rinaldo spoke in a calm, serious voice. We understood very little at the start. Abramov's questions evidently centered around why Tanyusha was covering herself in their presence instead of simply showing what she had, and if it did not border on being a tease to pretend such modesty and then slam-bang let the veils fall. Did she act that way at home, too, and was it even necessary, since she had quality goods to offer and no reason whatever to hide anything; on the contrary, she was a beauty with style, evidenced among other things by her choice of undergarments, in which choice respect for one's fellowman dictated that one not have any illusions about one's figure, and what about her personal cleanliness and what was her opinion on questions of birth control, what did she know about AIDS, and were her parents in a position to offer her a good home in the future, and what did she actually intend to do with the money she would be earning here in the future, and whom had she chosen as her role model, although she obviously felt equally drawn to foreign and Russian authors, why had she then never done anything to remedy human misery, all the more since she had neglected to approach them, by which he meant himself and his two companions, even if experience could not be exported lickety-split just like that, and had she been baptized, etc. etc.

As I said, I did not understand everything, but stared spellbound at the Chimp—the nickname most frequently used for Nikolai Stepanovitch—and watched as this same fellow, Styopka, brushed her hair behind one ear, winding a few strands around his forefinger, stroked the nape of her neck—her rosebuds blossomed—traced along her arm, switched from wrist to hip and stuck a finger down into her panties. Petrovitch pulled her chemise out and began pushing up the thin fabric until he had reached her navel, into which he inserted his forefinger, rotating it gently. Tanyusha laughed a bit, and he laughed, too, and held her towel out to her and said she should decide for herself what was right and wrong, since she already had, or so he hoped, eighteen years behind her and was a citizen of legal age.

Tanyusha had listened very attentively to Pogorelsky, agreeing with him several times. Her nods grew all the more fervent in the silence that followed upon Alexeyevitch's questions, like the long, full, inevitable resolution of a chord in which all the consequences of future events lay already determined.

Finally, Tanyusha managed to formulate the declaration that she was agreed on principle but asked all the same to be allowed to speak with her mother first. The trio had no objection and demanded that I, whom they called in by yelling for the "boss man," should show the girl the nearest telephone as quickly as possible.

I led Tanyusha into my office, where two phones and a fax stood at her disposal, pushed my armchair around in place, shoved a few papers to one side and closed the door as she began to dial. She seemed so lost in thought that it never occurred to me to speak to her.

During my brief absence, they had ordered Georgy to bring the three girls out from under the table and take them to the basin room. By his account, they were only semiconscious. What fate befell them is unknown to me. We in any case were told, with no explanation, to clear the table.

Upon her return, Tanyusha was received respectfully, not to say reverentially. Each of the three swept the palm of his hand across the tablecloth several times, removing the last traces of crumbs, while Tanyusha slipped her chemise over her head and tugged her panties down her legs. She placed her bath shoes beside the door and laid her folded underwear on top. The one they called Polutykin offered his hand as she raised one knee to crawl up on the table, and she then sat down in the middle, taking care not to rumple the tablecloth. With equal caution she stretched out her legs, cast a glance over her shoulder, shifted her butt a little to one side, lay back, put her arms behind her head and stretched to grab the table legs. Her ribs stood out clearly, and, rising above them, her firm breasts.

We were ordered to bring in the food. Tanyusha sat up once again, took several barrettes from her hair and handed them to Emur. We hastily set up a buffet and were just bringing in the last bowls when the three men sitting at Tanyusha's table joined hands and bowed their heads as if saying a prayer. Even Georgy and I stopped in our tracks. I had not yet counted to twenty when various sauces were poured over Tanyusha's feet and rubbed in like suntan lotion. Anton smeared horseradish sauce over her toes, dripping a white line of it up her ankle. He stepped back, and tall Ivan bent down and covered her right foot with garlic butter. Where-

upon Sergey gently sprinkled a tomato sauce—
which contained not only a great many herbs but
also wine, croutons, fine strips of ham and cubes
of cheese—over her right shin, clear up to the
knee, and softly massaged it into her calf.
Tanyusha smiled at first, but when asparagus with
mushroom gravy was dribbled on her thigh, she
yielded up a sigh that sent a shudder of pleasure
even through the two of us in the kitchen.

At the latest, it was when the man who
claimed to be Mikhail poured saffron and pep-
permint sauce on her abdomen, rubbing the little
bowl against her hip to wipe off the excess, that
Tanyusha's passion was aroused. She tossed her
head from side to side. Her fierce breathing
spurred these singular waiters on. Particular care
was taken with her belly. An entire bowl was
emptied from a great height, landing perfectly
on target and spraying everywhere. Her bosom
offered yet another high point, for all three could
scarcely get enough of it, amid unending praise
for its firmness. Fricassee was applied to the feet,
cheese omelets to the knees, they stuffed Russian
cheese dumplings between her thighs and calves
and poured kvass over that. Her abdomen was
filled with roast chicken and mushrooms, her
belly layered with scrambled eggs and herring,
noodle casserole and a topping of smetana. One
after the other, each stepped back from the table
like an artist from his easel and admonished the
other two to be careful. Belyakov whistled "Buy
Mama Blue Silk for a Pretty Dress" to himself,

only to be drowned out by Chussev's tenor. "Who doesn't love a writer?" he repeated several times, and continued in a booming crescendo: "I would love him, he's a clever man. . . ." Nikolayev arranged the pelmeni in cream as best he could around her breasts, plastered on a ruff of creamed cabbage and laid trails of vegetable and fish sakuski along her arms. Although a great deal had now spilled off Tanyusha's body onto the tablecloth, they scarcely found room for the galushki and the pumpkin-apple zapekanka and finally laid them on her right and left thighs. For a finale, Leonardo scraped clean the little bowl of tkemali sauce. Only her face was still visible.

Grasping at the table legs again and again, as if searching for an ideal grip, Tanyusha sprawled her body. A lusty cry rose from her throat as the three began to lick the food from her skin. Here and there they now bit into a herring or a cheese dumpling. They worked slowly and with mouths full sang as they went the familiar hymn: "Glittering, sparkling railroad tracks! And an embankment, too! Look now, the train is leaving its tracks, and plunging into the goo!"

Like well-mannered waiters, they kept their hands and folded napkins at their backs. Except for Eugen, who evidently had bad teeth, they made good progress. Valentin was crazy about the pelmeni in cream, which he greedily devoured from Tanyusha's right breast. Yegor, however, regaled himself on the cheese dumplings between her thighs but had to make room for Kibok opposite, who was slurping a mixture of galushki and pumpkin-apple zapekanka from her left thigh. Sometimes they changed places, each recommending that the others sample this spot or that.

The one who from now on they would call only Timur suddenly began to suck at her right nipple, holding it between his incisors—and bit into it. Tanyusha screamed, several times, arching her back high yet still holding fast with her hands. Uspensky, who was raising himself up little by little, nibbled away at it. . . . Finally, the deed was done. Chekhuspekhov managed to tear off the entire tip and swallow it whole. His Adam's apple bobbed. Tanyusha's voice sounded soft and dreamy, so that I could not tell if she was whimpering or singing.

Roused now by what Lepashin had done, they each finally took heart and got down to business. Wherever some piece was licked off and laid bare, all three would take a good bite. They used their hands as well. The thighs were especially prized, particularly the tender inside, of course, so that Pierre and Yaroslav repeatedly banged skulls. They would reel back, but in the next moment dive into the delicacy with still greater determination, as if they were engaged in a contest. Their jaws had very hard work to do. "Battered railroad cars and corpses, what a gruesome sight," they continued in song.

Tanyusha no longer showed any reluctance, but moaned and cursed with a vengeance whenever the trio took too long to chew or dabbed at their mouths and brows with their napkins or could not decide quickly enough where to start in again. She assisted the trio by turning her upper body now to one side, now the other, and was willing as long as it proved possible to turn or lift her legs. But she never released the grip with which she had chained herself, as it were, to the table.

At the latest, Tanyusha died in that moment when the one who insisted on being called Palermo snapped three or four times to get her heart into his mouth and by savagely twisting his head ripped it free from arteries and veins and, his mouth stuffed full, chewed away uncouthly— and a bloody business it was. Meanwhile there was a little squabble between the other two— the only bit of dissension I was able to notice— over the liver. The backs of the knees were a final delicacy.

The radio alarm clock read 10:12 when the three finally stopped, a smeared-up mess from head to foot, not to mention table, floor and walls. Not one corner of a towel was still clean enough to wipe a mouth with. Now they vanished, one after the other. Kostodayev closed the door behind him.

While it was in progress it had all seemed such a matter of course that we somehow grew accustomed to the, to be frank, unappetizing sight and felt no agitation when regarding the eviscerated body, its ribs arching above a puddle of blood and what was left of the entrails. Only Tanyusha's feet with their painted toenails and her head had survived this singular repast. Her eyes were closed, and her mouth had a relaxed smile. She was in a better world now.

We did not dare leave Banya No. 43. We were too tired to clean up. Instead, we went to work on the chicken drumsticks and shashlik spits that Georgy himself had prepared and left in the oven. After that we passed the time playing cards. Around 11:30 we stretched out on the kitchen floor to sleep. Although Georgy hardly snored at all, I could find no rest.

A little after midnight, inspired by the secret hope that the three might have departed without our noticing, I put my ear to the basin-room door.

Not even the gurgle of the overflow drain was to be heard. But their things were still hanging in the locker room. It stank of beer. Shura had done the right thing to flee with the professor and Jesus. I went back to the basin room and debated with myself whether to awaken Georgy Mikhailovitch—if only I had done so! I curse myself for being so considerate! But we're always wiser afterward.

I entered alone but found no one. For better or for worse, the trio had to be sitting in the banya—what an incredible thought!

Trying not to make any noise as I shuffled, I crept to the wooden door. But as hard as I tried to listen, I heard not a peep.

All the rest I have told, have had to tell ad nauseam. No matter how often they have tried to set traps for me, including a great many hints that pointed toward Georgy, I have neither contradicted my testimony nor failed to answer any question, nor have I ever hesitated for a single moment before saying what I had to say, for it was nothing but the truth. And in what can I believe if not in the truth?

The heat was intense, but dry. Maximov and Burlyakov were lying on the wooden benches; on the floor between them, face to the wall, lay Yegorovitch. They were evidently dozing. I climbed up cautiously. Before I even noticed the pistols in their hands, I saw how their bodies glistened. They were sweating at last!

I turned around expecting at any moment to throw myself to the floor at the slightest noise. Even as I closed the door, I remained in a crouch. Georgy had awoken in the meantime and was anxiously waiting for me, which did not prevent him, however, from snacking at the onions and bacon on the shashlik spits. Back to normal, I told him. We were in no mood for chitchat and lay back down to sleep.

It was the police who woke us up. When they carried the three men out, dark outlines were left behind on the wood where they had been lying.

And I am accused of murder! Need I say another word to prove the absurdity of the charge? I shall say only this: Which of us could possibly have been able to save those three?

That is the decisive question that remains to be resolved!

I swear that all my statements have been made to the best of my knowledge and in good conscience. I promise never to rest in my attempts to compensate that upright person into whose hands this letter may eventually fall for efforts and moneys spent leading to my release.

With deepest respect,
Ivan Dmitritch Lipachenko
Veteran of two wars, member of no political party, director of Banya No. 43

This letter was sent anonymously to me at the editorial offices of the newspaper *Privet Peterburg* in September 1993. Banya No. 43 on Fonarny Alley was closed for renovations between July and October 1993. Until February of that year one I. D. Lipachenko was indeed listed as its director. My inquiries, however, have been met with a wall of silence at the banya. All I was able to learn was that Georgy Mikhailovitch died in an automobile accident last spring.

It took me several days to make my way up the ranks of the police to someone who could definitively tell me that I. D. Lipachenko has been listed as missing since February 1993. The search, however, is still on for him, since he is accused of seven murders—the three girls were found in the basin. By way of evidence, I was handed a flyer inquiring as to the whereabouts of the man pictured on it: Ivan Dmitritch

Lipachenko, age forty-three, of St. Petersburg. The photograph showed a man with longish hair, mustache and melancholy eyes. Major P. K. Matyushin of the police skimmed the letter printed above. It contained, he said, no information that might lead to the apprehension of Lipachenko. And with that he dismissed me.

(18)

I never visited Leningrad without undertaking an excursion to Novgorod, whether alone or in the company of others, to see the bronze doors of the Cathedral of St. Sophia, to walk in Yuryev Cloister, close to which the Volkhov flows into Lake Ilmen, and to gaze out over that broad landscape, where churches are scattered like geodetic points.

After a drive of barely two hours and already within the district of Novgorod, on the left side of the Moscow highway is a white brick gas station, along with a house of the same material but decorated with red cinder blocks and set closer to the road. When I first stopped there in the early eighties, there was a sign above the door that was much too small to be read as you drove past: STOLOVAYA. I can remember the bright interior in detail and how cozy it felt the first time I entered it. Clean, starched cloths covered the little tables, the ashtrays had been emptied, the curtains were freshly laundered, and fragrant wild-flowers were set on every table.

I sat down by the window and read the menu in disbelief, for along with borscht and sakuski, egg salad and bread, it offered pelmeni, schnitzel, and roast chicken. A reproduction of Rembrandt's *Prodigal Son*, perhaps the most beautiful painting in the Hermitage, hung beside the kitchen door. When it opened, all I noticed at first was that the waitress was short and on her shoulder carried a large tray from which she served ice cream and fruit salad at two tables. Then she raised her head. I saw a girl of no more than fourteen and of such beauty that it would be hard ever to forget it. Barely able to suppress her laughter at the guests' jokes, she tossed her ponytail back over her shoulder and, with her tray braced against her hip, came over to my table.

"Borscht, pelmeni, juice." She repeated my order, looked at me from under her bangs, turned and left.

From some business travelers who had raised their glasses to me and invited me to join them, I learned that Sonya practically ran the place by herself, with only her father, the grouch outside who pumped gas, to help her clean up each evening.

They called him "Leonid"—perhaps because it really was his name, perhaps only because of his bushy eyebrows. He had wiped my gas cap off and cleaned the windshield, but gruffly refused a tip. Three of my tablemates had first met Sonya the year before, while looking for a bed for the night. The girl and her punch had saved them from the cold, and worse. Normally only truck drivers were allowed to spend the night here, driving on the next day to the Baltic, Finland or Moscow.

"What an evening that was!" said the fellow with the flabby cheeks, propping both elbows on the table.

Sonya was her own cashier and gave correct change down to the kopeck. Each of the Muscovites left a ruble under the ashtray.

Visiting at two-year intervals, I watched the girl grow up. Her face became narrower, her movements lighter, her friendliness more distanced. But the ponytail remained. When I tried to remind her of our earlier meetings, she simply shrugged, arranged settings on the tablecloth and tugged little napkins to rights in their tumblers. She wore no ring. Her fingernails, however, revealed regular care.

From time to time the old man, who had quit working at the gas station, would peer inside as he shoved tea, salad or sausages in at the hatch, through which Sonya would then return the dirty dishes. When she added up the bill, checking it over again before finally tearing the slip from its pad, there was almost nothing to remind you of the girl who had once played her waitress games here.

Four years passed before I returned to the city that, once people recalled how it had been baptized, was now named St. Petersburg. I don't know whether it was more a longing for ancient Novgorod that made me rent a car or my curiosity to know what Sonya and the old man had done with their *stolovaya*. Whenever I recognized a landmark, I expected the white house with the red cinder blocks to appear any moment.

Then I would start to panic at the thought that I could have passed it by. The farther I drove, the more clearly I could see that fourteen-year-old girl, the way she suppressed a smile and tossed her ponytail back over her shoulder and tray. Finally, I arrived in X and turned left at the end of town, where the road grew wider for two hundred yards or so. I hastily grabbed the bottle of whisky from the backseat, hid it under my jacket and went inside.

Not five minutes later, following the waitresses' directions, I found myself driving down a gravel path leading toward a forest that from the highway had been only a thin streak. After driving a good ten minutes, I was about to turn back when, from above shrubs and grasses as tall as a man, a construction trailer came into view, with a set of rusty stairs leading up to the door. Lacking front wheels, the ends of the axle rested on wooden blocks. Half of the only window was covered with cardboard, the ventilator on the roof was turning slowly and thin smoke rose from the pipe beside it. Suddenly I saw a figure standing motionless in the doorway, watching me. I no longer recall what I said. The eyebrows had remained dark and seemed even bushier in a face framed by wisps of gray hair and a stubbly beard. With each step he took down the stairs, with each movement of his knee, his face winced with pain. Once Leonid was standing across from me, he did not hesitate to grab the bottle by the neck with one hand and press it like a stamp against the palm of the other. I asked about Sonya.

"*Herr,*" Leonid began. It was the one German word he knew. "So you knew my Sonyusha?"

I nodded.

"Yes, who didn't know her?" he said, his voice faltering. He held himself very straight, gazing right past me like a blind man but choosing simple words so that I understood everything.

"We didn't have a bad life. The work was hard, but we were glad to do it. Ira worked on the kolkhoz, I built roads. Sonya was two already when we got married. Ira never told us who Sonya's father was. Ira was beautiful, the most beautiful woman between Leningrad and Novgorod. I found work at the gas station, and we didn't have to be separated anymore. Then Ira left for Moscow with the kolkhoz director's oldest son, who had made a lot of money in Siberia. She said: Now she's just your daughter. You understand what I'm saying, *Herr?*

"I brought Sonya up to believe in the ideals of Communism. That's why I took her out of school early. She had to learn what work means, and I wanted to keep her away from bad influences. Sonya and I wanted to be examples. We wanted to prove you can do good work even when it's for other people and not for personal gain. Sad to say, only a few ever try it, far too few. We opened the *stolovaya,* and Sonya was happy that she could do good. Everyone who came in was glad to see her. But there were bad people, too, who complained about the food or told lies about us in town, said we were lining our own pockets. Our ideals were foreign to them. Even our central office was suspicious, because we were making so much money. Then came democracy—and now nobody wanted to really work anymore. Or if they did, then truly just to line their pockets. We didn't even have time left to go mushrooming. And Sonya loved to have mushrooms on the menu!

"One day the restaurant was full of people from Moscow on an excursion, all of them young. They ate and drank so long that they couldn't drive any farther and needed beds. The next morning they showed us their cars, new foreign models. I encouraged Sonya to take a little ride with them into the village to place our orders. Yes, I did encourage her, because we no longer had time even to go mushrooming, and she ought to have some joy in life.

"At first I was angry at her for making me wait so long. At noon she was still not here. Toward evening I notified the police. They wanted to know too many things about me. I closed the *stolovaya* and went searching on my own, wandered the stretches of woods to the left and right of the highway, peering into every car, and did not get home until late that night. I couldn't sleep, I was so worried about her. But Sonya never came home. I numbed myself with work. But I could no longer bear people's questions about her, and so I chucked it all."

The old man cleared his throat a few times. "Two years went by, I was helping out at the gas station, and suddenly there was Sonyusha smiling at me—from a magazine someone left behind. Five pages of pictures of her, dressed different each time. She looked me straight in the eye! So, *Herr*, now you know everything."

As if he had had to work for his bottle and had now finished the job, Leonid turned around and climbed back up the stairs, halting briefly on each step. I just stood there waiting, but not knowing for what.

Six months after this encounter, I got a fax from Petersburg, from Misha Izaakovitch, who is only in his mid-twenties but already a very successful businessman.

> . . . Actually I have a different reason for writing this letter. A month ago I was checking on a construction site, a development on the M river in the district of W, five hours' drive from Peter. On the way home it suddenly began to snow, at first only a little, but then in heavy flakes. The wind was howling, and when we finally reached the main highway, in an instant the dark sky and the snowstorm had merged. Everything vanished. We had no choice but to follow the example of the other cars: we stopped in the next best village and went looking for quarters to bed down in. We ended up spending the night in the house of two old people whose grandson happened to be visiting them. As it turned out, we were only a few miles from X, the village where you went looking in vain for Sonya. I must tell you that Leonid died four months ago. The old people made sour faces and could only say that they hadn't found him until much later. Seryosha, the grandson, a skinny, strange little guy, promised to show me the grave.
>
> He helped shovel the car out the next morning, and we took him with us as far as X. While the others went looking for breakfast, he led me to the cemetery and told me about how two

weeks before he had just been hanging around here when a woman in a long coat came looking for the same grave I wanted to see. So that he would leave her alone, she gave him a thousand rubles, or so he said. Seryosha led me here and there, up and down the cemetery, until I held a note out for him. Then he pointed to a spot directly at our feet.

As I swept the snow from the grave, I kept finding roses everywhere. The little mound was totally covered with them—a sea of roses! You've never seen anything like it.

Seryosha claimed he saw the woman fall to the ground, arms outstretched. Her coat had slowly billowed out until it covered the grave almost completely. He wouldn't tell me anything more, although I gave him another thousand besides.

**19**

. . . I would finally like to keep the promise I made to you.

By way of preface I must note that all I knew about Alexander Kondratenko was that he was fluent in German, English and French, worked at the Institute for Oceanographic Research in Kaliningrad and had been divorced three times, the last time against his wishes by a former Miss Kaliningrad, who was the mother of his youngest son but who is now married to a German from Kazakhstan and living in Hamburg. Alexander celebrated his birthday, November 8, in Petersburg, where he had studied biology with his friend Dr. Kolya Sokolov. (It would be equally rewarding to write about Kolya Sokolov! He works at the Zoological Institute of the Russian Academy of Sciences in P. and on his expeditions to Siberia has discovered more than forty (!) previously unknown species of butterfly. He, too, speaks fluent German. He looked after me during my week's stay in P.)

To the matter at hand: Kolya Sokolov (from here on, simply K.) had persuaded me to accompany him to visit his friend Alexander Kondratenko (from here on, A.). It was the eve of A.'s fiftieth birthday. During his stay in town, he was camping out near the Obvodny Canal in two rooms that had no heat, but that because of the location were still used as an artist's studio. I was surprised to encounter such a hulk of a man, who could barely fit sideways through one leaf of the narrow double door opening onto the stairwell. A. paid no attention to my outstretched hand, drew me to him and kissed me on the brow.

"My brother!" He had been drinking. "Where shall we go?" he asked, and pulled the apartment door to, squeezed between K. and me in the dark and, holding a cigarette lighter out in front of him, started down the stairs in quick, booming strides. Whenever the distance between us became too great, the racket ceased all by itself. A. would turn around and hold out the lighter for us. Each step we came closer, he held it still lower, until his hand was touching the stair immediately in front of us. The stairwell smelled of potato peels.

Moving through back courtyards and down long, narrow driveways, in the middle of which A. kept stopping to hold out the bluish yellow flame at knee level as if searching for something, we made our way out onto a wide street and, once across, suddenly took off at a run toward a bus stop. A. braced open the bus's jerking doors while we slipped in under his arms.

Two stops later, we got off and walked on in the same direction. A. talked about his trips to the South Pole and about the museum at his Institute, where the fetuses of the world's only Siamese twin sharks were displayed. He smiled, little dimples formed at the corners of his mouth, his eyes disappeared inside slits. Despite his suit and tie, despite the unbuttoned overcoat that billowed at his calves, he looked like a clown, a stately buffoon.

Of special interest were his reminiscences about an Atlantic crossing during which butterflies had flown around the ship several hundred miles from the coast. An incredible sight! A. described the insects' length and wingspan by touching thumb tip to thumb tip, forefinger to forefinger, then crossing them over one another—for smaller species—or moving them farther apart for the largest.

Meanwhile we were passing dark, empty store windows, above which stood big letters telling if the shop sold groceries, milk, bread, or fruit and vegetables. In between were squalid doorways and, by way of variety, a fish store, a dry cleaner or sometimes even a kiosk, until it would begin all over again: groceries, milk, bread, vegetables. We had been walking a good while now, K. silent at my side, when A. knocked at a door with a cardboard sign stating business hours. Glimmering through the window beside it was the meager light shed by a single bulb, which was dyeing the bottom third of the curtain orange.

You can believe me when I say that by now I had given up on the idea of champagne and a birthday party. But once eyes appeared in a hole about the width of a thumb and the door opened at the same moment and we were even invited in, K. began smiling again, too. The coat-check attendant brushed our coats smooth over his arm. The waitress, a woman with a broad mouth and short red hair, led us in and used a napkin to sweep crumbs from the only free table. We were shown our seats and given ample time to order. I shall spare you the details of the menu. Although it was after ten o'clock, everything was still available and the prices were more easily converted into pfennigs than marks.

Never failing to keep up with us as we ate, A. went on talking uninterruptedly about those butterflies on the expedition ship, the Schiller monument in Kaliningrad, about fishing trips, old Baltic beach resorts and the village of Tharau.

After an hour and a half I noticed some strange movements in the room. At regular intervals someone would stand up, walk over to a table, bend down and after a brief conversation return with a lit cigarette. No sooner was he seated than another guest at the next table stood up, walked over to the person who had just sat down, bent forward and then returned to his own table. Once there, he would be visited by someone else. . . . That was more or less the pattern. Finally, someone asked us for a light as well. K. had only two matches left. As if by way of apology, the waitress laid her green lighter on the table. A. picked it up and shook it, scratched his thumb several times over the wheel, then handed it back and stood up. He staggered.

"I'm afraid," K. said out of one corner of his mouth, "that A. will fill your ears with his woes tonight yet. . . ." He put his bowl of stewed fruit to his lips, drank and dabbed his mouth with the starched napkin. Then he leaned back in his chair.

The first guests to leave bumped into A. at the door to the entryway. He had looped his tie like a bandage around his right hand. It is not an uncommon thing with big bears like him: suddenly they just capsize. The waitress, who had a bottle of Armenian cognac in her hand, first had to let A. by—that's how doggedly he came walking toward us. His brow was damp.

"I've lost it. . . ." He held himself steady, first on K.'s shoulder, then on the back of his chair.

"I've—lost—it . . ." he repeated disjointedly, and once again was standing in the redhead's way. He even picked a fight—that wasn't real cognac, it had been watered down—until K. took the bottle from her hand and poured. A. gaped down at us. The skin around his cheeks had suddenly gone slack.

"I shouldn't have done that." He dropped into his chair. "I shouldn't have done that!" he wailed, trying to take out a cigarette, but instead he kept shoving the pack farther away with his fingertips. K. finally gave him one of his own. And then the tragic scene began.

"Do you know what that means, to be a friend?" A. asked. I let him have my left forearm, on top of which he had laid his hand, as if I might run away from the question. "I'm having trouble with him, with my friend." A. stared at his hand, which was still grasping my arm. Then he raised his head. "Tell him he should wear it. He'll listen to you!"

K. bent down across the table as if to drink from his glass without using his hands and explained: "A. was in Hamburg, to see his son—"

A. interrupted at this point, but K. went right on, saying that A. meant a coat Irina in Hamburg had given to A. to give to K., a coat just like the one A. was wearing.

"He won't wear it!" A. blurted out. His cigarette was dangling so precariously from his lips that it looked as if it might drop at any moment. Ashes drizzled from it as he spoke. And then, before we could react, he stamped the cigarette out.

"Uh-oh!" the waitress said, and put her cigarette back. Even A. realized in the next moment what he had done. K., however, stood up and went out onto the street to find a light. A. grabbed me by the arm again.

"She opens the door, and there I stand," he began, as if he had to make good use of K.'s absence. He spoke of how his son had recognized him and asked him if he knew how to drive a car.

"I slept there," A. said. "Her in one, and me in the other. Each in his own room. She wanted me to understand her. And there was a new coat for Kolya, too. And three days later—whoosh, gone, before the Kazakh got home."

He was close to sobbing. And suddenly he said, "I'm a German, and I mean a real German!" and his forehand sank onto the hand that held my arm tight. The best thing, it seemed to me, was to just let him weep.

K., having returned now, gave his cigarette butt to the waitress, clapped A. on the back and explained to me that A. was not really named A. at all, because A. was not a real German name. No one knew A.'s real name, because as a German orphan he had been raised in a home. "His birthday is May 8, because all the kids in his group have May 8 for their birthday." Which was why A. celebrated his on the day that was furthest away in the year. He knew only that his mother had once put dyed eggs under his pillow. That was the only German custom he could remember, which was no help to him at all.

We were the last party that the waitress asked to pay its bill. A. raised his head as if he wanted to show his tears and said in English, "But I have much more rights to live in Hamburg than this bastard!"

Then he let go of my arm, braced himself on the table and got to his feet. He stumbled to the coat-check room between the two of us. He wept. Never before had I seen a man weep as he walked and not even bother to wipe the tears away.

A. eventually got his arms into his sleeves. K. gave the coat-check attendant, who also removed the iron bars from the entrance, a couple of notes. A. stood swaying in the middle of the entryway, holding the hem of his coat in his hands. We waited. The coat-check attendant placed his feet closer together and stood with arms crossed, rubbing his biceps. A. was so busy thrusting his left hand—which he had evidently stuck through the pocket and in under the lining—down into the hem of his coat that he stopped crying. His fingers groped along in tandem, and now a look of happiness flitted over his face, the dimples appeared and the slit eyes, too. Slowly he pulled his hand back out through the hole, stretched out his arm and opened his fist in triumph. "There it is again, our aurora butterfly!" K. said, a cigarette already in one corner of his mouth. I gave the coat-check attendant a bit more money, since it was already twenty past midnight. . . .

It was a sunny April day. Below the office windows the guys with the shell game were shouting. Florian Müller-Fritsch was wheezing. He felt the end had come. Ever since this morning, when over the obstacle of his belly he had had to roll his socks inch by inch up over his sweaty feet, he had smelled death. It was no longer his own stench, which had so often substituted for the company he lacked, not that foul odor whose essence remained on his fingertips after he had clipped his toenails, not the aroma of his own farts, which he liked best to sniff from under the bedcovers or inhale from the bubbles rising in his bathwater, and most certainly not the fetor like old vase water that was his own breath, or the delicate bitterness of his sweat when he scratched his back. What Florian Müller-Fritsch now smelled had finality.

All the same, he didn't call a doctor but went to the office. He didn't want to go to a hospital or crawl in a hole like an animal; he wanted at least to have the German language around him, even if he couldn't stand the people who came with it. He would lie down in the middle of the office and die. That would shock even the Russians.

He was surprised at his own inner calm despite his shortness of breath, and at the lack of any un-usual thoughts or feelings. Nothing that changed his view of the world. The time was long past for some achievement, something permanent. For what Florian Müller-Fritsch had dreamt for himself had always been granted only to others—to his boss, for example, who had not even been born yet when he could already write and do sums. Florian Müller-Fritsch had never given much thought to death. For years he had been a believer. Later he had gritted his teeth and survived one thing after another and put that all behind him. And now he was done with life as well. It all went too fast. Maybe that was why he was so composed.

Florian Müller-Fritsch did not touch the work on his desk. He would not last until the afternoon confer-ence in any case. Just the walk had devoured his ener-gies. It was also hard to comprehend that you were seeing everything for the last time: the nail clippers, the doormat, the driveway entrance, the dairy shop, Sennaya Square. To enter a building for the last time, to climb the stairs, to say good morning and get no answer. At least his Russian colleagues had opened the window. Did they smell his death, too? His shirt and undershirt clung to his back. He shouldn't have leaned against the wall. Spots were even coming through his tie, and white rings were forming under the sleeves of his jacket. He didn't have to be embarrassed by that anymore. This wasn't even him anymore.

Florian Müller-Fritsch hesitated to stand up. Neither his boss nor the boss's deputy looked in on him. No one spoke his name. And yet they surely had to notice something was wrong with him.

The files crinkled under his hand. He tried to slip off his shoes—with no luck. He pressed his teeth together till they gnashed—then quickly opened his mouth again. No air was getting through his nose. But he could smell death all the same.

Florian Müller-Fritsch braced himself and got to his feet, gave the desktop a slap and staggered to the window. He wiped his throat and the back of his neck with a handkerchief, used a sleeve for his forehead. The sweat, or whatever that was, trickled and itched. He reached for the backs of his knees and almost fell. He sank down across the windowsill, heavy and soft. Maybe sunshine would help.

He stuck his head out and dripped on the shell-game players, without their noticing. They would make perfect sales reps! The way they accosted strangers and enticed them and did not let them go again. The way they could alter their tone of voice, facial and body language from one moment to the next, depending on how they intuited their victim's state of mind. He neither had any idea of how they made their money, nor had he ever placed a bet. My God, Florian Müller-Fritsch thought, what am I doing with my last hour of life? He tried to imagine all the passersby coming to his funeral, and that trees were still growing in those little curbed enclosures along the street.

Suddenly board, tumblers and ball vanished below him. A woman screamed, wailed. Mouth wrenched wide, she reeled back into the semicircle of onlookers. People pointed at her. His thoughts accelerated. A carousel of images began. The woman had lost everything, everything, a whole month's wages, if not more. You didn't have to know Russian to understand that. She knelt down beside the little puddle of his drops and pulled her cardigan off. Slipped her sandals from her heels. But no one wanted those, either, and her arm fell again. And then something happened to him, something unexpected and without any great to-do. Florian Müller-Fritsch felt the warm easing between his legs and understood: He, too, could be someone's destiny.

In the next moment he pushed himself back into the office, groped for the door. Intoxicated, he followed the eddies of his thoughts, crashed against the railing on the stairs, propped himself on it. Half falling, half pushing, down he went. People made way for him, flattening themselves against the wall. If only she's still there, Müller-Fritsch thought, kicking open the door and stepping outside. The wet sole had loosened itself from his right shoe, his teeth had sunk deeper into his gums, his tie cut into his neck. The woman was still crouching there on the sidewalk, wailing and pulling at her hair. He would put an end to her hell, now! But no sooner was he standing in front of her than his shirt began to unravel across his stomach and at the collar. With renewed energy, the woman let out another shriek, tried to stand up, staggered back, pulling others with her.

Florian Müller-Fritsch smiled at her, however, even though his teeth were now only stumps. She didn't have to think him handsome or attractive, she didn't have to do anything for this. He had chosen her. His sacrifice was for her. He reached for his wallet, which was stuck to the fabric; he ripped it free—in his hands the leather softened, paper mush oozed out. His right trouser leg dissolved.

Russia, thought Florian Müller-Fritsch, Russia. Images were whirling faster now: wide landscapes, scudding clouds, distant horizon, trees and meadows, sun and water. His lips melted, his shoulders caved in, the leg bearing his weight grew shorter and shorter. He had only a few movements left. . . . Florian Müller-Fritsch managed just four more steps, then toppled slowly, landing on his side. His fat legs twitched. Knees up against chin, he covered his smiling, grimacing face with his arms.

Passersby came crowding over, stood around the tiny enclosure beside the curb, nothing more than dirt and dog turds and, sometime long ago, a tree. The windows filled, people pointed at the cowering mountain of flesh, and someone blurted out: Müller, you walrus! But he heard nothing now.

When the ambulance came, Florian Müller-Fritsch was already so soft that they had to send for plastic bags. But that took too long. By the time those arrived, the rest of Florian Müller-Fritsch had just oozed away, leaving behind a fresh dark spot on the ground and a sweetish, sweaty odor.

The following year a tender sprout emerged inside the enclosure not far from the shell-game players' spot, a young poplar, which by May had met its end under the wheels of a police van.

O h, her . . ." Alyosha groaned to himself as the short woman opened the door. He never thought of her until she was standing in front of him. And as always, it startled him. "No need to be afraid, he's in a good mood today," Vera Andreyevna said, standing on tiptoe to take Alyosha's coat from his shoulders. But then he held the heavy thing in one hand by the collar and waited until she gave him a hanger.

Alyosha knew the apartment as well as if he had once roomed here. The same jackets and coats were hanging from the red Peg-Board; he saw the same shapkas on the hat shelf, and beneath it lay the same dark green rubber mat from ten years before, when, following his last exams, he had been invited to visit Semyon's home for the first time.

"Happy New Year, dear Vera Andreyevna, my best, best wishes. . . ." He presented her with the roses wrapped in cellophane, three long-stemmed yellow roses, for which he had spent more than for the two bottles of vodka in his shoulder bag.

"Oooh, Alyosha Sergeyevitch, how marvelous, roses at this time of year, such marvelous roses. You are out of your mind!"

Three splendid roses—and he had now given them to this woman to whom he felt no connection, about whom he knew nothing more than that Semyon never spoke of her. Shouldn't he simply grab the roses away from her again, right here and now, the first long-stemmed roses he had ever been able to buy for his friend and teacher? They even still had their leaves. And he had simply given them away.

"Come, come, Alyosha, down along here," she whispered.

He put his comb back in his jacket and picked up his cream-colored shoulder bag. Vera Andreyevna opened the living-room door a crack. Semyon was lying down, one leg crooked and resting against the back of the sofa, the other under a plaid wool blanket. He was wearing his dark green crewneck pullover and squinted in that same nervous way he had always done when searching the audience for Alyosha at the start of a lecture.

"Who's there?"

Already at his side, Vera Andreyevna took his glasses from the tea table beside his pillow and tucked the side pieces behind his ears.

"Look here, my dear, Alyosha Sergeyevitch Anukhin, your favorite, and these roses here—for me!"

Semyon raised himself up from his pillow. He cast the blanket off and maneuvered his long legs around to the carpet. Vera Andreyevna helped him sit up.

"Alyonushka!" Semyon fought back a belch. Alyosha waited until he had folded his bathrobe over the legs of his pajamas. Vera Andreyevna held his house shoes under his feet so that all he had to do was slide into them and, alternately setting out one foot, then the other, push until his toes were firmly in the tips.

They greeted each other in silence. Not until Vera Andreyevna had left the room with the roses did Alyosha squat down and clasp Semyon's hands, pressing them to his lips. He was close to tears. Semyon kissed him on the brow.

"Three years, Alyonushka, three years." Semyon withdrew his hands in order to push himself farther forward.

"Come now, stand up!" He ran a hand through his student's hair. Alyosha remained in a crouch.

"Fetch that chair there, or wait, we'll sit together. . . ." Semyon pointed to the table and pressed his lips tight. His neck tightened again in anticipation of another belch.

Alyosha did not know what to do. He would most have liked to say: I'm sorry! And yet what reason had he to blame himself? He had phoned Semyon, written him letters. Before Alyosha's mother had moved from Petersburg to be with them in Kharkov, his visits had always been a matter of course.

"You made her very happy, dear boy, come, sit down, here," Semyon said, and stood up.

"I have something else!" Alyosha patted the cream-colored shoulder bag. Now he could smile. Semyon smelled of vodka. On a round plastic coaster with the symbol of the Tenth World Festival Games, Berlin, 1973, stood a water glass with a black rubber band stretched around it, exactly halfway up.

Semyon opened one door of the sideboard with his fingernails, took one bottle from the table and shoved it behind the other door. His hands trembled as he clasped two of the fancy green glasses between his fingers. He pushed the door closed, pressing his knee against it. Glass and china gave a familiar jingle.

"Enough is enough!" With a shake of his shoulders he fended off Alyosha, who had stood up to embrace him.

They were sitting silently side by side when Vera Andreyevna entered with a vase in which the three roses pitched to and fro.

"We don't have anything that's right for them," she said as if to herself, and returned to the kitchen.

Semyon pulled the tinfoil cap off the bottle and poured. "Here's to you, dear boy."

"To you, Semyon."

They drank it down. Semyon poured another.

"I'm always trying to ambush sleep," he said after a pause. "I've become a regular hunter." He laughed and shook his head a few times.

"How are you, Semyon? Your health is good?"

"Why ask. Healthy, sick, what's the difference? I don't complain."

"I've heard you spend a lot of time in bed."

"You've heard?"

"You told me yourself, on the phone."

"It's more comfortable than sitting. What is there to say on the telephone?"

"Yes, what . . . ?"

". . . nothing." Semyon pouted his large, slightly bluish lower lip, until his mouth was nothing but a splotch of bright red flesh.

Alyosha searched for questions and was afraid he would break into a sweat. "And because you can't sleep at night, you're tired during the day," he said at last.

"I'm not tired, that's the trouble."

"And so . . ." Flicking his chin with his right forefinger, Alyosha tried to smile.

"Enough . . ." Semyon turned back to the table so that their knees no longer touched.

Alyosha blushed.

"Come, Alyonushka, let's drink to our reunion," Semyon said to cheer him up, and raised his glass between two fingers. The vodka sloshed from both glasses onto the white crocheted tablecloth.

Alyosha wiped his forearm across his brow. "Semyon," he blurted out, "Semyon—all I wanted to tell you is simply that I love you." Alyosha knew exactly how he looked now. He told the truth. "We just have to get used to each other again, you know what I mean?"

Semyon did not reply and refilled the glasses. "Then let's drink to our getting used to each other."

More vodka spilled on the tablecloth. Alyosha put his finger through a crocheted blossom, trying to rub off the drops. "You're alone a lot?" he asked.

"It's not so bad." Semyon drummed his fingernails against the empty glass. "That's no vase for roses," he said, without turning his head. "A few days ago they wrote about our Antonova. You remember her, don't you? The girl who used to work the library desk? There was an article in *Vedemosty.*"

". . . it's been an eternity since I was here last." Crossing his arms, Alyosha propped himself on the table. The empty glass stood before him.

"Antonova visits me regularly." Semyon was still staring at the vase. "You didn't read it then?"

Alyosha shook his head.

"She comes once, twice a month, whenever Vera happens to visit her sister."

"She helps you out, does she?"

Semyon laughed. "She helps me out, yes, yes. She has a folder of newspapers that you're supposed to look at while she crawls under the table. Plus some Mussorgsky or Glinka." Semyon whistled a few notes.

"Under the table?"

"How else? I don't want to watch her at it. I read sometimes, and then it takes longer."

Alyosha stared at Semyon's profile.

"I assume she spits out her false teeth first." He laughed, and as he leaned back he stroked the flat of his hand across the crocheted cloth to the edge of the table. "*Vedemosty* didn't even change her name. How about a game?" They both stood up together. The door handle jiggled several times before Vera Andre-yevna's elbow pushed the door open. She entered with the tray. Semyon pulled the chair to his right out from under the table and picked up the chessboard, bent down for a plastic box and poured the figures out. They were too small for the board. Then he shuffled off to the bathroom. Vera Andreyevna hurried to set the table.

"Well, is life still exciting?"

"If you only knew how we suffer, Alyosha Sergeyevitch, this isn't even living anymore." She put the lids to the varenye glasses upside down on the tray. "Him most of all, he suffers so, Alyosha Sergeyevitch, help him!" She was now holding the empty tray in both hands.

"Do you suffer, too, Vera Andreyevna?"

"Sometimes I think that it's all just a bad dream. I can't get used to it, Alyosha Sergeyevitch. When we spoke of how the system of the socialist state was just a temporary first foot in the door of capitalism, for me that was more like a tribute, you know, as if they were trying to tell us that the struggle goes on, that you're the vanguard, you're carrying the banner now, it all depends on you. And suddenly, just like that, reaction rears its head everywhere, and there's no longer supposed to be any place for us and it was all in vain? He suffers from all that. Help him, I beg you, Alyosha Sergeyevitch, help him and us, tell us that it was not in vain and that the struggle goes on, I beg you, Alyosha Sergeyevitch."

"Yes, Vera Andreyevna. But you must promise me something, too," he said, clearing his throat and crossing his arms over his chest. "You mustn't let your courage flag, either. It does depend on you, now more than ever, surely you know that, Vera Andreyevna."

Alyosha spent the few minutes he was alone in the

living room walking around the table, stroking the backs of the chairs like a railing and stopping out of habit at Semyon's desk.

How often he had squatted down beside it, trying not to miss a single title of the books piled there in leaning towers. Back then, he had pulled out the précis and excerpts, the articles and lectures, from between the pages, and then smuggled them back in place. All that was left now was a desk lamp and a paperweight, as if Semyon had just recently rented the place.

Alyosha went back to the table a second time. He found nothing he could pick up in his hand. Not even a newspaper. Only the chessboard, the water glass with the black rubber band and the old coaster suggested that someone lived here. Bending down over a chairback, he arranged the chess pieces and then sat down.

"Dig in, dear boy," Semyon said, closing the door behind him and laying a hand over the light switch. "Like this—or maybe this—or—or leave it on high?"

Two dull yellow globes shone above the table and were reflected in the pastry plates. A flame flickered under the glass teapot.

Over his pajamas Semyon was now wearing his dark green cardigan instead of his bathrobe. He smelled of soap and the toilet. Still standing, he passed the bowl, from which Alyosha took one of the cookies decorated with marmalade. Semyon, however, tipped it now, letting half the pastries slide onto Alyosha's plate, and poured tea. Alyosha closed his eyes for a moment.

"Say it, Semyon, please," he uttered in torment, as if he had to invent each word anew. "After our—"

"Alyonushka?" Semyon leaned across the table and gave Alyosha a kiss on the mouth. Then he drank. "What else is there to say? You know it all better yourself. And now you know about Antonovna, too! But whether I can still afford to pay her now that she's a celebrity . . ."

"What do I know better?" Alyosha asked, and took a sip from his glass as if that were one of his duties.

Semyon set his cup back down on his plate. "Why do you act as if nothing has happened?"

"I couldn't come before this, believe me. . . ."

Elbows on the table, Semyon put his face in his hands. His large, fleshy ears stood out. Now that his hair was longer and unkempt, they weren't so noticeable anymore. "Alyonushka, this is not about me and not about you and not about Vera. Isn't it enough for you that everything we lived for is gone, collapsed, has turned to dust, to crap! Isn't that enough?" He rubbed his eyes with the balls of his hands. "Three years, it took less than three years. It makes me sick!"

Alyosha dunked a cookie in his tea and, bending over his cup, bit the soggy part off. As he took a second bite a corner of the cookie fell into his tea. He fished it out again with a spoon. Alyosha shoved another cookie in his mouth. He ate quickly and with a good appetite. The clock in the hall struck three.

"Let's play," Semyon said, and sat down with his glass at the other end of the table, near the window, where the chessboard was. His eyes were bloodshot. Still chewing, Alyosha moved down two chairs to face him and now settled in front of the white pieces.

"I haven't played for an eternity," Alyosha said.

"Doesn't matter."

"We never played chess."

"Hm."

"What should you care if people want sausage and then ham with their butter. Do you think your ideas will lengthen their lives?" Alyosha said.

"What do you mean my ideas . . . ?"

"They were mine, too. . . ."

"One first has to consider and then make a move. This is my move."

"Stop believing, then it's easier. You drink too much."

*Mens sana in corpore sano, mon ange.*"

"Listening to you at the university and afterwards, the whole world seemed understandable and I thought I knew how a man is supposed to live."

"You've forgotten it. That is our fate, and there's nothing anyone can do."

"Man is meant to work, you said, to strive for knowledge, to educate and perfect himself; in that alone would be found the meaning and goal of his life, his happiness, his fulfillment. I believed you."

"We worked like oxen, like beasts, like horses."

"Just like our ancestors. They built the seven gates of Thebes, they pulled ships up the Volga."

"My past has vanished. I know no one who would not behave like the rest, not one fighter from the old days."

"There is no happiness in Russia, and never will be,

we merely wish it for ourselves. Perhaps you want to keep the wish alive, is that it?"

"Sorry, sorry, you can't make that move. Well? Where do you want to move now? Ah, that's different."

"I am unwilling to let my feelings perish uselessly like a ray of sunlight in a ditch. I no longer suffer."

"Oh go on! Our situation, yours as well as mine, is hopeless, whether you happen to be suffering or not." (Semyon takes a large gulp of vodka from his water glass. They stare at the chessboard.)

"It seemed to me that a man must have faith, he must trust his ideas and ideals, believe in them, otherwise his life remains empty, empty. . . ."

(Pause.)

"To live and not know what for . . . either one knows what one is living for or everything is utterly absurd and has no meaning whatever."

"Nonsense. Sense . . . it's snowing outside. What's the sense of that?"

(Pause.)

"Let me think." (Semyon touches several pieces, one after the other.)

"Careful, the knight."

(Pause.)

"I know, I know—I drink my little glass down, my fine little glass, hurrah, life, life is rosy red, just as long as you're not dead!"

(Semyon finally makes his move. Alyosha at once captures his queen before Semyon can pull her back.)

"Sometimes I want to live like the Devil lives. . . ."

(Pause.)

"If I could start all over again, what would I do

differently? Nothing, presumably. No wife maybe. What should I do differently? I wanted a different world. One that could be changed." (Semyon pours himself another. With his thumbnail he nudges the black rubber band up the glass.)

"I think that's . . . check!"

(Pause.)

"Take the pawn. I can hear everything coming to a standstill. Soon nothing will be moving. And when it has been very still for a while, then you'll hear a thudding sound that just won't stop, boom, first the standstill, then the crash. I am a prophet, keep that in mind!" (Semyon yawns.)

"And—check."

(A longer pause.)

"You rascal you."

"You drink too much."

(A longer pause, during which they play.)

"I fight boredom with agony. Leave me my agony."

"Check."

(A longer pause.)

"Otherwise there's only boredom." (Semyon yawns.)

"You're not paying attention."

"There is nothing more ridiculous than a clock." (Semyon yawns.) "Where has it all vanished to, where is it now?" (He yawns again.) "Tell me, am I a traitor, too, if I find my only pleasure between the toothless gums of our Antonova?"

"Everything today frightens me somehow."

"That thought strikes me sometimes like an ax." (Semyon yawns.)

"What?"

"This standstill. Only victims and wheeler-dealers."

"Check. You're not paying attention."

"To go to Volgograd, just once I'd like to see it, that hill, Volgograd."

"Your turn."

(A longer pause.)

"I'm tired."

"Three more moves, Semyon, another three or four."

"Oh, enough. What a damned unbearable life."

"This is your only move."

"I was happy once, it didn't matter if it was summer or winter in Leningrad."

"Let's finish this."

Semyon tossed down the rest of his vodka. "Some other time, Alyonushka, some other time." He was on his feet now.

"Look here, you can't do anything else." Alyosha began to place the pieces, looking up at Semyon with each move. "Here's check, here's check, and this man's covered, see, the only possibility is here. But there is the knight. . . ."

"I must heed my exhaustion, enough. . . ." Semyon staggered with his empty glass to the sofa, sat down. "Some other time, some other time . . ." He rubbed each house shoe off with the other foot and put the empty glass on the tea table.

Alyosha walked over to him, the chessboard like a tray on his palm. "Three more moves!"

"Hand me the blanket, please, no, some other time, next year or whenever you come back, Alyonushka, hand it to me. . . ." Semyon lay on his side, his face to the back of the sofa. He still had his glasses on.

Alyosha slid the chessboard back on the table, spread the blanket over Semyon and pulled it up to cover his shoulders. Nothing betrayed his rage. He even lifted the old man's feet up and folded the blanket under them. "Do you want to sleep?" He listened to Semyon's breathing.

The old man had underestimated him. Alyosha finished all the moves. It was inevitable—an elegant checkmate with the knight. "What did you say?" He was back beside the sofa at once.

The old man was breathing more easily. A dark shadow was visible at the glass door.

"What?" Alyosha couldn't understand the disjointed sounds.

". . . the mathematicians died as well, many talented young men, but not the zoologists. . . ." The old man went on muttering incomprehensibly. Alyosha bent down over him and winced. Spittle was dribbling from Semyon's mouth. "Against England, against England. . . ." Then he began to snore.

Alyosha stood up, pulled his cream-colored shoulder bag from between the legs of the chair and looked around once more to the chessboard. When Semyon woke up he would have to see that elegant checkmate with the knight. He pushed his chair under the table, cleared his throat and walked to the door. The shadow vanished.

"Very nice, very nice, thank you so much," Vera Andreyevna said. "Come back often. Your encouragement does him good." She clasped his right hand. "At some point quantity simply has to turn into quality, and then"—Vera Andreyevna began to weep—

"then we'll still have a lovely year or two to look forward to."

She suddenly stepped closer to Alyosha, who was putting on his shoes, and stroked his hair until he got to his feet.

"That is my hope as well, Vera Andreyevna," he said, and shook her hand and hung the cream-colored bag over his shoulder.

Alyosha went down the stairs, while Vera Andreyevna stood in the doorway. She watched him go and thought: If he turns at the next landing and waves, then everything will be all right.

Viktoria Federovna opened her eyes as the eerie singing began in the panes of her bedroom door, spread to the wardrobe and bed, and finally set even lamp and ceiling jingling. She lay there without stirring, but noting every detail. Once this singing was over, she wanted to be able to say where it had first begun, the exact volume to which it had swelled, whether there were words for describing it or sounds for imitating it—she did not want to be limited to speculations.

Then the lamp stopped ringing, the song died away, left her bed, retreated, leapt from the wardrobe to the panes in the door, loitered briefly and vanished. Only in the ceiling was there still a whimper, a high, almost shrill tone that would not calm down. It lured the song out of hiding again. Already it was clinging to the panes, and quickly took hold in the wood of the bed and wardrobe and reached the ceiling again, as if returning to its nest.

Viktoria Federovna stared up at the net of black lines, which she had divided into six zones. She did not notice any new cracks. "Good morning," she said, and repeated, "Good morning." Even after her third "Good morning," she was not sure if her voice could have been heard in the entry hall.

She put her right hand to the wall—the vibration was there. If she held a hand over her left ear, the song was softer. It hummed and scurried back from the lamp, across ceiling and wardrobe to her bed, halted, before fleeing to the door, and out.

"How peculiar," Viktoria Federovna said, and thought that someone in the corridor might have understood her. Since she had been living alone, her hearing had grown more acute. Which was why she could not claim with certainty that this singing had never existed before. But she could not recall it.

The alarm clock showed three minutes past seven. Normally she awoke at half past. She turned over on her side and snapped her fingers: the song started up in the panes, reached out to the wardrobe, across the bed and as far as the lamp. She snapped her fingers: it ebbed but kept up the whimpering, didn't calm down. Snap: it leapt up at the panes.

Viktoria Federovna took exact note of the turning

points. If she waited too long, she got angry for foolishly missing her chance. After three such defeats, she put her arm under the blanket, stuck two fingers between the buttons on her nightie and drew circles around her navel. Her forefinger flicked—the singing died away. Her fingers circled her navel. "Practice makes perfect," she said to drown out the whimper. Now she thrust her middle finger forward—the starting signal.

She kept the rhythm going nicely. "It comes and goes like a trained wolf."

Then nothing more happened. She flicked her forefinger in the little dimple, tried a third time. She had never missed so badly. The whimpering fell silent. The clock ticked beside her. Viktoria Federovna raised her head from her pillow. "Amazing," she said to the silence, went on stroking her tummy, pushed her forefinger into her navel until there was no air left under the tip—and popped it out again, as if from the end of a bottle.

"If I get up, I'll have twenty extra minutes." And now she moved her legs out over the narrow runner, beneath which loose pieces of parquet clattered, and pulled back the curtains. The thermometer read a few degrees above freezing. In the street were tanks standing in the rain. Tanks as far as she could see.

"Uh-oh, uh-oh, uh-oh!" Viktoria Federovna pressed her face to the window and drummed her fingernails against the pane. "Rotten weather!" Then she warmed the palms of her hands on the radiator.

The cup beside her bed reminded her of the night just past. She had drunk hot unsweetened tea to cure a chill and the feeling of little lumps in her throat and stomach, but the aftertaste had almost made her retch. It was part of the flu she had been dragging around with her for days now. The headaches, the queasy stomach, the weakness in the legs had all come on their own, so they would have to leave on their own. But they did not go away, and Viktoria Federovna had grown accustomed to them the way you get used to a heavy coat that makes you sweat and leaves you freezing when you take it off.

The sharp pain in her neck had disappeared, along with the fatigue, which as she was getting to her feet had congealed to its aching essence inside her head, right at the spot where it had last touched the pillow. Gently she lowered her head to her right shoulder, shifted it to her left, then right again, back and forth, laid her warmed hands on the little bulge of her belly and went to the kitchen. She had set as her first goal to have breakfast and nevertheless not be late.

Viktoria Federovna held a used match to the little flame of the water heater and lit the middle burner with it, turned the tap on; the pipes banged. She turned the tap wider and held the kettle under the jet. From the fridge she took butter, tvorog, a large jar of varenye and the white bread she had tightly wrapped in a bag on Sunday. She laid her knife on the plate and set the cup and sugar bowl beside it. It was fun to do for herself. Except she couldn't find the tea sieve again. From experience Viktoria Federovna knew that it would be a good idea to check the rim of the sink in the bathroom. And indeed the sieve was lying next to the soap.

She now climbed into the tub, threw her nightie over the two large hooks and balanced herself on her heels because the water was still cold. In her son's shaving mirror attached to the windowsill above her— through a pane in the door, daylight entered from the direction of the kitchen—she saw only her hairline. She had to stand on tiptoe if she wanted to look herself in the eye.

"Sick? Not a bit," said Viktoria Federovna, and looked to see if her smile could be read from just her eyes. It was finally turning warm between her toes.

She pushed her hair up under her cap, squatted and switched to "shower." Closing her eyes, she let the water fall now on her right shoulder, now on her left and held the jet over her nose. She relished two whole minutes of this. Then she began to brush her teeth and lather. Although she was a brunette of the darker sort, the hair on her forearms and legs was so sparse that she never hesitated to go without stockings in June. Bracing one leg on the edge of the tub, she gently massaged her calf, moving up and down the shin and rubbing her thumb across her toes, where a few flecks of red polish on the nails served as a reminder of summer. Rinsing off was the ticklish part of the schedule, for Viktoria Federovna enjoyed the warmth so much that she would often first be startled into action by the whistle of the teakettle. Getting out of the tub was worse than getting up: tea always woke her up, but she would freeze all day long.

She slipped her fingers under the bathing cap, tossed it deftly into the sink and dried the drops from her arms, legs and butt. She had goose bumps all over.

She ran her forefinger around the shaving mirror, making ever smaller circles. If she moved it and her son, Igor Timofeyevitch, arrived for one of his infrequent visits, he would grumble just like her husband used to. She caught herself smiling and pushed the mirror farther around, stepped back an inch or two, tucked in her belly, waved at herself with her toes and exhaled. She really had lost weight. Viktoria Federovna fished the blue bathrobe, her favorite article of clothing, from its hook, folded first one half in front of her, then the other, tied the belt and grabbed the sieve.

For ages now she had felt it incumbent upon her to behave no differently by herself than in the company of others. That was as much a part of the battle against a lack of culture as a well-set table. At five after eight she had eaten her tvorog with varenye, one slice of bread and butter, and had drunk three cups of sweet tea.

"If I manage to arrive on time, the week will have been a success!" She set the dishes in the left front corner of the sink, poured the rest of the hot water from the kettle over them, turned on the tap, put on her yellow rubber gloves and scrubbed with the brush. Once clean, the two cups, the plate, knife and spoon were placed in the right front corner. After that she wiped the table, rinsed out the rag and dried the dishes. As she was tossing her dirty underwear into the basket in the bedroom, she heard two thuds from the stairwell: ten after eight. You could depend on Marya Ivanovna. Since she was the last of her family to leave their apartment, you didn't hear the radio while the door stood open.

Viktoria Federovna wore the same wool panty hose as yesterday and the blue dress she normally thought suitable only for the theater. It was nothing special, except for the white collar embroidered with white thread. But the more slender she was, the better it looked on her. Before she pulled on her boots she went to the toilet. She hadn't dawdled, but her extra twenty minutes were gone. Shortly before eight-thirty Viktoria Federovna pushed a few strands of hair under her cap, picked up her handbag, closed the double doors to the apartment and gave the outside one a shake, just as she always did. After the first steps, she took hold of the banister.

"Never pays to overdo!" She could hardly feel her knees, they still had so little strength. Now she remembered her umbrella again. She had packed her marmalade jar and the plastic bag yesterday. She had to be careful and budget her energy. Viktoria Fede-rovna was crossing the courtyard in measured steps when she saw Misha Sergeyevitch coming toward her, carrying a covered washbasin at stomach height. He was always dragging something home. Although they lived all the way up top. His head tucked low from exertion, his key pouch between his teeth, he greeted her out of the corner of his mouth. Instead of nodding, she simply raised her right hand, and was about to turn around to punch the code to let Misha in when without stopping he turned around at the entrance and forced the main door with his back. Just watching gave Viktoria Federovna a headache.

She showed her monthly pass at the subway station and made sure the woman who checked really saw it.

Last year, in this same station she had used for eighteen years, someone had grabbed her by the arm and spun her around. She was cheating the state, a controller had shouted for all to hear. No one had stopped to testify on her behalf. And until she had dug her pass from her handbag again, so many people had gone by that those on the platform probably did take her for a cheat. It wouldn't hurt them to show a little understanding for people, she had said at the office in describing the incident, but uttered not a word about the fear that being grabbed like that had left her with. Even when she wasn't thinking of it, she sometimes felt that hand on her arm. How very different things were with the teenagers who leapt over the barrier in plain view, paid no attention to whistles and instructions, and weren't even afraid to give the subway personnel a shove at the bottom of the stairs. There had been a newspaper article about how one such lad had been shot by a policeman. The policeman got hauled into court. But where is the limit beyond which measures have to be taken? She was on the policeman's side. Otherwise everyone would be leaping over the barricade someday, and only the old and sick would pay to ride. All the same, Viktoria Federovna felt confident she could manage such a leap, only not today and not in front of all these people. She was also the sort who didn't stand on the right side of the escalator but walked down it on the left. That saved thirty seconds, which was sometimes enough for her to catch an earlier train, or at the least to make the first car. That way she was among the first to arrive up top at

Sennaya Square. Today, however, she joined those on the right.

As the escalator dropped Viktoria Federovna off, she had just enough time not to have to take the last car. She even found a seat before others squeezed in. One phase of her trip had been successfully completed. For the remaining fourteen minutes of the trip, she closed her eyes—not because she was tired but in order to protect her body from external stimuli and preserve as much of its energy as possible. Perhaps, however, she accomplished just the opposite, for she never failed to notice even the slightest contact with her neighbors. Each acceleration, each braking forced thigh against thigh, shoulder against shoulder. Before every stop the pressure of compacting hips increased and was released as the body shifted along the bench. On the other hand, Viktoria Federovna strove to avoid passing on the full impact of what she herself was experiencing. Today, however, she gave herself over to inertia. Except for her head. She would never understand how anyone could rest her head on a stranger's shoulder. It was already too much for her when, as sometimes happened, the long bench emptied out, but her neighbors to right and left remained seated, as if they were a family of three. She found that offensive. Whereas she happily recalled two men who had been so wrapped up in their conversation that their heads had banged together whenever the train started or stopped. They were discussing something, with each brushing the back of his hand across the other's jacket. They were still talking away as they got off. She had envied these men, for whom various models of a water pump had provided an inexhaustible topic of conversation. She could never come up with much to say about any topic.

Viktoria Federovna usually walked from Sadovaya station. The situation at the trolley stop was the same as always. Women and men ran in helpless confusion back and forth alongside the overcrowded cars and would not resign themselves to having missed the chance to board. One woman in a blue coat had only been waiting for the bell to ring. She threw herself at the back of a jacket standing on the bottom step and flung her arms around the neck above it. The doors banged, struck the shoulders of the blue coat and opened. A second time. The tips of her little green shoes touched the running board, she appeared to squirm, to writhe—the jacket's elbows hacked at her breast and stomach, a fist landed on her ear. She leapt back onto the street. From behind the high, narrow panes of the closed doors, passengers gazed down at her like stern icons. The trolley pulled away.

"Your nose is bleeding, my girl," Viktoria Federovna said, out of concern for the white blouse under the blue coat. Then she walked on. It was windy.

At the entrance Viktoria Federovna checked the clock. She had been walking for eight minutes, which left five to climb the stairs to the fifth floor, hang up her coat, remove her boots and turn on the computer. She took a deep breath, pushed the outside door open, pulled her cap from her head, pushed the second door—and exhaled. If she ever had a say around here, that blower would be the first thing to go. The

warm air in the entrance left her queasy. And Natasha
Ivanovna would not be allowed to work the coat
check in that getup. People took her for a cleaning
lady. And you had to wait, with her jabbering silly
trash. Viktoria Federovna had a lot of ideas. The security women needed only one barrier with a buzzer.
They could stay seated and press the button handily,
with no to-do. They wouldn't even have to wear arm-
bands. And anyone without an ID or a pass simply
didn't get in. One woman sufficed for that. But it's
boring all by yourself. Besides, the entrance and stairwell needed paint and the dings in the ashtrays and
wastebaskets should be hammered out. She took key
no. 421 from Semyonova and recorded the time. Her
knees did better at the climb, and she no longer broke
into a sweat, either.

Viktoria Federovna was already sitting at her computer, gazing out at a roof with new, shiny white tin,
when Vera Mikhailovna looked in. She never knocked.

"Have you heard?" Vera Mikhailovna was evidently
very pleased. Viktoria Federovna had just asked "About
what?" when the lights went out and her computer
screen faded with a soft click.

"Oh my, oh my, oh my," Vera Mikhailovna wailed,
pressing the balls of her hands to her cheeks and running off. The corridor was at once filled with shadows.
Only if a door opened could you recognize faces.
They all wanted to get to the canteen before the
coffee and tea ran out. Viktoria Federovna was not
particularly fond of Vera Mikhailovna, although there
was no one with whom she spoke more often. On
May Day, Vera Mikhailovna, who had the honor

of distributing their food coupons, had emerged out of the pedestrian tunnel at Victory Park, a flag over her shoulder. Viktoria Federovna had turned away in alarm—for no reason, quite automatically. She closed her door now.

She did not care if the power came back on or not, because the calculations for October, the new prices, lump-sum payments and hourly rates had all been entered. All she had to do was wait out the last two days of the month. It was a shame about her tea. Usually at this time of day she fetched a little pot of water, set it on an overturned tile on the windowsill and would wrap the immersion coil in a dish towel if Olga Vladimirovna came in.

Viktoria Federovna looked out the window to the Fontanka Canal, where the bank opposite was being shored up again. Man taming nature. A truck was parked on a steel platform out over the water. She liked to watch the workers pound steel beams into the ground with a pile driver. There were none to be seen today. Everything was quiet in the corridor. Whoever wasn't in the canteen line was out shopping. She pushed the keyboard back, spread her elbows, laid her head down on the back of her right hand and closed her eyes.

In such situations she was always reminded of Pyotr Petrovitch, a Budenny man, later a pilot, and asked herself what his assessment of the situation might have been and what his proposals for mastering the problem would have looked like. Pyotr Petrovitch was a passionate man through and through, but honest as well, and modest. His upper body sat like a jockey's

above his long legs, which were said to be pros-
theses—his contribution in blood to the Great Patri-
otic War. He had even learned to dance again. He had
always made something of his life. If he was con-
fronted with a false idea, no one and nothing could
hold him back. How often had he simply leapt to his
feet, not even asking to speak, grabbed his chair by its
back, raised it almost six inches off the floor and
banged it down again.

"Enough!" Pyotr Petrovitch had shouted, and Viktoria Federovna had winced. "Enough," he repeated softly,
and whispered in total exhaustion: "Enough." His face
was still trembling from shouting. With weary eyes
Pyotr Petrovitch surveyed the assembly. His gaze
swung from one wall to the other and back again. His
body stiffened.

"How can anyone talk like that! How can anyone be
so blind!" he cried. His upraised right hand fell wearily
to the back of his chair. He shook his head sadly.

"What sort of people are you! Truly, what sort of
people, I must ask myself. And yet I must also ask what
have we done wrong. And that pains me." They all
could see how Pyotr Petrovitch reached for his heart
again, massaging it with one strong, hairy hand. With
the other he kept himself braced on the back of his
chair.

"You talk and talk," he began anew, paying no attention to the occasional sob. "You talk and talk, criticize
and criticize, and do not see the miracle transpiring
before your eyes at every moment. Are you blind or
just pretending to be?" Pyotr Petrovitch paused and
scowled at his chair in disappointment. He had to

clear his throat. "I'm not in the habit of making long speeches, I'm a simple working man. But if I'm asked, I speak my opinion, openly and honestly, so that everyone knows where he stands with me." Once again Pyotr Petrovitch cleared his throat.

"I would like to ask you a question that you can perhaps answer better than I. My question for you is: How many people live in our hometown?" After a brief silence, the hall showered Pyotr Petrovitch with numbers. Everyone was relieved that Pyotr Petrovitch had asked such a simple question.

"Fine, that's enough, fine, fine, many thanks, thank you, many thanks. I would like to choose the lowest of the numbers given. If I recall correctly, it was two point eight million. It's true that many more people are now living here with us, but fine, I'll not get into another argument. Just picture it. . . ." Pyotr Petrovitch's gaze scanned the room. "How do you organize things so that two point eight million people can live together? They want to eat, drink, they want housing, work, something to wear, they need transportation and streets, schools, stadiums, hospitals, factories, newspapers, museums, libraries. A gigantic task. But our society accepts the challenge, does not close its eyes to the problems. What is more, it is there for each of you. An example: When you get up in the morning, what do you need first? Well? No! What you need first isn't water or toothpaste, or the toilet, either. Stop and think: You get up out of a bed. You turn on the lamp on your nightstand, there is light. You see a room, a cupboard, the door, curtains. Have any of you ever taken the trouble to think about what that means:

a home? Your assumption is that the first thing you want to do is likewise the first thing you need. But how many other things don't you notice, although each is so precious? Have you never thought that it is not simply a matter of course that you have a bed to sleep in and a switch to push so that there is light? Perhaps you no longer even think about its being warm in your apartment. You don't know any different. Have you ever frozen at home? No, the heat comes into the building like the air you breathe and like the water that runs from the tap into the bathtub, hot and cold, just as you like and as much as you like. You've not been awake five minutes and have only just left your bed, but you've already made a thousand claims on society—as if things had to be this way. And because I am not a subjective idealist, I must add by way of correction: Even while you sleep you lay claim to society's achievements. That is my opinion, but one that, as I shall show you, accords with objective reality. An example: warmth. It is ten degrees outside, but you have it warm, in the kitchen, in the bath, in the living room. You have heat. What does that mean: we have heat? It means that you live in a building for which land was found and surveyed, its subsoil tested. Excavation crews arrived, followed by specialists for setting up cranes. And where did these people, architects and construction workers, get their knowledge? They went to school, they read books. But where do books come from? Where does paper come from? Cranes? The steel for cranes and antirust paint? Where do those many, many bricks come from, the window frames, the glass? Have you any idea what a miracle a building is? So far, so good. But that still doesn't make it warm. What's missing is the line to the power plant. And so the pipe itself is laid, insulated pipes welded together in the ground. Quickly a power plant is built. How is that done, what all do I need for that? Tell me. Where do I get the huge boilers and the special concrete? And even when it's finished, where do I find people to operate such a complicated plant? Ah! And the coal that's needed to heat it? On which ship, by which train will it be transported? Do you realize what boundless labor, what boundless cares and difficulties are tied up with it? Only society is in a position to solve all that. And I have just picked out one example among thousands upon thousands. I could have spoken about a loaf of bread or a pair of pants. With us, everything is organized so that the products of agriculture and industry reach the people for whom they are made. Everyone has food and drink. Fruit need not be dumped in harbors, grain need not be burned. You never thought about that, eh? And nevertheless, society gives you everything. Even though I'm telling you nothing new, and in coming here did not think it possible that it would be necessary to explain such simple things. I thought we had come further and could move on to the next stage.

"And now tell me yourselves: In view of this miracle, is there any point in continuing to talk about how the bus was late one time? Maybe there was tire trouble. Or to complain about a power outage? Maybe lightning struck the line. If you can buy only dark brown shoes instead of light brown—are they not more beautiful in any case?"

They all sat silent and stared at the floor. Pyotr Petrovitch modestly took his seat again, placing his hands on his knees. Finally, after clearing her throat several times, the chairwoman took the floor.

"I believe I speak in the name of everyone here in expressing to you, dear, honored Pyotr Petrovitch, our heartfelt thanks for your remarks. Surely I speak for us all when I say that each of us understands better now that he was unable to see things as they are in reality. You, dear Pyotr Petrovitch, first had to teach us to use our eyes at last. We are deeply ashamed. And for that I would like to express our thanks to you, Pyotr Petrovitch. You have shamed us. Please accept our thanks, accept our many thanks, dear Pyotr Petrovitch."

"Oh, don't mention it," Pyotr Petrovitch said merrily, stood up and walked to the door as if measuring the floor beneath his feet with every step. From there he lustily waved with his cap. "Good-bye, children, until next time, many thanks, good-bye, good-bye."

"Are you feeling better, Viktoria Federovna?" Olga Vladimirovna asked after knocking at the open door.

"Oh . . ."

"Are you feeling better, Viktoria Federovna?" Olga Vladimirovna's forehead again showed that same wrinkle between her eyebrows that always reminded Viktoria Federovna of the emblem of the Moscow Olympic Games. She nodded.

"I'm told they're sending the kitchen crew home. We're leaving, too," Olga Vladimirovna said, removed the rubber band from the ledger, opened it and pressed its bouncy front cover down against the desktop with her middle finger.

"That would be lovely," Viktoria Federovna whispered, and added her calligraphic initial to the first of yesterday's balance sheets from M-III. Olga Vladimirovna thumbed here and there. She didn't have to explain anything. Usually by this time the water had started bubbling. She closed the ledger.

"I have to go now."

"Me, too," Viktoria Federovna replied, but at the sound of sudden screeching and stomping in the corridor, she exclaimed, "Like schoolchildren . . ."

They nodded to each other one more time.

She could be home by twelve, lay one blanket around her legs, the other over her shoulders. And when she woke up, she would eat some smetana and varenye and turn on the television. From her handbag she took a book she had wrapped in a newspaper cover. She had already read two thirds, but a headache had forced her to quit in the middle of an episode that went on and on without much ever happening. She paged through until she found the pale green ticket and read: "A businessman who must travel abroad for an extended period writes and faxes a letter every evening to his best friend, who is very ill. But soon he has described everything from his workaday world. Which is why he begins to write fables and invent things. Since he needs a new idea daily and this isn't *The Thousand and One Nights*, he asks colleagues and acquaintances to help. The sick friend, however, collects the faxes, improves on them here and there, and puts the pages into a folder. He dies and the stories come to an end. Numbed at first by the news, the businessman who wrote them only gradually realizes what the loss of his friend means. Suddenly alone, he roams his apartment and can do or not do as he pleases. Never before had he felt so lonely in this city—the anticipated pleasure of seeing his friend, the waiting, had kept him company. The stories had forced him to observe and to invent, and prevented him from feeling lost. Not long thereafter, his penchant for gambling and picaresque adventures landed him in desperate straits and ruined him. He was last seen by a woman on the Berlin–Petersburg train. But after a tempestuous night he vanishes, and every trace of him is lost. All that is left of him is the folder containing the writings collected by his friend."

Viktoria Federovna sighed softly, closed the book again, unplugged everything, picked up her coat, cap and handbag, and left.

In the Dieta, which was on her way to the subway, she paid first and then joined the line for dairy products, which began right next to the cashier. Those ahead of her had taken over the room by executing a wide bend to the right, making a U-turn back to the entrance and then lurching forward at a sharp angle that ended in a loop and landed them parallel to the counter, on the other side of which was a saleswoman who studied each receipt. Viktoria Federovna grew increasingly weary from standing in line. Yet she was not one of those women who sat on the bench beneath the window and stood up only when their turn came. She didn't know what to think about and so carefully observed two saleswomen heave the dull-silver vat up on a stool. While one thrust a broom handle under the protruding edge of the black lid, the other, her face turned away, held the vat tight. Viktoria Federovna had watched them pry the black rubber circle loose countless times before, and she now heard the whoosh even before the lid opened like a mouth gasping for air. She knew that smetana would drip from the porous underside. She thought there was no need for standing in long lines. If the line were just half as long, she would have been home five trains earlier and would have missed nothing. All the same, she was convinced that everything in life balanced out.

The tin ladle dipped, stirred at what had settled to the bottom and banged against the inside of the vat. Viktoria Federovna pushed her marmalade jar at the saleswoman, who put it on the scales and waited till the pointer came to a stop. She squinted to read it— two hundred grams.

The overflowing ladle, lifted vertically from the vat, hovered there until the dripping thread thinned, tore, formed again, white yarn, tore again. In the very next moment—and this was critical—the ladle had to be above the jar. Viktoria Federovna loved this coup: soundlessly the helicopter moved in, set down, and in a flash they had grabbed the attaché cases and Angelina and escaped. The impossible had proved possible. The ladle descended along a new thin thread into the jar, touched the rim and tipped, an upended dome. They were safe now. Two taps with the handle—the signal to turn around. Without wasting a drop, it moved back to the vat. They banked away—and suddenly they were plunging, dipping down into the cream. What had happened? Had they taken the wrong briefcase? The wrong Angelina? It seemed to her an eternity before they began climbing again. Reaching the edge of the jar, the ladle yielded up the difference to the agreed amount only in little gulps. Viktoria Federovna was satisfied with the angle of the pointer. Anything over remained irrevocably in the glass. She licked at the screw threads on the jar. And as she did, her eyes fell on the white-and-green sign pasted to the tiled wall behind the saleswoman: AMERICAN CHEWING GUM. The saleswoman wiped it off with the leather rag used for cleaning the scales. Viktoria Federovna screwed the lid on her jar. How quickly times change. Three years before some jokester had pasted a map of North America on the wall here. People had scribbled the names of the cities in Cyrillic letters and had pointed and tapped at them so often that they turned into white spots, like the YOU ARE HERE on orientation maps.

Viktoria Federovna had counted on a seat on the train. She was disappointed and tired. Shopping had exhausted her, and it was no fun with her bag in one hand. Otherwise she liked to play captain and could stand in place for the whole trip without holding on. Power was out everywhere, apparently. But the subway always ran.

Each time the train pulled out, she felt a pain at the back of her head, reminding her of the whimpering. She had to take care of herself, she had to stay quiet. Tomorrow was Friday. On Friday evenings Timofei Alexeyevitch and Igor Timofeyevitch had played chess together. Rain or any sort of foul weather left Viktoria Federovna in a buoyant mood. The chess game between father and son created a festive atmosphere, and she always hurried to be done preparing supper before those two had ended their match. She would wait at the well-set table and study the television listings. She knew all the movies. Nevertheless, she felt a tickle in her tummy at the thought of three upcoming evenings with sweets. The game over, father and son shook hands—she never learned who won. After supper they would arrange the chairs. Viktoria Federovna sat in the middle, Igor Timofeyevitch on her left, and Timofei Alexeyevitch on her right. Igor Timofeyevitch waited beside the television until his father and mother had taken their seats, hesitated a moment, pushed the red on/off button and scurried back to his chair in order to watch that first image along with his parents. When Timofei Alexeyevitch would lay his hand on Viktoria Federovna's arm and shove a piece of nougat in her mouth, she was happy. And what you have once experienced no one can ever take away. Of late, however, she often compared herself to a prime number that always remains isolated, while the people around her shared their life with one another.

Viktoria Federovna moved toward the left door of the subway exit, which was easy to get through because of the marble paving stone beneath it. At a kiosk she bought a small loaf of white bread and 24-*Chasa*, her weekly paper. And she dare not forget soap, either. It used to be that she had only to lay her new bar on the rim of the sink and she would later find it fused with the old thin piece that barely separated your hands. Her son had not inherited his father's frugality. And if she did not use up the old piece herself, it turned brittle. But if she pushed it down the drain to let it dissolve among the struts, she would soon find it back on the rim of the sink, and so she went on using it. Now that she was alone, she simply threw it out. While Viktoria Federovna packed the soap in with the other articles, the saleswoman took her fingers from her mouth to give her change. It had turned cold.

Viktoria Federovna paid close attention to the pain at the back of her head—a little hammer that rapped every two seconds. First she would run water for a bath, empty the sieve and teapot down the toilet, fill the pot with water and keep her hand over it so as not to spill. Otherwise it was never enough for the plants in the entry hall. Then it would be time to eat buttered bread and cheese with sugared smetana for dessert. Then a bath, then sit in the living room with her legs up, read, watch television this evening and keep her head still. Tomorrow was Friday. She thought of Olga Vladimirovna, of Timofei Alexeyevitch, of Igor Timofeyevitch and Pyotr Petrovitch. Her biggest fear was her boots. When she bent over to pull the zipper all the way down, the back of her head would be a pin cushion. And before that came the stairs. The door seemed to unlock itself. She always thought of what Timofei Alexeyevitch had said when they moved in: first comes the dark key, then the silver, and the golden one for the inside door, and then comes our apartment. The golden key had turned dark, the dark one had been worn shiny. The silver one had stayed that way. She differentiated them by their shapes.

As the singing began again around one o'clock, Viktoria Federovna's boots were lying beside her bed, her coat and cap had slipped from the armchair to the floor. The bag with white bread, soap, smetana and her favorite paper stood in the hallway. Next to it lay her handbag, with her bundle of keys on top. The singing leapt from the panes in the door to the wardrobe, to the bed, and from there to the ceiling and lamp. There it lingered, soon lost its energy, retreated by way of wardrobe and bed to the door and the panes, ebbed away. The whining remained. In those moments, however, that preceded its commencement and fading, one could have heard a snapping sound, though very muted, from under the blanket beneath which Viktoria Federovna lay sleeping.

Hm," Lorenzen said, "and then?"

"Right," Graefe said, "he grinned and left."

"With the money?"

"Right, and the rest of them applauded."

"You don't say?" Lorenzen leaned across his desk to the intercom.

"Masha, can you hear me? Tell security we're finishing up here, roger?"

"Okay," Masha's voice said from the intercom, "roger."

"Masha, and tell them they damn well better keep their eyes open, roger?"

"Okay," Masha said, "I'll tell them."

Bracing himself with one hand on the desk, Lorenzen moved back to his chair.

"Let's go through this point by point, so there's no screwup. I don't like the taste of this."

"Right," Graefe said, and pulled his chair so close to the desk that he had barely enough room to cross his legs.

"You have to know how to take on types like Shigulin, or they'll take you for everything," Lorenzen said, "including your shirt."

"Right," Graefe said, "including your shirt!"

"We simply have to know how to take them on."

"Right," Graefe said.

"You're certain, then, that Shigulin was our man?" Lorenzen asked. The pencil he had been holding wedged between the tips of his forefingers dropped to the desk. Graefe winced.

"What's ever certain . . . ?"

"That's why I'm asking you!" Lorenzen shouted. "So we don't have any fuckups!"

"Got it," Graefe said. "It's just that you can never be certain here."

"But we have to be," Lorenzen said. "But we have to be, my friend."

From the middle drawer he took a Browning and laid it on the blotter, next to the pencil. Then he removed the magazine and leaned back.

"He's money-hungry, that's all," Graefe said.

"And a good thing, too, for crying out loud," Lorenzen said. "There's something you need to know. Only money is going to help these people. Money and competence. Nothing else. That's why we're important here, understand?"

"Right," Graefe said, "I know. I only wish it was as clear to them as it is to us."

"Yes," Lorenzen said. "Bullshit gets you nowhere." Lorenzen looked at the palms of his hands. Then he played with the magazine some more. "How much did he ask?"

"He said he knew somebody," Graefe answered, "who would repair it for twenty dollars."

"That's crazy!"

"Right. And I just bought it yesterday for twenty dollars."

"And today it's broke!" Lorenzen said, shaking his head. Suddenly he bobbed forward. "Masha, what's with the car?" Then he called to the door: "Masha?"

"Sorry," they heard Masha say. "I was rinsing up."

"What's with the car?"

"They got the message."

"Thanks," Lorenzen said.

"Right, his prices were good," Graefe said. "We've bought a lot from him, but there's an end to everything."

Lorenzen pushed the magazine back in and hit it with the ball of his hand.

"So why is his job camouflage? What did you mean by that?"

"Have you seen his Moskvitch, the red one?" Graefe asked, and gazed at Lorenzen's heavy hairline, which began low on his brow. He had something of a hedgehog or mole about him.

"How did he come by a car like that, I ask myself,

even if he's delivering to the Finns and the Americans like he is to us?" Graefe rubbed his dry hands.

"And so?"

"Now he has a gold chain bracelet, like some Austrian." Graefe crossed his arms in front of his chest. "Now he thinks he's somebody."

"And so that's what you did with the money then?"

"Right. That's what I did with the money."

"How much?" Lorenzen asked. "Fifty?"

"Yes. And then I added a ten, too, sixty."

"And then you made him sing for you?"

"Right. I told him that for sixty marks—"

"Oh, marks!" Lorenzen interrupted.

Graefe smiled. "Sure."

"Folk songs?" Lorenzen asked.

"More cabaret stuff, pop tunes, almost chansons. . . ."

"And meanwhile Shigulin repaired the thing?"

"Right, and sang."

"In front of everybody?"

"Right. Even Masha applauded."

"He conned you!" Lorenzen said, and threw himself back in his chair. "A total con job!"

"How was I supposed to know that he has an act . . . in a club over on the island?" Graefe stretched his legs to the side. "And he danced, too!"

"As an encore, so to speak," Lorenzen said, looking up from below at Graefe—whose chin was on his chest now.

"Right."

Lorenzen bent down over the intercom. "Masha, is the car up yet?"

"All A-Okay."

"Thanks," Lorenzen said, stood up and opened the wardrobe. "Next time we'll have to figure something out together."

Graefe buttoned his suit jacket and took his coat.

"Wonder if there's any point in my talking to him?" Lorenzen asked.

"Right. I don't know."

Lorenzen put the Browning in his jacket. "You are coming along, aren't you?" He frowned as he looked at Graefe. His hairline slid down even closer to his eyes. "I've got a reservation at the Chaika, corner table."

Graefe opened his hands as if he were about to catch a ball and then said, "Love to."

Lorenzen bent forward one more time. "Masha, tell them we're coming now. They damn well better keep their eyes open. Tell them that, Masha! Can you hear me, Masha?"

"Roger and out," Masha said.

There was a crackling sound as Lorenzen turned the intercom off. Graefe winced.

"After you," Lorenzen said, and let Graefe through the door first.

24

Around eleven Henry Jonathan Ingrim entered a restaurant on Nevsky Prospekt for a snack intended to forestall the first stirrings of hunger. The best thing would be to take care of it now, and that way you had the whole day ahead of you. Half an hour later, fortified, he left, took in several shops and even found something worth buying. As it got to be half past twelve, he entered a restaurant on Nevsky Prospekt because who knew if he would find one again all that quickly. To his surprise, he merely sawed at the edges of his schnitzel and asked for the bill. Then he recalled his snack.

The lion's share of the day *still* lay ahead of him.

25

W ho's there?" I asked, and tried to put on my pants as quietly as possible. It was nine. Since the middle of June we had had no hot water, and of a morning I need at least the prospect of a shower to get me out of bed. I had shrunk back at the rattle of my doorbell.

"Who's there?" I called for the second time, louder now, the way my landlord had taught me. I was determined not to open up without some answer and was content for now to button just the top and middle buttons on my pants. Since I could hear feet scraping on the landing, my question likewise had to be intelligible out there. I pulled on my shirt, unlocked both locks of the first door and—truly annoyed now—called out: "Who's there?"

"I extend you my greetings," rang out a bright female voice that would have enhanced any chorus.

The Communist, flashed through my mind. At that same moment I peered through the outer door's peephole. As if she had decided to risk the joke, her face swam closer to my porthole. She opened her gigantic maw.

"Good morning, good morning," she called in a voice of bell-like clarity. She had come for revenge. Presumably she was armed. It was not for nothing that everyone said she was crazy, meshuga, had run amok. Anyway, where had she got my address? And how had she got into the building if she didn't know the code for the entrance? To consider her harmless might well cost me bitterly.

"What do you want?" I called, noticing too late how weak my voice sounded.

"I have an article for you," the Communist replied, as friendly as ever.

Actually I liked her, this plucky little matron who set everyone's eyes rolling whenever she stood at the door to our editorial offices. It was easier to handle astrologers, fortune-tellers and preachers of doom. We had never printed so much as a single line of hers. Never! Naturally, she was going to lose patience at some point. The connection between the police and the Communists still functioned impeccably, or so we were constantly told, so she had easy access to information and, if she wanted, to weapons as well. One could presume that much for starters.

"Why have you come to see me?"

"They sent me to you, for you to decide." She

waved a sheet of paper at me. But where was her other hand?

"You'll have to wait for me to dress," I replied, and walked back through the living room to the bedroom, where she couldn't hear me. On the nightstand stood a red plastic car—my telephone. With one hand I picked up the roof, plus hood and trunk; with the other I punched the number—it had buttons where the seats should be. I heard it ring through the hood. I now announced to the trunk lid that I was being besieged by the Communist and asked how she had come by my address, but from under the hood came only laughter—I hung up.

"I worked late yesterday," I said to the Communist by way of greeting, asked her in and put the kettle on. With her, I was not embarrassed by the disorder in my living room that came with drying laundry. On the contrary. That way she could see that I did my own housework, and perhaps she might even like the scent of fresh laundry. She was holding her article in her hand like a flyer.

"But, please, have a seat, do sit down, please. . . ." I shoved the big armchair over, removing damp socks from it as I pushed, and sat down on the couch, where my underpants were drying along the top of the back.

Without a word she laid the article on the table between us. She must have been holding it in her hand all the way here, because the sheet had not been folded and she wasn't carrying a purse.

"That's for you," she said. "May I take a seat?"

She pulled her kerchief from her hair. Tanned and wearing a simple dress topped by a faded cardigan, she looked like a peasant woman who rises early to make good use of the morning hours. Her movements were youthful, her features had a lovely clarity, and the liveliness of her eyes had to rouse people used to nothing but the dull, tired faces on the subway or bus.

Clasping her hands, she waited for me to finish the article. Both sides of the page were written full, in fountain pen, and signed by Tatyana Ivanovna Kutuzova, retiree, twice honored as a Heroine of Labor.

"You are German, correct?" she asked as I looked up.

I said I was and laid the page on the table. "Would you like some tea?"

With a wave of the hand that brooked no contradiction, she refused. She fixed her eyes on me and nodded a few times.

"My opinion does not please you?" she asked, as if we were not alone at the table. "Please, tell me what does not suit you, we can speak openly about it. If you do not wish to publish my work as an article, then as a letter to the editor, signed with my name and address." She took her ID from her cardigan pocket and laid it open before her, the passport photo at the bottom.

"Would you really not like some tea?"

"I do not wish to impede your work," she said, "but I do not understand your refusal. Help me to understand it. I could be your mother, your grandmother."

"It's propaganda, agitation, these aren't facts," I explained, staring at the page.

"You're right there," she observed, never taking her hands from her lap, "but the facts and particulars are known. I restrict myself to essentials and save space."

The kettle started whistling.

"And you really don't want any tea?" I asked, already on my way out.

This time no one would call me out of the room for a conference or a phone call. I removed the kettle from the stove with a towel. The whistling grew softer. Having no means of escape, I felt paralyzed. I would have to go back to her soon.

At that moment I chose rebellion, however absurd and pointless it might be. I filled the casserole with water and put it on the fire. I took the kettle across to the bathroom, used half the boiling water to rinse the tub, put the plug in the drain and poured in the rest. Returning to the kitchen, I lit the second burner, refilled the kettle and put it on. I did not even have chocolate or candy in the house.

As before, the Communist was sitting bolt upright in the armchair. As I took my seat, she began:

"I don't deny we made mistakes, that there were unnecessary hardships, that human lives were pointlessly sacrificed. But we weren't given time to discover the whole truth, the world was against us. What's important is that oppressors and traitors were exterminated, at least most of them. There was no one left who lived off exploitation, and everyone had the chance to do honest work. Why am I telling you, you know all this. We conquered illiteracy. The same possibilities were suddenly available to the children of workers and peasants that the children of the educated enjoyed. We replaced the brutality of the market with planning; instead of dog-eat-dog capitalism there prevailed among us, more or less, the togetherness of comradeship. If we did without something, there was some benefit in it for us as well. There was no room for individual egoistic interests. We were at the threshold of defeating imperialism with our productivity. But they forced us into an arms race that demanded our greatest sacrifice. They made money at it, but among us there was truly no one who got anything out of it. Just the opposite! And nevertheless: We lived without fear of tomorrow. Where do you find that! Do you think a working woman anywhere else would have gone to Sochi for vacation? Do you suppose palaces would have become orphanages without Soviet power? Did old people have to starve and beg? Was it necessary for girls to sell themselves? We made mistakes, yes, we didn't crack down hard enough. It was only because we weren't hard enough that Jews and revisionists were able to overthrow Soviet power and put Yeltsin on the czarist throne. The principal question of our time, however, is: Is the capitalist form of society even rudimentarily able to solve the problems confronting humanity, all humanity, today? That's what we should be talking about!"

A hiss was coming from the kitchen. The water in the casserole was boiling and splashing on the flame. I sloshed what was left into the tub, filled the casserole and set it back on the stove. I emptied the whistling kettle, too. I held the spout to the tap and realized at that moment the entire hopelessness, indeed the absurdity, of my plan. And yet once you take the first step, there's no turning back. The Communist was waiting for an answer.

"Do you know," I said, "that as a Young Pioneer I always found it intolerable that when we delivered the old rags we had collected, we were given money. That negated my contribution to the communal effort. I didn't want money."

"I understand that. I understand it very well!" Her eyes shone. "Even if we were doing better now materially than before—let us go ahead and presume as much, it isn't true, but let's presume it is—I ask you, would it be a better life? No, absolutely, emphatically, no! It would not be a better life! We had an idea, do you understand, an idea!"

"Yes," I said, "of course I understand that."

"The enthusiasm that inspired us all after the war! And how quickly the successes followed: our stores were museums, and the things we could buy! And then our theater troupes! We could travel everywhere."

The Communist pulled a folded photograph from her ID wallet.

"This is me, in the stadium, alone on the stage. And here, these are a hundred thousand people. And these here, marching in formation, ordered according to professions and brigades: first the architects and engineers, followed by masons, carpenters, excavators, roofers. All of them with flags, balls, scarves, ribbons and flowers, framing the athletes, both men and women. The finest women athletes handed so many bouquets up to the chairmen and his deputies on the platform that they could no longer even applaud. How that made us laugh. And I struck up a song, at the microphone, and the chorus behind me fell in, and finally the melody was taken up by all the people around the stadium." The Communist leaned back and sang a few bars. A hiss was coming from the kitchen.

"Do you know why I wanted to marry a pilot? Because from up there he could also see everything we had accomplished!"

"One minute please," I said. The Communist had leaned so far forward that I was afraid in the next moment she would grab my hands.

The whistling kettle was spitting water. One trip with it was equal to two with the casserole. In my haste I couldn't decide whether it was better to prepare my bath by bringing water to a boil and then mixing it with cold, which decreased the number of trips necessary, or if success might not be sooner achieved by using only warm water at shorter intervals and not running any cold at all, since, given the fact that there was no telling how long this would take, it was logical to expect a cooling off of the water already transported. I knew no formula by which to calculate the efficiency. In any case, it helped to hold the hot, indeed almost boiling, water close to the surface of the water already in the tub so that as you poured you avoided the unnecessary cooling of water cascading from higher up.

The Communist tied her kerchief back on.

"Sleep on it. Then we will discuss it again. That goes for my other articles as well. It's the only way we shall make progress."

She waited in the entry until I had unlocked the doors.

"What doesn't kill me makes me stronger!" She extended her hand in farewell. "Do you understand this proverb?"

"Yes, I understand it." And after I had waved to the Communist twice, I closed both doors.

Barely an hour had passed, but when I looked at my half-filled tub I suddenly understood: my pointless, reckless rebellion would succeed! I would take a bath today! The certainty of it was so unexpected that it overwhelmed me, and in the same instant I felt the excitement that would come over me as I slipped into the water, where, wrapped in its warm security, every travail would be transformed into happiness.

Tucked at heart level, the passports lent my jacket the quality of a bulletproof vest. That did not, however, imply invulnerability. Our car followed the asphalt that had been poured over the sand from the broad swath cut through the forest. The little light next to the tachometer started blinking every fifteen minutes, and within barely half an hour it glowed before our eyes as red as a brake light. We poured oil and water either simultaneously or by turns into various openings under the hood and kept the signaled danger in check for fifteen minutes. But then the paved road came to an end. A few hundred yards ahead someone lay sprawled across the road. We drove more slowly. When we had passed the body, one of us got out and made sure: not a corpse, just a woman who had been drinking. To our left the sea glistened through the trees, and then the pavement began again.

Every car we passed or that came toward us was an ally. We were particularly fond of Finnish trucks. Every car that approached from the rear, with passengers who gawked at us as they passed, made us uneasy. We counted every mile we had driven since the last village and at the same time kept track of the distance left till the next name marked on our map. We hardly noticed it had started to rain. After driving for three hours, we reached the lovely town of Vyborg.

The moment we left the car we were encircled by men of all ages. They crowded in closer and closer, making various offers, partly in Russian, partly in Finnish. At first they almost whimpered, whined. But as we retreated and opened our car doors, the tone abruptly became demanding, abusive, even menacing. They chased the children away. Quickly we locked the doors from inside and drove off—slowly at first, so as to let them jump out of the way, then faster. Someone kicked our fender. When stones began flying we accelerated to full speed. People were yelling now, cursing us.

On the other side of Vyborg we came to a high, narrow suspension bridge patrolled by a soldier. As we crossed it we had a magnificent view of the country-side: the town with its towers behind us, lakes and the river's many arms stretching out into the distance on each side, and the endless forest up ahead. We were still dazzled by the contours of this landscape when a band of young booted fellows camped beside the road brought us to a stop—just passing the time, it seemed. Legitimized by nothing more than a barrier across the road, they demanded our passports.

Their captain, or whatever he was, bent down to the driver's partially open window and, as if snatching at gnats, motioned for him to turn off the motor. He ordered him to roll the window all the way down. Only now did he seem comfortable. He kept flicking a match between the corners of his mouth in a steady rhythm. This offered hope that his intervention would end happily. We said nothing. Suddenly, however, the match stopped moving, was clenched between his front teeth. Whose passport was he checking now? The other guys sauntered up and down the shoulder but never took their eyes off us. Two of them leaned against the barrier and grinned.

What would they demand in order for us to pass? We were prepared for anything. The captain spit out the match and dropped the passports in the front-seat passenger's lap.

As we pulled away we could not help extending a word of greeting, out of relief and gratitude. During the next segment, the forest drew close to the road. Despite an urgent need to relieve ourselves, we drove briskly on.

The second obstacle was visible from a good distance. To our left was a wide moor, with dead trees sticking up out of it like poles. No life left here. To our right, the forest floor looked as if it had been swept clean. The car rolled to a stop. With indifferent faces the guardhouse residents approached us, surrounded our car and without further ado pushed the grid aside. Out of the corners of our eyes we could see the finely raked stripe of sand that formed a fire lane through the forest.

We drove on, taking care not to exceed the speed limit, and reached barrier three. This one opened all on its own, without our even having to stop. Then we sat in a line of waiting cars, including some with jovial tourists. The sky was slowly clearing. We quickly took care of formalities, walked through customs on foot and then picked up our car. There had been no challenges. Before continuing our journey, we availed ourselves of a little outhouse.

We jauntily passed the raised barrier and enjoyed the way the asphalt smoothed out to form a road with center and shoulder lines. To each side were guardrails and parking places; the cars were clean and free of rust, the meadows lush, the houses well cared for. We had made it!

Not twenty minutes later, we were sitting on the terrace of a pretty restaurant; we ordered steaks, duchesse potatoes and mushrooms, a Greek shepherd's salad as an appetizer, accompanied by a splendid Chianti Classico, and finished off with coffee and sautéed bananas over vanilla ice cream. Only now did we realize what tension we had been under.

While we smoked, enjoying the sense of having eaten our fill, we talked about how our mission had turned out to be a success after all.

To be sure, we had to admit that not everything had gone absolutely perfectly. For example, they had pulled Boris from the car. And the man across from me now found the energy to say that through the rear window he had seen Boris stumbling under the blows of their clubs as they forced him in the direction of the moor. We all agreed that this did not bode well for Boris, since for a good while now he had been suffering from heart trouble.

No, no, I don't have any, I don't have any other tickets!" I repeated. "Excuse me—no, believe me!" And that is how I forced my way, step by step, through the crush of people thronged at the entrance to the palace and stretching out into the street clear back to the railing along the Fontanka Canal. No sooner had one of the black-clad doormen spotted the invitation I held high above my head than with upraised arms he plunged in my direction, parting the crowd like a swimmer parting water. His white gloves grabbed me by the shoulder. I was dragged under the archway. Here, however, he let go of me, smoothed my jacket, tipped his top hat and demanded to see my invitation, as if I had just popped up before him that very moment. Then he bowed, the portal opened, and in I went.

While I was perfunctorily frisked for weapons, a brass fanfare was struck up that then accompanied me as I proceeded alone up the marble staircase. At every second step, girls and boys at either side welcomed me with a curtsy or a bow, nodding as if we were about to begin a minuet. At the first landing, where the staircase curved and divided, a pair of children stepped forward and escorted me up the right-hand side. To the final chords of the fanfare, I bent down over the hand of the lady dressed in blue satin, kissed it cautiously and took the last stair.

"You are welcome here with us!" The older gentleman in tails beside her, a red sash glittering across his vest, scrutinized me with blue eyes. I took his outstretched hand. He knew my name and presented me to his wife as a German art historian who had received a stipend for a three-month stay in the city. With sincere interest he also mentioned the title of my dissertation: "Color as Style: The Influence of the French Impressionists on Repin."

But even before I could put a question to him, the brass took up their fanfare of greeting again. The grand seigneur wished me a pleasant evening of interesting encounters and conversations. As I accepted a glass from the hand of a buxom Italian woman, he said that, should his time as *maître de plaisir* allow, he would love to converse with me, in German if possible—he had kept up with all my published articles and was extraordinarily interested in conditions in my country.

"To your health!" With a wave of his hand meant to urge me to drink, he and his wife now both turned away. I emptied my glass and gave it back to the Italian woman. I knew her from somewhere. Taking my hand, she now escorted me into the entrance hall, but she vanished before we had exchanged a single word.

Searching for familiar faces, I strode through three rooms on my left, one opening onto the next, although mirrors placed between the marble pilasters transformed them into a labyrinth. The ceiling with its rich plaster embellishment provided the best orientation. The curtains at the tall windows had been closed to heighten the effect of the chandeliers.

Despite such splendor, there were also small anterooms between the large salons, with little nooks like the snack bars you find in museums and palaces used by Pioneers, where all sorts of people crowd around Formica-top tables to devour sandwiches and sausages and chat over a cup of tea. The people most at home in these latter-day implants in the palace were the sort I found it impossible to imagine making it past the grand seigneur and his wife. Robust guys with buzz-cut hair held their heads close together. When they spoke incredible gaps were revealed in their teeth. The lower echelon had been put into light-colored suits stretched so tight across the shoulders that the arms dangled from them like foreign bodies. Their bosses' jackets, however, fit well. Out of the corners of their eyes the guys with buzz cuts sized up the neighborhood and fell silent whenever one of the couples whom they had to count among the grand seigneur's immediate circle walked by. These aristocrats—and I call them that simply because there is no more apt word—strolled past the mirrors or stood in groups together, although the ladies, all of them wearing massive jewelry, took a seat on dainty armchairs. Their movements spoke of reserve and caution, as if all their lives they had touched nothing but crystal and porcelain. The gentlemen kept their heads tilted in a fashion that at once revealed to me the origin of the expression "to lend an ear."

The guys with buzz cuts and the aristocrats kept their distance. The artists, however, surfaced like emissaries first with the one group, then with the other, and attempted to play host to all and sundry.

"Enjoying yourself?" Scipio brushed a shiny strand of hair from his brow. He always reminded me of a handsome horse. His wife, Anastasia, in her cork shoes a good half head taller than either of us, had shown up in tight green overalls. For a purse she carried a green bottle under her arm. She kissed me on both cheeks, and Scipio passed out cigarettes. We drank one after another of her green cocktails, smoked and got caught up in a conversation concerned solely with whether those attending this "Bonaparty," *the* event of June, were more at home in the nineteenth or eighteenth century, laughing louder and louder till a photographer took Scipio by the elbow and dragged him off to the next room. Anastasia followed them.

I put out my cigarette and strolled on. Ten minutes later, I found myself standing again on the little gallery that overarched the stairwell, not six feet from the grand seigneur.

"You seem to have found no one to chat with?"

I shrugged and tried to smile just as sincerely. The grand seigneur took three glasses from a tray held by a waiter attired as an elevator boy, handed the first to his wife and waved me over to them. We drank to one another's health one more time and toasted the success of the "Bonaparty."

The fanfare rang out again. New guests were constantly arriving, for the most part couples or families with grown children, and as I bent over the gallery railing, all I saw at first was hairdos and shoulders. More and more people from the Petersburg business world appeared, who could not be classified among either the aristocrats or the buzz cuts and whose quick grace of movement set them off from the representatives of various consulates. I carefully observed the degree of attentiveness with which the grand seigneur received his guests and compared myself with the men who were leading beautiful women up the stairs. In the background the waiter stood at the ready with new glasses. But no hand waved for his services. For no sooner had one fanfare died away than the notes of a new chord were struck. By now the two children who played the role of escorts were starting to look flushed—and then I froze!

The railing melted under the palms of my hands, my body weight tripled. That balding head, the long nose, the skinny legs . . . as long as he had not yet reached the landing, I could still flee, hide, escape at my next best opportunity. Absurd hope—a stranger's face would turn to me any moment now. I saw his pointy knees moving up the stairs. A scandal was brewing, maybe even a scuffle. Of course, I was prepared to apologize with all due decorum—or to hurl myself at him.

Vladimir, in a tux no less, stormed up the stairs, tak-

ing them two at a time now. Both children pulled
back. He was laughing wildly. I stood ready. . . .

Now he bent down low to the grande dame's hand
and prolonged his kiss in order to give her time to run
a hand through his sparse hair. His next move was
immediately to spread his arms wide. The old man
pressed him to his sash, kissed him.

I stepped toward them. The grand seigneur gave
my name and repeated his flattering words from
before. Vladimir, he said, was one of the most important artists not just in the city but in the nation, perhaps in Europe. We should become acquainted.

"Pleased, I'm sure." Vladimir took my hand and
shook it vigorously as if we had never met till now. I
laughed, but did not know what to do next. He pre-
tended, however, that everything was quite all right;
yes, even invited me to his studio, and the grand
seigneur placed his hands on our shoulders as if we
were his sons. I was embarrassed by the oafish impression I had just made, simultaneously cheered by the
honor such a gesture signified—and still felt I had
been rescued when the Italian woman began to sing.

We ended up at the far right of a semicircle that had
formed around the singer. The more urgently I sensed
a need to find just the right words, the more miserable
I felt, the more hopeless my situation appeared.

"I'm glad to find you here."

"What?" Vladimir asked out of the corner of his
mouth, nodding to the beauty, whose aria was now
heading into its final leaps.

"I'm glad," I repeated.

The Italian woman's eyes widened, the motions of

her jaw became abrupt and jerky. Her hair—parted at the front but with many braids woven into an extraordinary pattern at the rear—quivered. Her white pleated dress, only barely concealing breasts, shoulders and neck, was so tight that she could sing only coloraturas.

"I'm glad to find you here!" I whispered, and thought I detected a certain rejuvenation in Vladimir.

"Funny," he retorted softly and, as the first to break into applause, stepped out from the audience to raise the Italian woman's right hand to his lips. The way he straightened up again, stepped to her side, escorted her back step by step, released her fingers now to rejoin the applause, while she lowered her head to each cry of "Bravo, Giulietta! *Da capo!*"—it all was done with infinite grace. His wooden movements appeared to have relaxed over the past few weeks into a perfect suppleness. As if sleepwalking, he opened the French doors behind him to admit the singer, who moved backward in little mincing steps, and now soundlessly closed the chamber from inside. The applause broke off and the semicircle of guests dissolved into little groups.

Suddenly Scipio was standing next to me again. He measured me from top to toe in a glance that embedded all his concentration between his eyebrows.

"You know Vladimir?" he asked, not letting the least display of emotion escape him.

"Yes," I said, "I'm staying with his sister."

"With Svetlana?"

"With Svetlana," I confirmed, and smiled the same smile he was smiling. "With the sister of the second Cézanne. . . ."

Scipio gave a whinny and moved closer, crowding me.

"Out with it!" he said, and relit a half-smoked cigarette. Anastasia laid a hand on my shoulder.

"As a rule, I do not accept invitations to artists' studios," I said. "They entail too many obligations. But in this case I had no choice." There was nothing I would rather do, nothing could be more liberating, than to talk about my visit to Vladimir's studio. These two would understand me.

I told about how six weeks before, on a Saturday afternoon, Svetlana had taken me to Vasilievsky Island, to one of those comfortable artists' studios built on the top floor of some new buildings. Vladimir had greeted me at the entrance with just a brief, limp handshake. Without looking at her, he proceeded to give Svetlana all sorts of instructions about preparing for the visit of a French collector.

"Do you know what his name was?" Anastasia asked.

"No, he never showed," I said. Smoking was permitted only in the stairwell. I was left on my own, was glad to be. In a low voice Svetlana explained that what I saw here were only the commercial pictures, the artistic ones were in the loft, reached by some narrow wooden stairs. I watched as Vladimir wandered among carved frames, large bowls, little stools and his own paintings—all of them groups of women in French (spring) or English (autumn) parks. He positioned one picture after another on his large easel. Sometimes the ladies were tossing a ball, sometimes gazing at swans, and sometimes they stood solitary in the moonlight.

The longer the wait for the Frenchman, however, the chummier Vladimir became. One of the first things he shared was: "Anyone can claim to be an artist nowadays!" He offered a list—and at each name he pressed a finger of his right hand against the ball of his left— of those incapable of drawing a nude or a still life. "But they are the talk of the town," Vladimir declared, and helplessly raised his empty hands. "Naturally, if one is no good at it, it is difficult to make daily calls on gallery owners and journalists and offer them valuable gifts. But," he continued, serving his left palm several punches with his right fist, "one can fight back with work, hard work, and shut their mouths with something of quality!"

"Do you like Svetlana?" Scipio asked.

Anastasia cast him a sparkling glance and suddenly broke into laughter.

"If someday there were no more artists," Anastasia said, and took a pull on her green bottle, "Svetlana would create new ones!" She was right. Svetlana's adoring devotion to her brother included everything even vaguely related to him and might itself be called creative. After painters, sculptors, writers and composers—the geniuses per se—she still had lots of empty space in her hierarchy. At some point, then, came the philologists, the art historians, a selection of musicians and actors. And after them, the devoted servants, votaries, sisters of the greats of this world.

"But we ought to be fair and not make fun of her," Scipio said. "For in our dark hours a Svetlana is often our only consolation."

I said nothing. But Anastasia, too, remained serious.

"Did Vladimir talk about his projects?" Scipio asked, passing the green bottle back.

"Only about the machinations of his enemies," I said. "For he is firmly convinced that they have left no stone unturned in their attempt to defame him as a man and artist and drive him from his studio, or, better yet, from the city, or, even better still, from life itself. With their false promises people had even tried to alienate his wife, his muse, from him."

Both gazed at me in great earnest.

"His defense is his work," I said, dispensing with any ironic undertone. "Do you know his article 'Where Are Our Artists Headed?'" I asked.

Vladimir's manifesto had been abridged beyond recognition, his ideas and convictions turned into something almost incomprehensible. That, too, had been an intrigue of his enemies. "He has been called a second Cézanne," I can still hear Svetlana's voice saying, and adding in defiance: "And there will never be a third!"

Scipio and Anastasia listened to me without moving a muscle, and I went on with my story, saying whatever came into my head.

Presumably it was as a result of Svetlana's enthusiasm that, despite the Frenchman's failure to appear, Vladimir began to show me his artistic works. His abrupt, repetitive gestures and faltering gait made him seem old. He kept brushing strands of his long dark hair across his bald spot. Steadying himself at every step, he brought one painting after the other down from the loft, placed it on the easel and stepped back until he was standing beside my stool. Squinting his eyes, he wiped his hands on his shirt and wheezed.

"The surface of the sea is still too drab! Don't you think?" He bit his lip. "This gesture is not convincing! Don't you think?" Not one of the pictures—they had titles like *Women in a Discussion, Brezhnev—a Madman, The Gulf of Finland, Georgians Drinking Tea, Farewell, Death of a Cosmonaut, Sakharov in Moscow, Table in the Artist's Studio, Beggars on May Day, The Nevsky*—not one of the pictures vanished again without Vladimir declaring it bad, flawed or, in the best of cases, unfinished. The only exception was the portrait of his wife Julia: a perfect painting!

"What do you think of his work now?" asked Scipio, who had lost every bit of his joviality. I said something about how I liked his colors and that indeed a great many things reminded me of Cézanne. And in passing noted that Russian customs exacted six times the purchase price upon export.

"Even in the West," Scipio mused, "people will still be able to grasp that a tanned human body is more beautiful than some black square. But do go on."

In conclusion, Vladimir, Svetlana and I toasted the fact that great painters should not have to wait to be recognized after their death, like van Gogh, for example, but ought to live to receive some portion of the thanks that posterity always extends so richly.

"Which is why I offered him money for the portraits," I said, justifying myself to Scipio and Anastasia. "A major mistake!" I added.

After showing his work, Vladimir had drawn two sketches of me and, having signed them and rolled them up, presented them to me. And I had offered him a hundred marks, so that he could buy some paints, canvas, frames, etc. Svetlana's response was to clap her hands to her face. Vladimir pressed his lips together, hard. It seemed quite impossible for me to pocket the money again. He was astounded, Vladimir said, that I had so misunderstood him. Suddenly, however, he shouted, "If not with my work, how then, how then am I to do battle?"

Now he exploded in a volley of insinuations and curses. I, too, was being used by his enemies to insult him. And he swore revenge. He would sweep them all away, with his work—and with force, yes, if necessary with force, too.

Sobbing now, Svetlana clung to him, pressed his left hand to her breast, tried to kiss, to caress him. I held his right hand, begged him to believe me that I hadn't the least thing to do with his enemies, on the contrary, I wished him only every conceivable good. . . .

After ten minutes I had not only pocketed my money again but also promised to return in order to continue our interesting conversation. I asked whether Vladimir was prepared to paint my portrait during my next visit. . . .

"I simply haven't been able to find a free day for it," I admitted. When in fact my plan had been to have Vladimir paint me, buy the portrait and then give it to Svetlana—as a farewell present.

"What sort of man are you!" Scipio said bitterly, and turned away. Anastasia clamped her idiotic bottle under one arm and linked the other in his.

Suddenly I was standing all alone in the middle of the room. Even someone who had not known the importance of these two, and thus had failed to notice the person they were talking to, would have had his attention drawn to me simply by their gruff, not to say demonstrative about-face. It was clear to me that I had to react, and at once. I took a few steps in the opposite direction, but caught myself, thought better of it and turned around. Surely I'm simply mistaken, I thought, and followed Scipio to the buffet. I would clap him on the shoulder and ask when I could pay him a visit. He was annoyed, of course, that I had paid so little interest to his work. The moment it comes to recognition and money, artists are insufferable!

And how they stared at me, the ladies and gentlemen all around! Out of the corner of my eye I could tell exactly what was going on. It even seemed as if people were whispering my name. I almost looked behind me—but was just able to suppress the urge by slapping the back of my neck as if I had been bitten by a mosquito. Rubbing back and forth with the flat of my hand, I used my fingertips, so to speak, to keep my head from turning. "Might I introduce myself," I rehearsed under my breath, and added, stressing each syllable, "Hans-Jürgen Göbel, Ph.D." And my next thought came as a relief: I was not an unknown here, a nobody.

Having subdued my inner conflict, I had advanced to within two arm's lengths of Scipio's back when I happened to glance past his left ear—and was startled to see Vladimir, in the best of moods and with his shoulders hunched forward, mimicking the Italian woman and the way she had lost control of her lower jaw while squeezing out her last bit of breath. And as he gasped for air and repeated the same grimace, this time even clacking his teeth, I came to a halt beside Scipio. He, however, suddenly laughed so shrilly that the attention of everyone in the salon was drawn to the small group to which I now belonged as well. Spurred on by success, Vladimir offered a third imitation of the Italian soprano, even doing a slight knee bend now. Scipio laughed longest this time, too, revealing so many little teeth in his mouth that I could not help thinking of a dolphin. I barely managed a smile, and held on to it that much longer, punctuating it with two very audible snorts. Naturally, that in no way sufficed to signal the delight and high spirits that would have proved me to be an intimate friend—or a mere member—of this artistic circle. "Wonderful, wonderful," I said tentatively now, annoyed that Scipio and Vladimir were so deeply engrossed in conversation that they refused to acknowledge my presence between their shoulders.

"May I introduce you to Dr. Göbel?" Scipio asked, as if repeating an exercise in a foreign language or offering a cigarette.

"Yes, please do," Vladimir replied, gazing expectantly at Scipio.

"He's standing just to my right, but don't look yet, wait a bit," Scipio said.

In that same moment I surprised even myself by laughing. I laughed loudly, heartily, and found that I suddenly felt quite happy. Any other reaction would have been inappropriate. For the second time now, I took the hand Vladimir extended to me. "Pleased to make your acquaintance, Vladimir Maximovitch," I said, yielding yet again to the laughter rising up inside me. "Extraordinarily pleased . . ." and, unable to manage anything more than that, I went on laughing—quite as impressively as Scipio had done just now.

"Dear Max, this is Dr. Göbel, an art historian from Frankfurt," Scipio began again. "Dr. Göbel, this is Mikhail Olegovitch, a cult figure, an installation and performance artist."

Since no one joined in my laughter, I quickly calmed myself and reluctantly shook Vladimir's hand yet again—he was evidently a man of many names. "I have a very peculiar sense of humor," I muttered, and then greeted Vladimir with these words: "You seem to be quite a chameleon!"

"You should attend one of his performance pieces sometime," Scipio said, as if looking at me in a rearview mirror somewhere up ahead of him.

"Do you mean me?" I asked, automatically pointing a forefinger at my chest.

"Who else could he mean?" Vladimir responded in a friendly voice, and took me by the hand. We were now moving diagonally back across the salon. His intimate gesture had once again made me the center of attention. He kept nodding to me as well, as if hanging on my every word.

Now I recognized the double door in front of us as the one behind which Vladimir had vanished with the Italian woman. Without hesitating, he kicked the right side open and with a gesture of his hand bade me enter the almost dark room. He followed, shut the door and pulled the curtains aside. And now the night's whitish pink light streamed in, illuminating the room.

"Well, how do you like my work?"

"Congratulations!" was the word that burst from me. He must have been stricken by a creative frenzy over the last few weeks. All the flaws in his work had been removed as if by some divine hand. Here again were the *Women in a Discussion*, their backs turned to the viewer: the ornamentation of their colorful shawls now had the rhythm Vladimir had found so sorely lacking that day. Next to it was *Sakharov in Moscow*, where by the use of subtle facial expression, a barely noticeable lift of the eyebrows, he had been able to abandon all conventional gestures. Even *Beggars on May Day* had new depth, the red was less insistent. I walked from one painting to the next. What had happened? Why all of a sudden did these Cézanne-like narratives touch me so? Was it the light or perhaps merely their elegant frames or the splendid room itself?

To the right of each picture was not only the title of the painting in Russian, French and English along with the year it was painted, but also a price in dollars. Julia's portrait, the only painting that had forfeited quality, cost $6,000; *The Gulf of Finland* bore the same price; *Sakharov in Moscow* could be had for $20,000, *Beggars on May Day* for $12,000. The still life *Table in the Artist's Studio*, the smallest of them, was also the least expensive, at $4,500.

"Giulietta!" Vladimir cried. Head tipped forward, arms and legs stretched out, the Italian woman was sitting sound asleep on a settee. Her mouth hung open.

"Giulietta!" Vladimir repeated, clapping his hands. "May I introduce you to a German connoisseur of art? . . ."

Giulietta retied the open laces above her bosom and pressed the fingertips of both hands to her temples.

"It's time," Vladimir said, and gathered up the countless little jars, combs and lipsticks that lay beside her on the sofa, while she stood in front of one of the many large wall mirrors, raised first one arm and then the other, and thrust a deodorant stick in her shaved armpits. With a little flask, she sprayed herself from coiffure to hips, crossed the room and put her hand in Vladimir's. They both were standing again in the same pose they had adopted for their backward vanishing act. Vladimir pressed down the door handle—and Giulietta floated off like a bird freed from its cage.

"To the matter at hand," Vladimir said, closing the double doors. "These works are the starting point for today's performance installation." He cleared his throat. "I have worked on them for almost three months. They are all painted in my middle style, that is: they are good, but not exceptional. But they far outdo the original versions! Surely you would admit that, wouldn't you?"

I said that an artist's view of such things was much more interesting than any impression a nonartist might have. I was not familiar with the term "middle style."

"This very night," Vladimir proclaimed, not responding to my remark, "will, in the truest sense of the term, mark the fulfillment of an artist's dream. A man who for years now has sold not one painting, who ekes out a penniless life, reviled and misunderstood, that man, the true artist, will become famous overnight without having shown a single painting, without his having done anything at all. In honor of his paintings— exhibited in the most beautiful palace in the most splendid city in the world—a party attended by the most eminent guests is being thrown. Yet even that is not enough. What he had always secretly hoped for, what in mad despair he would have sold his soul for, has come to pass: his paintings have become beautiful. What had secretly left him dissatisfied has been set to rights. What had merely been an intent has now been carried out and brought to a certain perfection, as if its elements were acting of their own accord. What every man desires as his creation must bear his signature. What modern art so bitterly lacks has risen here anew, and in its purest form! Instead of meaninglessness— something existential. His is a fabulous career, and in the next few hours we shall experience its culmina- tion. Tomorrow his name will be on radio and tele- vision; by the next day newspapers, magazines and publishing houses will vie for him. Last but not least, he will become rich, and all within the next few hours! Buyers have assembled here for a good half of his paintings, some will be presented as gifts to the Russian Museum, a few he will have to hold back. The high point will be Giulietta—with the opening of the exhibition she will return to him."

He was silent for a moment.

"Well, what do you say? Is that not a performance of artistic genius? I call the whole thing *The Artist's Redemption; or, The Conspiracy of Dilettantes.*" Vladimir cast me a triumphant glance. "I merely have to open the doors to the salon," he added, "and everything will take its course. Only the artist himself"—and here Vladimir laughed aloud, as if mimicking my greeting—"can still steer it in a new direction. Which is also why he is an artist."

With no hesitation, I grasped the goblet he held out to me, put it to my lips, and drank. The wine raced down my throat like flame, igniting such a thirst that all my bliss seemed to depend on chasing it down in one gulp. His babbling burst like a dream that a mere second before had been a meaningful whole. Relieved, I set the empty glass down on the malachite console table in front of Giulietta's mirror.

In the adjoining room the fanfare rang out louder than ever, the shuffling of feet, the chinking of glasses, a murmur—and then silence, and the grand seigneur, whose sonorous voice I thought I recognized, gave a speech. I understood nothing, but knew he was looking for me in the audience. He had wanted to greet several important people by name. In vain would he raise his head and crane his neck up out of his collar. But even the few steps to the door, to the keyhole, were too much for me. It was Vladimir himself who had put me in this situation.

"You're not feeling well, are you?" he inquired as I took to the nearest bench and stretched out on my back, my head resting on my crossed hands. I listened attentively. And indeed I now understood single words, whole phrases and finally the sentence: "The artist must be free for the sufferings of others!"

"Stay here, Dr. Göbel," Vladimir said in a voice that

sounded as if he were offering a toast. "Be patient. Your reward will be a favored spot from which to observe it all." Then, leaning his thin body against one of the doors, he listened, opened it and stepped out as if on cue. There was a swelling of ah's and oh's that burst into applause that reached its peak as the door slammed shut.

I was glad to be left alone. It felt good to lie there. It was not long before the people in the next room settled down. Amid the silence, Giulietta began to sing—a melody in a fervent andante, simultaneously lamenting and wooing. Was that the same voice that had so heartlessly hurled its coloratura trills? I closed my eyes and listened. A chamber orchestra accompanied her ballad of love and death.

I was startled awake by a ghastly racket. Vladimir was smashing a painting to bits—he was flailing away at his own *Farewell* with an ax. The final stroke split the frame and ripped away a piece of canvas: the girl at the window was now gazing at a black hole. He was already at the next painting—the ax got caught in a frame strut of *Death of a Cosmonaut.* He yanked the painting along with its hook from the wall and trampled around on it. In a fury he slashed away at another. *The Gulf of Finland* took a glancing blow on the beach. As a left-hander, he held his right arm across his eyes. *Sakharov in Moscow,* his masterpiece, was separated from him by a thin sheet of glass—a crash like a vitrine hurled from the sixth floor, an earsplitting burst of flying glass, and the tower of Spasskaya Gate dangled free. Frenzied applause from the next room.

Vladimir was deaf to my cries. He swung the ax. I saw my own body reeling. Balanced atop it, my heavy head fell forward, to one side, backward. And all the while, sitting there wide-awake on the bench, I felt the mass of my brain congeal, grow heavier, and it seemed merely a matter of time before my skull toppled, ripping me along with it. More noise, a bedlam of voices, shouts, footsteps, a bang—the doors flew open. I slumped, fell headlong off the bench, thinking as I went that I had finally succeeded in getting my feet into my shoes. Striding at the head of the procession was Giulietta, escorted on her right by the grand seigneur, on her left walked Vladimir. From deep in my head what felt like sharp icicles stabbed at the fiery, pulsing network of my nerves. Shoes, shoes of every imaginable sort, were pointing at me. Lying there before the guests, I looked up. Her waist held tight in the embrace of two hands, Giulietta was showering Vladimir's face with kisses.

"Julia!" a shrill cry rang out. "Julia!"

She whirled around. To my right stood Vladimir with the Italian woman, and to my left . . . to my left stood Vladimir without the Italian woman.

What sort of creature has no reflection in a mirror? I thought. Like a restive herd, the partygoers jammed into the room. The two Vladimirs and the Italian woman were frozen in place. But the longer I gazed back and forth between them, the more apparent my mistake became. For the Vladimir on the right, in contrast to the one on the left, showed traces of Giulietta's kisses on his face and neck. And instead of aping the gesture of an embrace, the Vladimir on the left stood with balled fists and was bent forward as if someone had just taken a wheelbarrow out of his hands and replaced it with an ax.

The guests in the front rows appeared totally occupied with comparing the two Vladimirs; those pushing in from behind were becoming ever louder and ruder. As a murmur rose up and words like "fire department" and "police" were heard, Giulietta screamed and tore herself away from the Vladimir on the right and threw herself at the Vladimir on the left, clung to his neck and kissed him wildly.

Slowly Vladimir's fists relaxed; he hesitantly pressed the woman to him, stroking the back of her white dress with his dirty painter's hands. She gave a sob, pressed her mouth to his shoulder and let her tears flow freely. Now the Vladimir on the left looked like the one on the right. No. It was as if the room had merely spun around. For now it was the Vladimir on the right who was wiping his face with his sleeves and balling his fists.

"Giulietta, come to me!" he cried. "Giulietta!" he repeated in a menacing voice. The guests stood silent. And now what no one had thought possible happened. Giulietta's weeping ceased. Slowly she raised her head, stood up straight and threw her shoulders back. Vladimir's hands fell limply from her waist. Her eyes blank, her lipstick smeared, she turned around and, as if inventing each step anew, began to move from the one Vladimir back to the other. Her mascara ran in dark streams down her cheeks to her chin. As if suddenly released, I leapt to my feet as Giulietta failed to execute her next step and collapsed—either faint-ing or dead.

I rushed to her. But even before I had so much as touched her dress, someone grabbed me by the shoul-ders and yanked me back into the crowd. No one, not even a Vladimir, was doing anything to help her. I tore myself away—and again someone grabbed me. Guys with buzz cuts twisted my arm behind my back. They had finally found someone they could demonstrate their skills on.

"Don't you like your paintings?" The Vladimir on the right flung his arms wide as if trying to prevent the crowd behind him from pushing even farther forward. "Leave everything just as it is! Don't touch anything!" he cried in a strident voice. Only now did the shouts and threats of the guests show that they had noticed the actual vandalism.

"And you have nothing to say?" the Vladimir on the right asked the one on the left.

"I'm a painter, not an orator," he answered, wiping a hand across his cheek.

"Then you should let others speak for you!"

The Vladimir on the left seemed solely concerned with wiping his face clean.

"Why did you do this? You were almost at your goal, all your wishes fulfilled!"

"Bastard! What do you know about my wishes!" the enraged Vladimir on the left shouted, and raised the ax above his head as if it were a torch. "Get out!" He took a step forward, the veins on his neck were popping.

The guests understood words like this and backed

off. Only two women, apparently prepared to be chopped to pieces for art, did not budge, until Vladimir, the one on the right, gave them a signal. Or was he already directing a pair of policemen who were now dragging in a section of railing as a barricade?

At that moment I tore myself away, dashed over to Giulietta and undid her silly hairdo. How beautiful she was, despite the runny makeup. But I could not find her pulse. Quickly I picked up a round hand mirror that had fallen from her pocket and held it to her mouth. Thank God! She was alive. I tore at the laces constricting her bosom. . . .

Vladimir, however, the one on the left, had vanished. Between the remains of *Farewell* and the only slightly damaged portrait of Julia was an opening in the malachite paneling, a little door, not three feet high. Only the ax remained behind.

"You see?" Vladimir shouted to the partygoers who were pushing up against the railing now and taking pictures. "Don't you see," he proclaimed, "that what we have here is an installation, a perfect installation! We should not change a single thing, not add anything! For could we ever create any better sense of 'alienation'—a new, higher standpoint of consciousness from which to view this event? Has not a vastly more important point of meaning been revealed here: artistic despair?"

The guests behind the barrier said nothing, their eyes wandering thoughtfully between the mangled paintings and the beautiful Giulietta lying in my arms.

"Write something about this!" Vladimir called to me

gaily, and leaned against the black railing as if intending to have his first good, calm look at it all.

At that moment Giulietta opened her eyes, smiled at me, threw her arms around my neck and pulled me down to her lips.

"Bravo!" I heard the voice of the grand seigneur cry, and the applause behind the railing swelled to a deafening roar.

Thank God!" Svetlana groaned as I awoke. I could tell from the way the sun was shining in through the red curtains that it was already afternoon.

"Drink," she said, propping up my head. Chamomile tea. "Drink, it will be all right." She took a compress from my brow and replaced it with another cold washcloth. "The doctor was here, it will be all right," she repeated.

I painfully sat up in bed, and the washcloth fell on the blanket. I took the cup and drank thirstily. I automatically reached for the hand mirror lying on the chair beside Svetlana.

"You lay there as if you were dead, dead," Svetlana said, shaking her head.

I did not look good. Moreover, there were smeared traces of bright lipstick around my mouth.

"Julia called," Svetlana said. "Vladimir is finished with your painting."

"What painting?" I asked.

Svetlana gazed proudly down at me. "Your portrait . . ."

I had difficulty keeping my head raised.

"He painted it from memory," she explained. "He's a genius!"

"What style did he paint it in?" I asked, closing my eyes.

"In his high style, his very high style!" Svetlana gushed, taking the mirror from my hand and wiping my mouth a few times with the washcloth.

All paths lay in darkness. Only those who went shopping on their lunch break walked beneath the pallid light that between ten in the morning and two in the afternoon seeped through clouds hanging low above the roofs as the natural upper limit to our world. Rare snowfalls brought no more than a fleeting brightness to the streets. We worried mainly about dry shoes and coat buttons. Weariness could not be overcome with sleep.

Faces were shown only at work or in murkily lit shops. The old people standing in doorways were so bundled up that you never knew if they were waiting for a bit of charity or for one of their own kind. Often their only choice was between starving and toppling over.

Strides had deteriorated into the mincing steps with which we risked the icy sidewalks. We slid toward one another, collided, held one another upright, skidded away and in a sudden balancing act tossed shopping bags and arms into the air. Not until the dented sewer covers began spitting ice cubes up onto the sidewalks like well-licked pieces of candy was our normal gait restored to us.

Cloudless light struck the yellow wall of a building. We had not even missed the sun. The sky's dark blue matched the breadth of the boulevards. Houses and palaces revealed color and proportions. Statues stepped forward. Odors crept from courtyard entries and stairwells. The day was given a morning and an evening.

The river moved. Green water coursed through the city's arteries. Pale as naked bodies, floes of ice drifted below the bridges. Up above, along the railing looking out to sea, garlands of people were hung. Fishermen shoved forward and past one another with shoulders and elbows, but never cursed. Others pulled together on a seine like sailors weighing anchor. There was a smell of oil and fresh cucumbers.

Days passed before we realized we didn't need coats anymore. A child laid the palm of its hand on the asphalt and patted the scarred giant's back. All at once the wind from the subway was cooler than the air outside the station, filled now with gulls, doves and flies.

In a burst of high spirits, we rolled up our sleeves. The warmth took a seat on stones and shoulders, got tangled in foliage and hair. We could grasp it.

Of an evening, shadows like tendriled plants climbed the walls, then faded, only to reemerge out of the twilight and wander up a neighboring building. Night was abolished. The sun still dazzled above the bridges after eleven, softened to a white light on the northern horizon and not long thereafter embraced the silence as rosy-fingered dawn. To see it was to find sleep no more. When at the stroke of two the street gazed up into the sky, just standing there we took flight, found ourselves lifted into the air above the drifting dust, until the streetlamps stood motionless below and we could touch their tips with our hands. It was five-thirty in the morning before I was standing by day's garish light, alone on the broad Nevsky.

And besides, Misha Sergeyevitch is a man who always buys flowers!" Polina said with a hasty upward glance. "Why, he wouldn't even step on a spider."

"And Moni knew that, you suppose?" Grambacher asked, nodding in my direction and pushing back the chair next to him. "Come join us, Martens."

Polina sipped at the green liqueur glass she held between two fingers. The tips of her red nails touched briefly. I sat down.

"And what's with him now?" Grambacher asked, his hand still resting on the back of my chair.

"He's hiding, in Irkutsk. He knows a lot of people there."

"You don't say," Grambacher said, laughing, as if finally learning what he wanted to know. "Crazy story!" He turned to me without letting go of my chair.

"Nasty witch!" Polina hissed, and pressed her glass to her lips. She looked out the window.

"Off to Irkutsk! Siberia, ha! Nobody's going to buy that!" Grambacher gave a thrust of his right thumb, as if Misha Sergeyevitch were just behind his shoulder. He had not yet lit the cigarette he held between forefinger and middle finger.

"Misha's a good person." Polina tried to catch his eyes. "She's a witch."

"Ha, you don't say!" Grambacher roared, and was seized by such a sudden fit of laughter that he let go of my chair, wrapped his lighter in his fist and, putting his whole body into it, banged twice on the edge of the table. "Crazy story!" He wiped his brow with his other hand. "What a lotta bull!"

"Would you be so kind," Polina said, as if reciting verse.

"Oh, beg pardon," he apologized, leaning out over the table with his lighter.

By the time I had ordered, there was only Grambacher's red face to recall his amusement. Like Polina, he had both elbows propped on the table. He lit a cigarette and said nothing.

I had made his acquaintance two months earlier, while writing an article about his airline. There was a lot in it about Grambacher's passionate decision in favor of Russia, about his love of Petersburg and his pledge of full service, which would give the rest of the world a taste of Germany, of *Allemande en miniature*, as it were. I had also written about his firm's generous support of the arts, about Grambacher's personal involvement with Petersburg children suffering from cancer, etc. In such an article, Polina had to be mentioned as well, of course, because the airline created jobs and with her excellent knowledge of German—her father, a lieutenant colonel, had been stationed in the Naumburg area—Polina ran the office all by herself sometimes. From personal experience, she could report that many customers were pleasantly surprised to learn just how price-competitive the Germans were—when you considered the extensive service. Galina, Alya and Maxim Ivanovitch confirmed this. Warmly welcomed by Polina and her other coworkers, the lovely Monika, a twenty-seven-year-old brunette from Baden whose job it was to train this dynamic and harmonious team on new computers, felt right at home in this splendid city. Early on, Grambacher had enjoyed being seen in the company of this beautiful German, but by the time I showed him the completed article, which was then translated into Russian, he was back to calling Monika "Fräulein Häberle." Instead of snapshots of the team taken by Anton, our photographer, Grambacher requested that we publish a portrait photo of himself, which came wrapped in clear plastic and which he urgently requested I return to him.

I soon got very tired of calling Grambacher twice a week only to be told that the proofs had not yet arrived from Frankfurt. Nor had he placed one inch of advertising with us! Which was why I wasn't sure what Grambacher wanted now.

Polina, who had a round face but was actually quite trim, suppressed a yawn, stubbed her cigarette in the ashtray and pressed the embers out with the filter.

"Enjoy!" Grambacher said. On my plate lay two large schnitzels, four pickle slices and a mountain of French fries crowned with mayonnaise—my favorite meal.

"You do know, don't you," he began, "that in four months I'll be in Paris, I mean for good?"

I said I didn't. This necessarily led Grambacher to talk about Paris, about the city's incomparable atmosphere, the importance of being based there, the good connections to Munich, the charm of the language and the colorful street life. Far greater responsibilities lay waiting there for Peter Grambacher.

A perfect triumph. First he had got an article out of me and then he kept stalling me like some amateur. Now I had accepted his invitation and was letting myself be won over again, although it was absurd to invest anything more in Grambacher.

I squeezed lemon over my schnitzels but found no napkin to wipe my hands.

"When all's said and done," he said, "the Petersburg–Paris axis is truly Europe's main corridor, no matter how hard the rest of 'em may try." He winked. Leaning over the table and no longer gazing out the window, Polina now placed palms and fingers together like a wedge and slowly stretched her arms across the tablecloth toward Grambacher. I proceeded to eat with sticky fingers.

"The Louvre is the world's greatest museum," Grambacher continued. "You can lump Berlin, Munich, Cologne, Hamburg and Frankfurt all together—nothing can touch Paris. 'To Paris, to Paris'—Chekhov said that, way back when."

Grambacher had paid no attention to Polina's hands. She went back to staring out the window. But then, as if she had been waiting for just the right moment—he was talking about the unpredictability of the ground personnel at Charles de Gaulle—Polina stood up, flung her purse over her shoulder and pranced away.

Grambacher waved the hand with the cigarette, as if to say he knew what was up. "Let me tell you the story real quick," he began, elbowing his way closer.

I went on chewing.

"You know Moni, the girl who works for us, the lovely Fräulein Häberle?"

I nodded and pushed half my French fries from the middle to the edge of my plate. I didn't want to stuff myself again.

"She's been out snacking on the local cuisine," Grambacher said. "She's been busy getting laid, here to there, and had a grand old time with her Russians. All her money's gone for that. Wine, cognac, cigarettes, tons of 'em, fruit, chocolates, that sort of stuff. Not that I have anything against it, but she was always claiming to be the Good Samaritan, know what I mean?"

I had my mouth full and started chewing faster, but he was talking again.

"For Moni the Russians are all nature boys or anar-
chists or suicides or artists, that sort of riffraff, and
they of course were hot for a girl like that from the
West, you can imagine. She crawls into their beds and
plays Saint Nicholas. And she's not bad, Moni isn't,
even Polly will admit that—as a woman, I mean."

I forked up a couple of French fries from the edge of
my plate.

"I noticed it myself. The calls to the office, the
euphoria, the way the others talked. They don't like it.
She's frittered away their goodwill."

Grambacher finished his beer, held the empty glass
up for the waiter to see and pressed his lips together to
keep from burping.

"If it weren't for Polly, Paris would be easy," he said,
and asked for the bill.

The size of the schnitzels they served you here was
simply incredible. I used my knife and fork to squeeze
the second lemon slice.

"Now here's the point. Our Häberle tells Polly she'll
check around in Germany for work for Polly's cousin,
Misha. Which is why he comes to her hotel." Grambacher had edged so close that it looked as if he
wanted to eat from my plate. "He speaks a little German, Polly says, but you don't have to just talk, right?"

He nudged my elbow and then apologized. I went
on eating.

"And the devil only knows what the truth is. Our
Häberle told Polly it wasn't work he was looking for,
but that he jumped her and ripped her clothes off.
And then she screamed—Häberle did, that is—until
somebody came and he hightailed it. But Misha told

Polly, on the phone, that he had just sat there at the table while she poured him one glass after the other and kept playing up to him. She hadn't had any work to offer him at all. And now here's the point," Grambacher announced, and paused.

I had eaten only one of the schnitzels, but my pickles were all gone.

"She had torn off her blouse, button by button, or so he told Polly, and then groped for his underwear. Our Häberle must have gone off like a V-2. She was hot for another roll in the hay. And when she saw his tool she told him it was as big as a horse's or an elephant's or whatever. So then he smacked her in the mouth, she started bawling, and he took off. But now here's the point," Grambacher said. He had pushed his right hand to the edge of my plate again.

I grabbed a couple of French fries off the tablecloth.

"She told the police that he had attacked her, that he had tried to rape her. And they believe her, because he's gone. They don't believe Polly, because she's his cousin. She wasn't there anyway, and he's gone."

Grambacher lit another cigarette but remained sitting so close to me that I barely had room to use my knife. His bill arrived.

"I can't lower the boom on Häberle, not the way Polly imagines. What do you say to all this?"

"Fascinating," I said, "downright fascinating."

"Is that a story or ain't it?"

I nodded.

Grambacher put his cigarette out by pinching it between thumb and forefinger and stuck it back in the pack. "Well, gotta be on my way!" He laid money on top of the bill. "Polly's waiting for me." He braced himself on my shoulder as he stood up. "How sweetly drops each moment of farewell . . ." he recited, picking up Polina's cape and his coat.

Now the moment had come.

"Yes, right, sure, tomorrow, great, I'll call, super, bye now, ciao. . . ." Grambacher waved with the hand just emerging from his coat sleeve.

I waved back. The waiter took my empty plate and asked if I had enjoyed my meal. I nodded again.

Were you serious? You don't even have to write new stuff nowadays—if only to save the forests! But I'm happy to pass the following fax on to you. The fellow who sent it to me is a strange character who worked for me for less than three weeks—just as he had planned. This Yegorovitch was intelligent and more flexible than other Russians I know, but a dreamer and unreliable in a management position. He writes in German. You'll have no trouble reading it.

Best, your ———

Dear Herr ———,

You are surprised to hear from me, are you not? And yet it is inevitable that I should write you. Who can share my experiences? I know of no one besides yourself. And I have infinite respect for your opinions. Please read this.

As is my habit, I was strolling down Nevsky Prospekt between two and three in the afternoon. Across from Gostinny Dvor, more toward Yelisseyev's, between the ice cream and lottery vendors, I came to a halt—because I saw him. Which is to say, I even walked back a few steps to get a better look. As if engaged in conversation, he was sitting on a low stool with legs spread wide, blinking up into the May sun. His forearms were propped on his knees; his dangling hands touched at the thumbs and along the forefingers. These pointed downward toward a little slanted box with a raised oval surface.

You of course know what I mean. But just as inflation for us was something that had once happened to the Germans, I knew bootblacks only from reports about child labor in Italy or South America.

As I pushed my way closer to him, it began: from my lower abdomen, from the groin, there came a surge of joy such as I have only felt, and even then very rarely, when entering a book or record shop. You rush over to something, stretch out an arm and are still convinced that somehow you failed to notice the long line or the sign with special instructions.

Quickly I put a foot on the box and hitched up my right trouser leg as if out of long habit. He was so careful about tucking the ends of the lace under the tongue that I almost pulled my foot back, but then he spread a cloth over the vamp, placed the palm of his hand over it and started rubbing back and forth between toe and quarter. Though he was scarcely older than I was, in his mid-twenties perhaps, his black hair was already thinning. I would not recognize him again, except for his hands, which moved as if each were the mirror image of the other. He had rolled up the sleeves of both jacket and shirt and pressed the brush into the crater of what polish was left in the can, daubed the shoe in three places and began to rub polish in, hands moving like a juggler's. As he labored his face constantly dipped close to the tips of my shoes, and when he reached for the heel his rear end lifted off his stool. I knew the moment had come to open a newspaper. For I had no part in the work being done on me down below other than to remove one foot from the box and place the other on it. Is that not monstrous?

A couple of kids came tentatively closer, but pulled back from the man's unpredictable flying elbows. Pulling paper off their ice creams, others watched us from a distance. At my back, across the street outside Gostinny Dvor, were duelling megaphones—swaths of words, the devil only knows who versus whom. They don't realize that their poverty, their torments, their dreary joys are nothing more than their own failure of will, or maybe its misdirection. Nothing more and nothing less, very simple. What else could have brought them to the life they lead today? Children have more sense.

Before he beat me, my grandfather would always say: You knew. It was your decision. Ultimately, that is how I began to school my will. My first task was to stay awake and, as soon as my grandparents were asleep, to smoke a cigarette in the stairwell, and then I had to toss the butt in a mailbox in the entrance to the building next door. After a week, I decided that the first number that came to mind while I smoked would determine the number of steps I had to walk until I was allowed to toss the butt away. Like a man under a sentence, I would walk around till morning, even taking the butt to school with me. Bit by bit, however, I got hold of myself. If I was wavering between two numbers, I would pick the higher one. A member of a secret Olympic cadre, I was addicted to my training, to making myself a slave to my own will. The greatest difficulty, however, was knowing what my will was. Should I get up and smoke and walk, or would it be better to lie in bed with my eyes open till the alarm rang? Should I suddenly cross the street blind, or should I try to touch everyone coming toward me on the sidewalk? Was the will better schooled if I clicked my tongue after each word, or was it more effective to speak only every tenth word? At twelve, I basked in the feeling that I had myself perfectly in hand. Yes, things went so far that I could hardly do anything without turning it into a specific task. Given my chosen sport, I was inevitably a loner, of course.

When two men beat me up on the street because my touching drill led them to assume that they had spotted a thief, I counted the words they yelled at me and multiplied them by the number of blows and kicks they landed. I then screamed out each result that was divisible by five. Disconcerted, they left me in peace. Training of the will, therefore, is not necessarily linked to torment.

All the rest was a simple decision and absurdly easy in comparison with my previous self-imposed tasks. I fused my talent—and everyone has talent of some sort—with my will and could no longer be surpassed, either at school or at university or even now. I was not a grind, but my will demanded ever more incredible tests, a constant stream of new victories.

And now—as I switched back to my left foot and a taut black velvet rag scurried back and forth across the toe of my shoe and then was quickly laid around my heel, so that as the rag slid higher, his hands mimicked not the vertical but the horizontal gestures of a boxer—I stood in silent happiness. You understand. I realized my victory. I had made it! I had entered into a time that had previously been real only in my dreams. This moment, as I switched from one foot to the other, placing one shiny shoe back on the sidewalk and letting this man below me polish the wax on the other—this moment was the capstone of everything I had wanted, had worked for and lived for.

And yet in the very next breath, as I searched my pocket for money, I realized: My life until now had been only my apprenticeship. What I had taken for fulfillment revealed itself as a step back to the beginning—or, better, as the closing of a circle.

You understand: I am rich. My real estate dealings alone bring me more per week than you earn in two months—and I am a Russian. Money, however, is merely a milestone on the road to our will. From that point on, everything grows muddled. Those who keep going, and they are few, become either religious or, like yourself, cynics. And yet everything is possible. I repeat: everything—if, that is, within a nation there are only a couple of people with strong wills, who can sweep the rest along with them! No one will deny that the state is borne by those who think and work and create all those things by which a nation lives. Economic and political strength, however, are solid only if they are based on moral strength. But what is the goal of our communal human life if not to erect a moral order? From which follows, as our great Stolypin once so inimitably said: Without independent citizens one cannot create a state of law and order. And yet there can be no independent citizens without private property. From here, if you will, the path comes full circle back to utopias and for the first time is filled with life. From here, I greet you as my comrade, in the Goethean sense of the word! The tapestry of human life is not yet nearly so boring and gray as you are forever imagining. Kiev was taken twenty times and destroyed, trampled in the dust. The rich man wept, but the poor man laughed. And thus will I transform the garments of beggars into grumbling, and the rags wrapped about their feet will I replace with mad roars. By my will shall roads and highways blossom like sunflowers. I shall create! The masters of this world shall be as little fish, pierced through by the keenness of my mind. I shall lay fires with the matches of fate. I shall read the Onegin of lead and iron to the deaf ears of the masses. The people dwell in the ship of idleness; warriors have replaced will with song, a hero's death with white bread. Pillage with foliage. Courts-martial with amorous courting. All wish to be lazy, languid and loved. Let the eagle but roughly spread his bowed pinions, longing for Leli, he shall fly hither, like the pea from the blowpipe—from the word Russia. When the people are transformed into elks, when they sustain wound upon wound, when they loom soft as lynxes, nudging the gate of destiny with wet black muzzles—then will they ask for mild Leli, love, for Leli and pure *L*'s, will ask to rest their flagging flesh. Their heads will then be lexicons of words all in *L*. He who lopes about as a weasel in a strange land lacks love! For who, as he falls, selects for himself his whither as well? Into snow, into water, into the ditch, into the abyss? The drowning man climbs into the boat ere he rows. Ere, Ra, Row! Raw, Rage, Revenge! God of Russia, God of Raving. Perun the Giant, your god, knows no barrier, railing, rudder, he rages, rides, he roots. Where is the swarm of green aitches for two, and the *L* of the clothing alope? From the furred felted trumpet of Perun, from the flaming fleece of Perun spelt husks and chaff spray upon paws of feathers of nakedness into time and space. Izum! O Izum! Against Vyum, against Noum, come, Koum! O Laum, O Laum. My Byum calls, Izum, Izum! Doom. Daum. Mium. Room. Choum. Chaum. Pertch! Hartch! Zortch! Hansioppo! Tarch paraka prak tak tak! Prirara purururu! Zam, gag, zamm! Meserese bolchitcha! Vyeava Mivea-a

Ah, here is our knight—bonjour!" Mme. Razumonova cried in almost accent-free German, stretching a large, skinny hand out to him. Smiling, she regarded Martens, who bowed, gently took hold of her fingers and pressed his lips to the delta of pale

veins on the back of her hand. She kept on smiling until their eyes met again.

"She's doing somewhat better," she began, passing a hand over her pulled-back hair.

"I am very pleased to make your acquaintance," Martens replied, tore the paper from a little bouquet of three-dollar roses and stepped over the threshold.

"For me . . . ?" Retreating into the small vestibule, Mme. Razumonova put her unkissed hand to her mouth—beneath her nose, dark amber set in silver.

"For you."

"They're worth a fortune!" Mme. Razumonova carefully laid the bouquet among the combs on the low table under the mirror, while with her other hand she held a hanger out in the air as if doing some sort of calisthenics. There was a smell of cigarettes, stewed fruit and old furniture.

"So this is Mashenka!" Martens looked as if he were about to bend down to the white cat that had lifted the hem of Mme. Razumonova's dress.

"Correct," Mme. Razumonova confirmed, and retreated even farther, which gave Martens a chance to navigate the narrows between wall and coat rack.

"Punctuality is the politeness of kings, don't they say?" Mme. Razumonova inquired, and pushed past him to the door, smoothing her dark blue dress with the palm of one hand and with the other clenching tight the cardigan thrown over her shoulders. The three locks rattled loudly. Mashenka had vanished.

Martens was still smiling as he adjusted the shoulders of his coat on the hanger and then flattened himself against the wall to let Mme. Razumonova whisk by. He wavered a moment, wondering if he should remove his shoes, turned his head in profile to the mirror until he could no longer see himself and followed her into the room.

"Did you know," Mme. Razumonova said, turning to him, coffeepot in hand, "that our Yekaterina has never been ill, never, only childhood diseases. And now, when it's so important, all of a sudden, a fever of a hundred and two, even higher."

"Isn't Yekaterina feeling better?" Martens didn't know where he should put the second bouquet, still in its wrapping.

"Oh my, yes! Much better!" Mme. Razumonova assured him, still hesitating to remove the colorful knit rooster from the spout and pour the coffee. "If it were up to her! We're so grateful to you! Come . . . oh, those books. Yes, if it weren't for books, that songbook! Hand those to me, we'll put them . . . marvelous flowers!"

When Mme. Razumonova returned with the vase her face was no longer flushed. "After you called yesterday, when Yekaterina told me . . . I am so happy you've come! No, no. It's truly extraordinary. Do you take sugar? Is that all right? Out of a clear blue sky, a fever of over a hundred and two, our princess."

When Martens spotted the cigarette between Mme. Razumonova's fingers, he bounded up out of his chair and leaned across the low table. He had to take care not to bang his knees.

"Once Yekaterina is well," she said, blowing smoke through her nose, "you'll have to come back. Yekaterina is such an excellent housekeeper. And she's such a good baker! You don't take milk, Herr Martens? I have so many questions! This one here is kulitch, and this is paskha."

Mme. Razumonova steadied a large piece of Easter cake between the knife and fork on his plate, stuck the flat wooden spoon in the paskha and passed him the bowl.

"Where did you study, if I might ask? But don't be so bashful, please help yourself, yes, that's it. . . ."

Mme. Razumonova accompanied the tale of Martens' career with enthusiastic shakes of her head and more questions. *"Magnifique!"* she kept exclaiming, and closely followed each of his movements as he lit another cigarette. His dark blue tie went well with his pastel shirt. His fingernails were large and well manicured, and that little mustache looked good on him.

"In that chair, the one you're sitting in," Mme. Razumonova explained, and took a sip of coffee—Martens looked at the shiny arms under his hands—"is where my mother always sat."

"Oh, is it?"

"I never heard her voice, you know, for she was already mute when I was born. But now, eleven years after her death, I hear her voice. Isn't that peculiar?"

"Yes, it is peculiar," he confirmed, "but why not?"

"It's sweet of you to say so," Mme. Razumonova replied, blushing a little again and holding the cup on her lap with both hands. "People have become so boorish."

"Was it hard for you to have a mute mother?" Martens inquired, leaning back.

"Hard?" Mme. Razumonova said, picking up on his

word. "I never felt as if my mother was mute, we had our ways of communicating. She even wished that I might be mute as well. Imagine that! It was already after the war, I was in school, when she first brought me here, to the Moika Canal. I can still remember it perfectly. It was the middle of October, and snowing. Green leaves and snow—strange, but beautiful. . . . Hand me your cup. . . . We gazed into the Moika. The snowflakes didn't even make rings as they touched the water."

Mme. Razumonova's eyes had the look of those infinity shots in films shown on early afternoon television. Through a haze of smoke that filtered the daylight like curtains, she saw everything she was talking about. "That boisterous laughter, their guffaws as they held our officers underwater with poles, like dirty laundry. . . . People hooted when the bodies didn't resurface. My mother, she was nine at the time, lost her speech." Mme. Razumonova paused, and Martens did not stir, either. "I never knew her any other way— should I fetch some milk? If my father hadn't married her . . . For a long time I thought: Nobility, those are all the mute people."

The trees in front of the building dulled the light bathing the upper stories. The desk lamp in the corner was on.

"When I think of just the jewelry they took from her," she began again. "I had an old photograph of her, as a child with diamonds at her ears, like this"— bending middle finger to palm, Mme. Razumonova peered at Martens as if through a telescope—"round, you know. Even as an old woman she had a way of rubbing her earlobes. . . ."

He blew air through his nose and shook his head.

"And do you know when I realized what we had lost? When I realized that?"

Mme. Razumonova bent almost double.

"I was in the seventh grade when a girlfriend showed me the first oranges I'd ever seen. And suddenly there were my mother's diamonds before my eyes. One of them would have been enough to buy out the entire shop. Isn't that awful?"

Mme. Razumonova put her cup down, stubbed out the cigarette she had left until it had burned down to the filter, and fell silent. Martens heard slow music but couldn't tell if he was just imagining it or if it was coming from a neighbor's radio, or from the street perhaps.

"Do you know what my one wish is, Herr Martens?" He saw now that her chin was trembling, as was the little mole beside her nose. She alternated biting her upper and lower lip. Then, from a seam in the chair she pulled a handkerchief balled up into a wad, peeled one corner away and blew her nose. "Oh, I'm sorry, so sorry." She gave a laugh and fled weeping from the room. Mashenka—the devil only knew where she had suddenly come from—ran after her, and the music ceased.

Left alone, Martens found the room smaller—two large armchairs and a coffee table in between. He took scant notice of the photographs, postcards, stones, glasses and little dolls set along the narrow spaces in front of the books. As if he were not even there, Mme.

Razumonova now passed directly from the bath to Yekaterina.

Martens ate his Easter cake with his hands; he let the paskha be. It tasted old. He would have loved to drink a cognac, toss the pillows from the sofa and stretch out, his head on the bolster. He could make out two different female voices but understood nothing. The only clear sound he heard was the shushes with which they cautioned each other to speak quietly. Martens crossed to the bathroom. With the door open—he could not find a light switch—he washed his hands, gargled briefly, wiped his eyes and brow, spat soundlessly into the basin and dried his face on a pink towel hanging from a hook above which it read "Yekaterina."

"Mama!" a choked voice suddenly cried, and broke off in the middle of the second *a*.

Mme. Razumonova was startled. She had evidently not expected him in the dark bathroom. "Please excuse me, but I must go shopping. And to the cobbler. Yekaterina . . ."

Between her eyebrows lay a vertical crease. Already in her coat, she slipped into her brown pumps and took two shopping bags from their hook on the coatrack. "An hour . . ." She left the apartment with a preoccupied look that grazed Martens only at the last moment. The door was now locked twice from the outside. Mashenka gave a woeful meow.

"May I?" he asked into the silence of the apartment, and rapped on the doorjamb to Yekaterina's room. The flowers were dripping. He knocked a second time, this time on the slightly open door, and heard a soft "Yes."

Not until Yekaterina had pushed herself up in bed a little, stretching her tucked-up legs out under the blanket, could he see her face. Her dark hair spread out over the pillow, curled in strands down over her cheeks and along her neck and disappeared under the bedspread.

"So beautiful," she said feebly, and took the roses from him.

"May I?" Martens pulled the only chair up into the narrow gap left between the two beds, at the head of which, below the window, stood a white lacquered nightstand with a vase.

"There's something I haven't told you," Yekaterina began at once, then closed her eyes and smelled the roses. Their chalices lay just below her mouth.

"Should I put the flowers—"

"I know!" she broke in.

"What do you know?"

"Why do you even ask?"

"Since Monday . . . ?"

"Yes."

"The bookkeeper told you?"

"It's not her fault," Yekaterina answered in the same weary tone of voice.

Martens leaned forward on his chair. "Is it really so awful?"

Yekaterina looked at him as if opening her eyes for the first time. Little wrinkles formed at the base of her nose and at the corners of her mouth; she trembled, she rolled onto her side. Her shoulders were quivering. Martens shook his head and edged closer, taking care not to touch the bed.

"The main thing is that you get your money, whether from the company or from me . . . so why should you worry?" Standing up, he bent forward, placing his hands now on his knees, now in his trouser pockets. "Yekaterina," he pleaded.

Martens would have liked to pull the roses out from under her left arm. Actually he had wanted to tell her about the two women and the man with an accordion he had met on his way here. He wanted to imitate them and sing:

> Dunka, Dunka, Dunka, yes!
> Dunka, oh my darling . . .
> Ah, Dunka, Dunka, Dunka,
> ah, Dunka, love me please.

The women had laughed so hard and pressed up against the man between them until he had had to stop playing.

"I'll be going then," Martens said. Yekaterina's shoulders were rising and falling regularly now. He pushed his chair back.

"Please don't," she said after a while. "You have to wait."

"Does she know?"

"She's visiting a friend," Yekaterina explained, and rolled over onto her back again.

"Well, all right . . ." Martens sat back down. With one hand he petted Mashenka as she brushed against the leg of his chair.

"I can read something for you in the meantime—

poems by Heine," Yekaterina said, and unfolded a handkerchief and held it up to her face.

"But what should we do with the roses?" Martens asked, bending down further still to Mashenka.

Please publish the following ad in your paper: 'Wanted: uniforms, weapons, watches, china, photos and similar items from czarist period for decor of restaurant in Leipzig.' Awaiting your reply . . ." Followed by a telephone number.

After several tries I got hold of Hans-Karl Schulz, whose signature was on the letter. On the recommendation of ———, he had come to me with the request that I make a selection of said items and, if possible, arrange for transport. He would, of course, defray all expenses and reimburse me for my trouble. "You should know," Schulz kept saying, "how much I envy you your stay in St. Petersburg."

"Reply: Leipzig" was a great success. I could select the best addresses from among the offers. Hall clocks, postcards, armchairs, porcelain bowls, silverware, ivory letter openers, fans, a dagger, tablecloths, ladies' laced shoes.

After a week I assigned "Reply: Leipzig" to Anton, our photographer, who treated each response with the same care he devoted to answers to his own ad in our MALE SEEKS FEMALE column. He was the right man for Schulz. Five days later, Anton presented me with a computer printout of several pages. There were tables listing each article, a brief description and suggested price, address and telephone number. Customs regulations followed on a separate sheet.

"Listen to this," Anton said, and read: " 'Collector's items. Looking forward to your visit. Boris Sergeyevitch Altman.' " He handed me the torn-off sheet. This Altman must not have put pen to paper very often. The letters were clumsily printed. The address said nothing to me.

"First-class landscape," Anton assured me, "Lake Ladoga, Schlüsselburg, the banks of the Neva. They trade goods for money. Afterward we can go mushrooming."

He fought for every address. I asked about the ladies he normally reserved his weekends for. His answer was unintelligible because he was plucking threads of tobacco from his lips.

On Sunday Anton appeared in a light-colored suit. He held the car door open for me, pressing his monogrammed red tie against his dark blue shirt. We moved quickly through the city and drove on under a cloudless sky amid the swarm of people on their Sunday outing: grandparents and grandkids squeezed into backseats, car roofs loaded with canoes, tubs, crates, canvas and fishing rods.

"If anybody here waves, don't ever stop." Anton sprayed crumbs on the windshield as he spoke. His sister had sent meat pirogi along for a snack. They had to be eaten warm. He sniffed and chewed and hummed "My Fate," his favorite song.

Sometimes Anton was so lethargic that you felt you ought to stir the sugar in his tea for him, and then again, something would get him so fired up that he could stamp our return address on pile after pile of envelopes and brush his teeth four times a day. At his suggestion, I had bought vodka and cigarettes.

The exit off the Neva Bridge into Schlüsselburg made several wide curves around a parking lot, where we pulled up in front of the bunker-like entrance to a diorama that Anton had been enthusing over during the entire drive. He put on his sporty cap, removed windshield wipers and sideview mirrors, and checked all the doors one last time. It was shortly after eleven. I was to let myself be surprised.

A half hour later we were driving downstream along the banks of the Neva, where from 12 to 30 January 1943 the Germans had been handed a defeat during Operation Spark. They had been caught in a pincer between the Sixty-seventh Army of the Leningrad Front under Lieutenant General Govrov, the Second Shock Army and a portion of the Eighth Army of the Volkhov Front under General Meretskov, supported by the Baltic Fleet. Anton knew all about it.

We stopped again at the monument to the Heroes of the Red Army and, with the car doors wide open, polished off the rest of the pirogi.

"The Germans were here, and we were over there," Anton explained with his mouth full again, and turned the radio off. I was supposed to listen to the crickets.

It was sultry. We got out to smoke and gaze at the Neva.

"Strange, isn't it," he said, "how you always want to end up at a river, or by the sea, or on a mountain? There's something that keeps pulling you on. Know what I mean?"

We walked across the road to a wood, where signs marked a buried cable. The sandy soil with its sparse grass was badly gouged, with freshly dug holes and little ditches everywhere. Next to sandy pits lay rusted hand grenades, cutlery, spades, gas-mask filters. Anton picked up something white and tossed it at my feet. "Either from here or here." He tapped his shoulder, then his hip.

I found a riddled steel helmet.

"Wehrmacht!" Anton exclaimed.

The pattern of the trenches was still clearly visible. Lost in thought as if gathering mushrooms, we pulled shoe soles and entire boots from the earth, showed each other bones and ammo belts, crouched to hurl rusted hand grenades. If it had not been for the plastic bottles and other trash, I would have turned around for fear of mines. We stood side by side in front of a steep railroad embankment and pissed on a gas mask until its round eyecups glistened, then we sauntered back. The steel helmet got tossed into the trunk along with our basket for mushrooms and a pair of old trousers. Anton spat on his fingernails and polished each with his handkerchief, which he then refolded.

"This is it," Anton proclaimed as we pulled into the village of P. Three white head scarves shone amid the dark laundry strung on a line in the front yard of a green frame house. Once out of the car, Anton doffed his cap, jumped the roadside ditch and leaned over the fence. While Anton spoke, the women grabbed at sleeves and pants legs. Then they looked in each other's brown faces and shook their heads.

"There are some Boris Sergeyevitches, but no Altman," Anton said, and adjusted the rearview mirror. Two boys were coming down the road.

"Can I bum one?" Anton asked, rolling down his window. In the shorter boy's jacket pocket a pack of Belomors was clearly visible. He eyed me, then the backseat and the dashboard. The other one carefully set down a bag between his feet.

"I'll give you a light and you can give me—"

"You've got cigarettes!" The shorter boy's outstretched arm pointed to the pack of Marlboros between the bulge above the tachometer and the windshield.

"Maybe I've got a craving for a Belomor, eh? We could trade, how would that be?" Their faces remained impassive.

"Does an Altman live around here?" Anton flipped the pack open.

"Boris Sergeyevitch?" the tall boy asked, and stuck the cigarette in his breast pocket. He was missing an eyetooth. The short one pulled out a Belomor.

"Boris Sergeyevitch Altman, exactly. Thanks."

"What do you want from him?"

"To get to know him. Does his family live here?"

"Why?"

"None of your business—seems to me."

Neither of the two said anything. There was something harried about the look in the taller one's eyes, something hard to describe.

"He invited me to come see him, okay? On business."

The one with the bag pointed down the road. "Turn right at the last house, there's a path."

Anton put his head out the window.

"Right, turn right before that green fence," the short one repeated. The women had stopped to watch from the front door. Anton tapped the bill of his cap. "Don't smoke too much, boys!"

Sea buckthorn had overgrown the wooden fences along the road, pushing them forward until in some places you could have touched both sides at once with outstretched arms. So we parked the car and proceeded on foot. After a hundred yards the path led across an open field. Despite the dry weather, it was still soggy here. Hitching his pants at the thighs, Anton walked ahead of me, balancing his way across planks laid as footbridges over puddles. Just one false step, and I had muck in my sandals.

Then we spotted the cottage. The name ALTMAN had been burned into a freshly painted pale board set above the lintel, exactly in the middle. All the rest seemed to be of the same rotting wood as the tree trunk that lay beside the front door and that presumably served as a bench. We heard voices—children squabbling.

The shingled roof had been patched with pieces of tin. A cable dangled from the listing antenna and disappeared somewhere. The window was dark, half of it a milk-glass replacement. Little rubber boots and *valenki* with gaiters stood on a board just outside the door.

A boy, maybe ten years old, shambled out.

"How's it going?" Anton asked. It got quiet inside, as if someone had turned off a radio. "Hello, big boy!" The boy pulled his shirt down over his pants and dodged Anton's extended hand. We scraped the mud from our shoes on two sticks nailed to a short crossbar, and knocked.

"May we come in?" Anton hesitated briefly at the threshold and stepped inside. There was a smell of rancid grease, but with a sour tinge, too. Light from the windows cut across the room in beams. Children were sitting around a table, two girls and at the head a boy of maybe fourteen. They were peeling potatoes out of a bowl set in front of them, its rim only a little lower than their heads. They did not interrupt their work or look up.

"Your parents aren't here?" Anton put his cap back on. The door banged shut behind me. Worn runners were laid across the floor. There were slices of dry bread and scraps of food in a plastic bucket.

"Are you here for Leipzig?" the boy at the table asked, letting his knife and a potato slip back into the bowl.

"Yes, Leipzig," I said. The girls glanced briefly our way.

"Welcome!" The boy rolled down his sleeves and winced as he buttoned his shirt collar.

"Boris Sergeyevitch," he said, coming toward us with outstretched arms. "Boris Sergeyevitch Altman, my pleasure." First he shook Anton's hand, then mine.

The girls removed the bowl from the table and vanished behind a curtain that blocked off one corner of the room.

"That can't be helped," Altman said as we looked down at our muddy tracks. He returned to where he had been sitting before and wiped drops of water off the table with the flat of his hand.

Anton and I sat facing each other at the long sides of the table.

"Would you like some tea?" Altman lit a Belomor and leaned back. "Used to taste better." He blew at the glowing tip, pulled his mouth down in disdain and spat into a bowl that stood against the wall behind me.

"What would you like to sell us?" I asked. One of the girls, now heavily made-up, set a samovar in front of us.

"This is Tanya." Altman was missing several teeth.

"So what's this about?" I asked again.

Altman smoked and kept checking the tip of his *papyrosa.* The absence of adults was eerie.

"He was still young then." Anton pointed to a poster of Van Damme, tacked to the wood of the unplastered wall, right next to Schwarzenegger, Abba and Michael Jackson. He accepted a Belomor and unbuttoned his jacket. On a shelf beside the door stood a collection of tin cans towering in a kind of pyramid.

"Not bad, not bad," Anton said in admiration and thrust out an approving lower lip. "Cozy, cozy."

"Is our guest right about that, Denis?" The little boy was now sitting with his legs pulled up in a chair behind Anton's back.

"Right," Denis answered.

"And your parents?" I asked.

Altman tossed the matches to Anton, who caught them with his left hand. "In the city."

"And you stayed behind here?"

"We're out of there, out of Peter. Will you eat with us?"

"Steak and French fries," the little boy said from his chair.

"Not bad, steak and French fries," Anton repeated, sliding the matches back across the table and nodding to me. "Not bad!"

"We always have French fries," Altman said. "Isn't that right, Tanyusha? Tanyusha!" She was setting out glasses and placed a teapot next to the samovar. "A good girl. Help yourselves."

"Thanks, Boris Sergeyevitch, thanks so much." Anton first poured a little of the dark tea into my glass, then into Altman's and finally into his own.

"I made the rowan jam myself," Altman said as the girl set the opened jar in front of us.

"Rowan berries, cranberries, blueberries, cherries," she enumerated, passing out spoons, then vanished again behind the curtain. Denis was sent with the garbage pail to feed the rabbits.

"First-rate, simply first-rate," Anton whispered. He batted the air with his teaspoon as if searching for the right word. "Wonderful, tastes like last autumn." Altman held his glass under the samovar and ran hot water from the tap.

I had a hunch that there was a story here and feigned surprise when Altman responded with a shrug to my question about school. "And that's no problem?"

"All depends on the police."

"What a guy!" Anton whinnied. "All depends on the police!"

"Are you friends with them?" I asked.

"We do some work together," Altman said.

"They help you out?"

"We help them, they help us." He went on sipping at his tea.

"And what work is it that you do?"

"I'll get to that."

Anton began to talk about the restaurant in Leipzig, about his expeditions, about prices, sabers and ivory fans. Altman asked no questions, he didn't even seem to be listening. When Anton fell silent, the boy called out something apparently meant for the girls. For behind the curtain they began unpacking something—a toolbox or the like. Anton went on spooning varenye and sipping tea. He no longer looked my way. Suddenly the door opened.

"'Bout-face!" Altman shouted. The two boys we already knew retreated. Only Denis, his face beaming, stumbled into the room in his rubber boots. Altman had jumped to his feet. In the next moment, empty beer cans were flying through the air, rolling along the walls and under the table.

"Filthy pig!" Altman slapped the boy's head. Denis stepped out of his boots and took them outside, smearing his muddy tracks with his naked feet as he went. No sooner was the door closed than Tanya appeared from behind the curtain.

"Incredible," Anton whispered, and stood up. "Incredible!"

"Our work," Altman announced, taking a submachine gun from Tanya and aiming it at me.

"Incredible . . ." Anton said in a husky voice. "Fantastic!"

"From the Germans—Schmeisser, 38/40!" Altman
presented the submachine gun to Anton. He stroked
the barrel. "Nine-millimeter—no problem with ammo."

"Not exactly the czarist period," I said.

Altman whipped his head around. I was about to
calm him when he pulled a pistol out of the back of his
trousers and held it under my nose. "Heil Hitler!" he
screamed. "Say: Heil Hitler! Or say: Sieg Heil! Heil
Hitler! Sieg Heil!" The corners of his mouth twitched.
He aimed lower. "Go on! Heil Hitler! Heil Hitler!"

"Walther, nine-millimeter, six-shot," Anton said,
bracing the submachine gun at his hip. "Wait outside!"

"Scram!" All of a sudden Altman's voice sounded
saccharine. "Out!"

I stood up, shoved my chair back and took a couple
of cautious steps. Altman's extended arm followed me.
The door was ajar. Before I reached it, I heard a click.
Then I was outside.

"You guys buying?" Denis asked. He pushed a rabbit
down into the grass, plopped a crate over it with his
other hand and laid stones on top.

I asked him where the other boys were.

"Digging, looking for treasure." He pulled an empty
St. Pauli Girl beer can from a bag. "Know what this is?"

I nodded. The other girl, as made-up as Tanya now,
stood in the doorway and waved for him to come in.

"What have you got there?" I asked Denis. It looked
like a birthmark peeking out from between button-

holes. He pulled his shirt open and stuck out his chest. At the level of his heart was a tattooed medal.

"You should see Timur sometime!"

"Who?"

"The boss. Timur. Got any cigarettes?"

I gave him a handful.

"Wow!" he yelled, and waited for me to offer him the flat of my hand. He slapped it with his own. "You buying?"

"Yes."

"You want German stuff? Ours is better!"

"I doubt that."

"Denis!" the girl called, and stomped her foot.

"Give me something?" he asked hastily. I gave him my lighter, which he at once held up to the sun.

I waited by the car. The heat was oppressive. Next door a babushka was chopping wood. I said hello two, three times—she stared at me, collected her logs and went into the house. Cars passed only rarely. On the other side of the river stood a dense cluster of unstuccoed villas with little towers and turrets.

When Anton finally arrived he was holding a longish package wrapped in newspaper and pressed against his body like a crutch that was too short. It took him a long time to load it in the trunk. Without a word, he took out the vodka and cigarettes. I waited another half hour.

"And what if we get stopped?" I asked.

We were driving back along the Neva. Anton smoked. Traffic was light.

"And don't say a word about this, you hear?" Anton's

right forefinger wagged at me in the air. "And what if you do," he burst out, laughing. "What if you do!"

In the weeks that followed, we hardly exchanged greetings. Anton reimbursed me for the cigarettes and vodka. He wasn't interested in the replies any longer. He had found something that drew his gaze into the distance and made him blink, as if he were standing with his face to the wind. Then he disappeared from our editorial offices, and I haven't seen him for six months now.

Although my article had to appear without photographs, it was a big success. The deal with Schulz fizzled out. He never sent any money. Although even today we're still getting letters addressed to "Reply: Leipzig."

I had figured it was merely a matter of time, that is, of the right moment, before I got a yes out of her for an evening or a weekend, maybe even longer. But she held up her hand to me like a photograph with just one significant detail, a narrow gold band—as if I weren't already on intimate terms with her fingers, didn't love the gentle arch bedding each nail and all the little wrinkles on her knuckles. Her ring with the pearl had suited her much better. Splaying her fingers, she picked up three glasses at once, held them clustered as she put them on her tray, and left.

I came here only for her sake. If the window tables she served were occupied, I would wait outside the door or at the bar. During the day the restaurant was full of tourists and their children scattering toys about, but in the evening it was crowded with businessmen, who laid their cellular phones on the table between the glasses and bottles. You ate well here: Kamchatka crabs for four dollars, Wiener schnitzel, stroganoff or a seafood platter for eight, beer and vodka for two. If she had a little break between orders, I would watch as she stood temple to temple with the head waitress, yet never taking her eyes off the room as she talked. Straight-backed but at seemingly perfect ease, she would stand at the buffet table, where the ashtrays and baskets of silverware in napkins were kept. I needed only to raise a finger above the table and she was at my side. She would immediately unclasp her hands held folded before her and nudge the napkin up her forearm. Her skirt was tight, which made her take short steps. Under the taut fabric, first one leg showed, then the other. A strand of her smooth black hair swayed between chin and neck. With her last step to my table she would toss her head back, but then her hair would fall into place around her face.

How I hated guests who asked her for her name, laid an arm around her waist and gave her a tip without it ever occurring to them that a man could be lost without that smile. Her smile—revealing a minute gap between two front teeth and promising that she was ready for anything, capable of anything, right here, in front of the guests and the head waitress. I wanted to lean my head against her, against that spot where she held her pad to the gentle swell of her waistband. She thanked me for the order. I had to control myself when she bent her knee slightly and picked up her tray! With every step, her foot trembled for the tiniest moment on its high heel and each time created that special line between shin and calf. I sucked in the air that she had walked through.

I had divulged my passion to no one. Not one of my coworkers would have suspected it had he ever chanced to spot me through the window, since the blinds were never closed at night. Anyone who wanted to could observe the black tables and chairs, the blue and red settees, the bar with its glistening taps and tropical plants, plus the festive lighting and the well-dressed people eating and drinking, talking and laughing.

If old women weren't leaning with their backs to the windows and blocking the view as they hawked their wares of dolls and scarves, records and egg warmers, you could gaze across Nevsky Prospekt to the City Duma, with artists hawking their works on the steps. At the bus stop in front of me, buses burst open, emptied out and sank back askew under the boarding throng. Next came beggars crouching on the stairs to the subway. And everywhere children— whose magic trick was to cover their hands with a kerchief and stick them in other people's pockets and who suddenly came to a halt for you to stumble over them. The staffs at the hotels shooed them from the entrances. You were safe here inside.

Anyone peeping in the window would never have guessed my yearning to awaken next to her, to stand beside her while she washed and brushed her teeth, to talk with her while she crooked up a leg and cut her toenails.

She set the beer down in front of me—not a hand-breadth separated her head from my brow—picked up my empty glass, laid the bill down in its place and was already looking for change, but she must have mis-heard the figure I mentioned and instead gave back the full amount, down to the last ruble note. I neither contradicted her nor looked up.

Then—yes, she had only been waiting for me to raise my head as if it were all just a misunderstand-ing—she smiled at me, her lips moving as if for a kiss, and vanished. I closed my eyes in happiness.

And yet only three, four minutes later, when I had taken up my post beside the entrance, I was tormented by the notion that I might have missed her. Despite my assumption that she would have to punch out for the day and change clothes, the temptation grew to ask the doormen in their gray suits. Not only did they have an eye and a nose for quality in shoes, excellence in coat fabrics and the latest model in glasses—"You are welcome"—but they also had good memories.

"A woman, a woman, he wants a woman!"

A few steps away, at the corner of Nevsky, several passersby were standing around a lanky guy flailing his arms. For a few moments, as the west wind ripped

open the clouds, you were blinded by the bright, clear
light that was an announcement of spring and filled
the endless Prospekt with sea air.

"A woman, a woman!" the tall guy repeated.

Even if she had taken another exit, she would have
to come past here on her way to the subway—and
past that little group gathered at the entrance to the
subway stairs near the corner of the building. The tall
guy's excitement was echoed in the uneasy movements of coats, necks and handbags all around him.

She appeared in the doorway, alone and with a red
wide-brimmed hat. The men in gray greeted her.
Without looking around, she walked off in the direction of the Pushkin Monument. Her high heels must
have been audible from the topmost stories. The tips
of my shoes almost touched the hem of her cream-
colored coat. I tried to breathe normally. She wore the
hat at such an angle that it hid her hair entirely on the
left side. At the hotel entrance she slowed down, her
coat fell around her ankles. Then she stopped to
search her handbag. For the first time I could smell her
perfume. I waited. Her fingers moved as if typing on a
midget keyboard. She pulled out a dollar, closed the
handbag and—my God! "Nyet, nyet," she scolded.
Between her front teeth—not the tiniest gap.

When I looked up again, the only evidence of her
presence was the bowing liveried hotel doorman and
the green dollar bill in his hand.

I didn't run back. I didn't ask anyone, didn't bribe
the men in gray. With no will of my own, I stared
at the red carpet at the entrance until some instinct
for the path of least resistance led me back to my

previous post, which saved me from the catcalls of taxi drivers and children.

The crowd had grown larger around the tall guy, who looked to me to be not quite right in the head. Chin jutted forward, he was staring at something I couldn't make out, even when I stood on tiptoe behind the last row of backs. I asked why people had gathered here. Instead of giving an answer, a man whose elbow was digging into my chest tapped the woman ahead of him, who, with a quick exchange of glances, signaled the shoulder ahead of her. And so on. I assured them that I merely wanted to know why people were standing here. My accent betrayed me. And so they urged me to make use of the path that with some effort had now been cleared for me.

The crazy guy eyed me—the cause of this disturbance—from head to toe. I shrugged, he looked away. "Go on, do it, go on!" the woman ahead of me scolded in an almost toneless voice, and I made my way to the center of it all.

An old man in rags and with an open wound above his right eyebrow lay on the sidewalk, gazing up at those around him. A woman knelt at his side. She was just raising his head to shove a cap underneath. He wrenched his toothless mouth in a truly mad way. Threads of mucus between his lips broke, and his pale blue eyes danced to and fro. An old woman bowed to him several times and made the sign of the cross with broad gestures, as if wrapping herself in a long cloth. Others followed her example, including some young men. But no one helped, except the woman— a doctor, presumably—holding the old man's head.

Holding one hand to his cheek, the doctor undid the knot of her head scarf and, wrapping it around two fingers, pulled it from her hair. She put an ear to his lips. What he said was inaudible. She kissed him on the brow.

"God bless you, girl!" Like most of these people, the man with disheveled hair next to me was here by himself. His gray scarf, neatly crossed at his chest, lent him a certain elegance despite his threadbare coat and unshaven chin.

"What a girl!" "A real Russian!" people whispered. A large, broad-shouldered policeman forced his way into the circle, demanded to know what was going on and cast the old man a quick glance. A hulk who towered above the rows of people, he kept both hands hooked at his wide belt, his billy club dangling from his left wrist.

The doctor calmly took off her cape and handed it and her scarf to the redheaded woman next to her. Paying no attention to the gawkers or the policeman, she opened the few buttons of her blouse and undid the ribbons gathering the sleeves at her wrists.

"A beauty!" The disheveled man bowed low and crossed himself along with many others. I was touched by a round vaccination mark on her upper arm. I would gladly have assisted her, yet she seemed neither to expect nor to need any help.

When the zipper got stuck, she literally ripped her skirt from her body, rolled down her panty hose and slipped out of her shoes at the same time.

"Hallelujah!" the policeman boomed, never taking his massive hands off his belt or his eyes off the doctor.

"Little dove, don't stop halfway! Don't you know anything about men?" I heard the tiny old lady across from me ask. Yet the woman she had addressed had eyes and ears only for the man whose cheek she was patting, wiping blood from his brow.

"Quiet!" a man admonished, and swiped a thumb across his fogged spectacles.

His face frozen in a grimace, the old man fixed his little eyes on every motion of her hands. She unhooked her bra and slipped the straps off. The old man let out a faint "Ahh" as she pulled her panties down and flung them with her right foot—to the disheveled man. He kissed them hungrily and tossed them to the redhead.

The doctor was now straddling the old man. Carefully she squatted down, placing her left knee on the pavement, followed by the right.

"God be with you, what a saint!"

"You're Russia's redemption!"

"A saint!" Many voices took up the cry.

"Your name, girl, tell us your name!"

A woman sobbed. The doctor grabbed the old man's hands, which had been lying lifelessly beside him, raised them to her shoulders, led them gently down over her body and pressed them to her breasts.

An elbow in my side turned me around. The woman I had bumped against offered me a bouquet of thin, honey-colored candles that she was having trouble holding together.

"Take one," she muttered. I had barely touched a candle when she demanded a hundred rubles, then bent confidentially closer. "Two for a hundred and fifty."

While I looked for money, the disheveled man wrapped a scrap of newspaper around the base of his lit candle. Wax dripped on his hand and up his sleeve. I was the only one standing erect amid a bowing crowd. But when the same fellow held his candle out for me to light mine, I no longer felt alone. A few women had begun to sing. Voice after voice joined in. The tall crazy guy timidly beat out the rhythm.

Before I realized it, I was weeping. Not since childhood had my tears flowed so freely. How long had it been since I had heard music like this.

"Your name, girl, your name!" Women held handkerchiefs to their mouths or dabbed their eyes. Prayers and hymns vied in competition. With goose bumps down to my thighs, I luxuriated in the crescendo, hummed along with the melody, sang what words I understood, and would have loved to cross myself and bow low. Yes, I wanted to kiss the ground, wanted to kneel down to keep this singing from ever stopping, and wanted this doctor never to leave our midst again—and resting now on the old man's legs, she opened his fly, nestled his skinny penis in her hand and concealed it in her mouth.

"The snake, the divine snake!"

"Everything, everything will change!"

And now the first voices bawled: "He is risen!"

"Yes, he is risen indeed!" others replied.

Cars along the Nevsky honked. Even the policeman accepted kisses, but then he tugged his uniform jacket taut under his belt and swallowed hard. Like a child, he smeared a tear on his cheek with the flat of his hand.

As the crowd cheered, the doctor released the old man's shaft, squatted quickly atop it and lowered herself—head thrown back, mouth a soundless scream.

At the same moment the old man's pale blue eyes went rigid, a shudder flitted across his face. Little bubbles formed at his lips, and burst. The singing broke off, the prayer dwindled to a murmur. People craned their necks, stood on tiptoe, edged closer together. The doctor looked stupefied. Gradually, however, her mouth relaxed. She began to smile and the spectators' faces grew radiant.

She kissed him. There was a sound like falling raindrops in the fervor with which her lips touched his brow, cheeks and mouth. She stretched farther forward. The tips of her breasts covered his eyes, the nipples brushing the lids three times. And with that she pulled her lower body from his member. It was all so still that this could have been the start of a swoon. Finally, however, she raised herself up from his head. The old man lay there in our midst, his penis festively erect, his eyes closed.

"Closed them with her breasts!" people whispered. "A saint, truly, with her breasts!"

Slowly she passed her hand between her legs, nodded, looked up, raised her arm, stretching it higher and higher and finally spreading her wet fingers in token of victory.

What a cry of jubilation pierced the air, what happiness, what thundering applause. And they all wanted to touch her, kiss her feet, press a cheek to her knees, stroke her black hair, moisten it with their tears. I couldn't tell if these were fierce embraces or pokes and shoves that pushed me forward now, causing me to stumble. But I did not fall, there was no room.

People stormed the redhead, tearing the doctor's clothes out of her hands in seconds. She managed to save only a scrap of panties for herself. As the first blows from the policeman's billy club landed, people incited him to really lay it on, others cursed him and provoked him with obscenities and grabbed his club away. Once he blew his whistle, however, several men rallied to him and with linked arms formed a phalanx of backs, shoulders and necks, pushing us back until only the policeman, the doctor and the body of the old man were left inside the circle.

The woman, who had not been left with so much as shoes for her feet, awkwardly covered her breasts and genitals. The tall crazy guy, however, who was still part of the cordon, stepped up to her like a lord chamberlain, bowed, kissed her hand and spread his coat out before her, the lining showing. From his pants pocket he pulled a sack, smoothed it out and proclaimed, "For our saint! For our good lady!" and cast a few rubles of his own into it, as if we were monkeys who needed to be shown how.

In a crush of backs, necks and shoulders, we waved at him with our money, as if placing bets. Those in the back rows balled their money up and threw it into the circle. "Here! Here's mine! Here!" they called to the crazy guy, a hundred voices shouting orders to him all at once. He did what he could, leaping here and there amid the applause, bending like a giraffe and raising his skinny arms in protest when instead of rubles people began to throw bundles of chives and butter, bags of farmer cheese and sausages, garlic, bananas and bread. They also took aim at the police-man and the doctor with eggs, kohlrabis, herring and their homemade maxims: "Honor she paid him, with her body she weighed him, in a warm grave she laid him." As best she could, she attempted to escape the hail of gifts, dodging and ducking the heaviest pieces, but finally crouched down, exhausted, as she was struck by cucumbers, tomatoes and cabbages. But even then they did not leave off. "Down her sweet young twat run juices from that old sot!" The crazy guy kept bounding about like a gouty old goat. But his limbs were obviously flagging. "Her cheeks are pale, her hole's a mess, the brat'll be born fatherless!"

The policeman, his face beet-red, rushed the crowd and blindly opened a breach in the dam that had been protecting him as well. The next moment he was grabbed by a dozen arms and lifted up. The crazy guy was soon caught and shouldered, too, but turned out to be so weakened already that he had to be propped up on all sides with canes and crutches. The sack of balled-up money was dumped out over the doctor, whereupon she willingly climbed on the shoulders of a kneeling Goliath. She now headed the procession that spread out over the pavement, inundating traffic. The light of several thousand candles bobbed back and forth, illuminating faces.

The doctor waved at us, blowing kisses in all direc-tions, and suddenly burst into bright laughter. Only now did I spot a tiny gap between her front teeth and notice the ring on her hand, which she turned until a pearl appeared on top again. Then all I saw was the cloud cover moving in over the city, thick and grayish blue. Only to the northwest was there a sharp burst of yellowish green light, directly above the Admiralty, whose spire towered heavenward, showing us the way.

# SELECTED EDITORIAL NOTES

*Story* 10

IVAN TOPORYSHKIN: Ivan Toporyshkin was one of the pseudonyms of Daniil Kharms.

15

WHEN THE COMMUNISTS: Allusions to the life of Saint Nicholas.

16

ABOVE THE YELLOW: Excerpts from A. Byely's novel *Petersburg* have been included here. Until 1991 St. Isaac's Cathedral contained a Foucault pendulum that demonstrated the axial rotation of the earth.

18

I NEVER VISITED: Adaptation of Pushkin's "Postmaster," from *Tales of the Late I. P. Belkin.*

21

"OH, HER . . .": Quotes taken from Chekhov plays: *Three Sisters, Uncle Vanya, The Seagull* and *The Shooting Party.*

27

"NO, NO, . . .": This story is obviously influenced by E. T. A. Hoffmann's "New Year's Eve Adventure," from his *Fantasies in the Manner of Callot*. The motif of iconoclasm, however, is somewhat puzzling, insofar as the story contains a definite analogy to certain events in a Berlin art gallery, as reported by I. Kabakov.

30

WERE YOU: In Nabokov's *Mary*, Ganin schools his will by awaking at night and throwing his cigarette butts in a mailbox. In the final section, allusions have been traced to the following works by Khlebnikov: "Zangezi," "The Gods," "Phonetics 1922" and "Perun."

31

"AH, HERE IS . . .": The song "Dunya" can be found in a similar variation in Bulgakov's *White Guard*.